COME AWAY FROM HER

a novel

Samuel W. Gailey

Relax. Read. Repeat.

COME AWAY FROM HER
Samuel W. Gailey
Published by TouchPoint Press
Brookland, AR 72417
www.touchpointpress.com

Softcover ISBN: 978-1-956851-32-8
Hardcover ISBN: 978-1-956851-37-3

Editor: Scott Bury
Cover Design: Brock Book Design
Author Photo: Amanda Demme

Visit the author's website at www.samuelwgailey.com

@samuelwgailey @ samuelwgailey @ samuelwgailey

First Edition

Printed in the United States of America.

For Ayn & Gray, Geoff & Robin

GOOD FRIDAY, 1988

Their mournful call crept in through the corners of restless dreams dulled by consumption. High-pitched and constant, their wail stirred a slow tug of dread—especially in the early hours after dawn when everything moved a little slower and the light of day was just beginning to make its way upon the horizon. If the feeling of despair could be embodied by only one sound, it would be the raspy cawing of a flock of black crows.

The screeching became louder, more urgent, as if the birds were trying their damnedest to get Cap's attention, but he was not yet ready for this day or its consequences. He rolled on his side and tugged the wool blanket over his head to block out the awful sound, but it proved futile. The crows had escorted him across the threshold between sleep and consciousness, and there was to be no turning back.

The back of his throat burned with thirst, and it was painful to swallow.

He reached for some water on the nightstand, but upon bringing the glass to his lips, the remains of the bourbon from the night before greeted him instead. He held the glass to his mouth. Considered the ramifications, then resisted the impulse to down the booze to keep the looming hangover at bay.

He swung both legs from under the blankets, rubbed at his temples, and tried to sort through the jumbled mess inside his head.

What day is it?

Wednesday.

Maybe Thursday.

Definitely not Sunday.

A silent thanks was offered to God that today wasn't Sunday—a day of rest for many, but to Cap, it proved to be the most taxing day of the week. How he'd grown to dread the seventh day, the irony of which did not escape him.

Then it came to him—it was Friday. Good Friday.

So little of the bedroom had changed from when he was a small boy. Stark and unremarkable; merely practical and functional. A dresser with a simple mirror mounted above it. A wooden chair stood next to the lone window—the seat seldom used, and the window rarely peered through. Hardwood floors recently swept and mopped with Murphy's Oil. The walls painted Navajo White, just like those of the seminary where he began his adulthood. A full-sized bed had replaced the set of bunk beds from his childhood, and above the headboard hung a carving of Christ handcrafted from black walnut. The crucifix hung from this very spot long before Cap took residence, affixed to the wall by his father before he had two sons. The question of its removal never a consideration. So, Christ's martyred depiction remained, holding silent vigil above his bed, watching, always watching.

Cap slipped into the washroom and ran warm water over hands free of calluses, cleansing his skin with great intent. He rinsed his face, fingers grazing the stubble on his chin before ultimately tracing the thick patch of whiskers above his lip. And as he did every morning, he inspected the split on his upper lip, ensuring that his whiskers grew long enough to conceal the ugly flaw.

Next, he brushed his teeth with eyes closed. Ran a comb under the faucet and pulled it through his hair. Slipped on a robe and cinched it tight. Routines made a man.

He shuffled down the steps to check the living room to see if Tess might be up and about, but the room stood empty. A glass of red wine was perched on the edge of the coffee table, as if it had been put down quickly and forgotten.

A draft of cold air nipped at his ankles, and he noticed that the front door swung back and forth. He secured the door, wondering whether Tess had slept in his room or down in the rectory. Had they quarreled about something? Had he said something that he might now regret? A few cups of coffee would be required to help him sort through a random collection of vague memories from the night before.

The crows started up again with a renewed sense of urgency. Louder and almost frantic in nature. Or, possibly, the birds had never quieted in the first place, and Cap had merely tuned them out due to his muddled mental state. He figured a flock of them had probably discovered a nest of mice under the house somewhere and were all riled up, desperate to feed on those tiny, soft babies.

In the kitchen, more routines were followed. He filled a kettle under the faucet, then went about boiling some water. Retrieved a jar of Folgers from the cabinet, refilled the sugar bowl, and grabbed a jug of milk from the refrigerator.

The kettle steamed and whistled. As Cap scooped three heaping spoons of coffee crystals into his mug, a flash of black blurred past the kitchen window.

"Damn crows," his voice rasped, dry as a salted cracker. He flung open the door that led to the back porch and was greeted by a wall of dark, thrashing wings. The sky mushroomed black as thirty or forty crows took flight the moment Cap stepped out onto the landing's concrete slab. The flock of pure ebony soared north, then looped in a sweeping arc before landing on the snow-covered ground, settling into an undulating mass at the base of the steps far below.

He shuffled forward and a spike of pain chewed up his foot and leg. Chunks of broken glass littered the concrete. Blood seeped from a tiny gash on the sole of his bare foot, and the sting of the cut nearly caused him to drop his mug of coffee. He picked the shard of clear glass from his skin and noticed that not only his blood stained the concrete, but dozens of frozen scarlet drops splattered across the landing as well. Spilled wine, maybe. His attention went back to the crows as they hollered amongst themselves, their hooked talons scraping against concrete and ice in a frenzied fashion, feathers whipping.

Cap peered down the concrete steps that had been built into the side of the sloping hill that his house perched atop. Thirty-three in all. They were too damn steep, and he rarely used them, especially in the winter months when ice coated their surface. He kept a sack of salt handy to scatter when the notion moved him to do so, but the bag had yet to be opened.

The murder of crows continued to swarm the ground, flapping and jawing at one another. Something had their dander up, that much was for sure.

"Go on. Get out," he hollered loud.

The tangle of birds paid him no mind, snapping their wings instead.

The wind cut through the flannel of his pajamas, and he decided to retreat to the warmth of the kitchen when something between the frenzy of feathers registered in the blink of an eye: a shoe. A shoe coated with something black. Something wet.

"Ah, hell." He limped down the steps, still lugging his mug of coffee, hot liquid splattering his chest and legs. A mounting panic blocked the pain, and he could no longer feel the cut on the sole of his foot, even though it left a dotted trail of blood behind him.

A few crows took flight, then a few more, clearing the way for Cap to see the lower half of a body, surrounded by a pool of frozen blood marring the snow. "Oh, God . . ."

The mug finally slipped from his hand, porcelain shattering on the edge of a step. The sound of it caused the swarm of crows to take to the air in an explosion, screaming that awful sound of despair as they fled into the Pennsylvania sky that grew darker by the second.

FIFTEEN DAYS EARLIER

1

Cap never poured a drink before a Sunday sermon. Never. Not once. Maybe that fact wasn't something to boast about, but at least it was something to cling to.

But today was not Sunday.

The bottle of Wild Turkey perched upon the edge of his desk exactly where he had placed it, the seal yet to be broken. He peered at the bottle and felt that familiar tug of want.

No.

Not now.

Not right now.

He stared instead at the black pulpit gown and dark purple stole draped across the leather chair in front of his desk. The robe and stole were well-starched and wrapped in a plastic dry-cleaning bag, as he rarely wore formal vestments to church unless it happened to be an occasion that called for special garments.

Cap always felt somewhat foolish when wearing vestments. Like he was a boy playing dress-up, pretending to be a pastor. Perhaps traditional attire looked suitable on older, more distinguished clergy long with experience, but on someone a few years past their fortieth birthday, a robe and stole, in Cap's opinion, looked ridiculous. One thing was for certain—he did not feel comfortable wearing them and probably never would.

Outside, a late season snow tumbled down from gray March skies and swept past the study's windows in sheets. Flakes stuck to the glass. Some melted. Others did not.

Cap gazed once again toward the bottle of bourbon. Rubbed his jaw and eventually tugged at his mustache like he always did when in a state of deep deliberation. After wrestling with strong desire, he shook his head and sighed, then picked the bottle up by the neck and stuck it on the top of a bookshelf.

Out of sight, out of mind.

He tore open the dry-cleaning bag and hung the garments on the back of the closet door. He wore black trousers and a black shirt and wondered if he should even bother with the gown and stole. Who'd be there to see him? Who'd care even if they were?

No one.

Despite that understanding, he slipped the neatly pressed gown over his shirt, draped the stole around his neck, and inspected his reflection in the full-length mirror behind the office door. He was neither a tall man nor a short one. Lean, bordering on being too thin in the opinion of many. He ate what he wanted, didn't pay attention to portions, but never seemed to put on any extra weight. He had a strong jaw, pronounced cheekbones, and a set of dark green eyes that were often difficult to read.

Then there was his mustache. The facial hair almost seemed like it was part of a costume—something that he could, and *should,* remove at a moment's notice.

He adjusted the stole so that the material hung in equal lengths around his neck, then bent down and retrieved a pair of simple black dress shoes and a wooden box from under his desk.

Outside, the snow fell harder, blocking the efforts of the sun and casting Cap in shadows. His office became a cave. But he did not turn on the desk lamp because the darkness suited him fine. Much preferred it, in fact. He was light-sensitive. Had been ever since he was a boy. His fair skin burned easily, and when emerging from the house into direct sunlight, it always sent him into a messy sneezing fit.

His father would shake his head at Cap as if disappointed by his son's affliction. *How many times do I have to tell you? Put on a hat, boy. Either that or stay indoors. It's not exactly rocket science.*

Cap took a seat, placed the shoes upon the leather desk blotter, then opened the wooden box. He took out a folded rag, a tin of Kiwi black shoe polish, and a horsehair brush. His shoes appeared to be recently polished, but Cap knew he'd polish them again anyway. He wiped the shoes free of dust, opened the can of shoe polish and ran a corner of the rag inside the tin, and thought about the dead man inside his church.

When he received the call that Teddie Salsman had died late Monday night, Cap knew that a specific eulogy would not be requested nor necessary, simply because no one from the community would be present to pay their final respects. It remained an unspoken understanding in Black Walnut that it was only a matter of time until Teddie met his Maker. The man lived in what barely passed for a shack down by the county dump. Most folks, including Cap, figured Teddie would eventually incinerate his dwelling from one of the hand-rolled cigarettes that constantly smoldered between his fingers, or even more probable, that the man's liver would finally shut down after being so heavily taxed for nearly forty years. But neither of those two fates had taken Teddie from this earth.

Instead, Teddie's life ended in a hit-and-run accident next to a barren cornfield on Route 6 between Black Walnut and Wyalusing sometime after midnight. Streaks of blood stained the centerline for almost a hundred feet as Teddie's body had been dragged and shredded before flipping into the ditch. Crushed cans from Teddie's last twelve-pack of Rolling Rock followed his trail. Death was instantaneous yet gruesome. Neither of the Army-issued boots that Teddie wore had been found. His body was barely recognizable. Even though Sheldon's Funeral Parlor did the best they could to patch him up, it mattered little as there wouldn't be an open casket at the man's service.

Cap ran the rag in precise circular motions against the leather toe of each shoe, then held them up to the dull light that filtered in through the windows and repeated the process once again.

Teddie Salsman had no family, no close acquaintances, and not one single friend. Cap fully expected to stand in front of a county-issued coffin and offer a eulogy solely upon the ears of a dead man. Sheldon's Funeral Parlor had delivered the casket the previous evening as he had requested. There was no logical reason to make Bernie Sheldon haul Teddie's remains to the church. But Cap knew sure as snow was white that not a single townsperson would drag themselves to Sheldon's to extend their respects. After Bernie hemmed and hawed about bringing the casket to the church, Cap offered to pay for the man's time out of his own pocket to deliver Teddie to his house of worship.

Cap swiveled in his chair and stared out the window to take in the tumbling snow. Even though it was mid-March, Old Man Winter wasn't yet done. He had a little bit more to say. Everything outside blanketed in a layer of white. The sidewalk leading up to the house, the yard's dead grass, and the limbs of black walnut trees that lined the front lawn.

He watched the snow swirl in a thousand different directions and thought about Teddie, searching for something meaningful to say about the man.

The truth of the matter was that Teddie happened to be a nasty drunk who slung rocks at kids who dared to venture too close to his shack and cursed those who blocked his path on Main Street. He reeked of booze and cigarettes and filth in general. His clothing and hair matted with grease, his face black from dirt and ash. The man never pretended to be lovable, or likable for that matter. Teddie was a man who asked for nothing and didn't take to accepting anyone's help, handouts, or social kindness of any kind.

Even so, he and Cap had formed an unlikely bond, one Cap never confused with friendship, but there had been a time or two when Teddie Salsman was the only person in Black Walnut who was there for him.

The shack didn't have electricity. No running water. Not even a window. Merely a place to sleep and not be seen by the rest of the world.

Flames crackled in a poorly constructed fireplace, and smoke from chunks of hemlock combined with the smell of a kerosene lamp that glowed on top of a cinderblock. Under the pungent stink of smoke, Cap couldn't help but notice the stench of urine and rotting meat.

Cap sat upon an apple crate that served as a chair and pressed a bloodied handkerchief to the back of his head. He heard a haggard cough, and then Teddie emerged from the shadows holding two mason jars and a jug of whiskey. Neither of the jars was even close to being clean.

Teddie's hands trembled as he poured them both a couple of inches of homebrewed booze.

"Thank you, Teddie."

Teddie merely grunted, took a sip of whiskey before sitting down on a crate warped with age, then reached down to the floor and lifted a tin box to his lap. He opened the lid, took another sip of whiskey, and one by one, removed a roll of gauze, rubbing alcohol, a needle and medical thread, and a few balls of cotton.

"Why don'tcha go to a real doctor?" Teddie's voice rattled with phlegm, as if he hadn't spoken in days. Perhaps he hadn't.

Cap took a taste of the homemade whiskey and felt the burn immediately. It tasted as bad as it smelled, but he drank it anyway. He peered at faded black and white photographs tacked onto slats of knotted pine: a stone-faced woman who looked uncomfortable holding a baby in the nook of her arm; a young boy sitting on the grass in between two German Shepherds; a woman in her twenties laughing at something out of frame; a clean-shaven portrait of Teddie wearing an Army uniform.

"You were a doctor, Teddie."

Teddie grunted again. Drank some whiskey. "Used to be a lot of things."

Cap removed the handkerchief from the back of his head and examined the crimson stains that dotted the material.

"Still bleeding?" Teddie asked as he threaded a needle, both hands trembling.

"A little bit."

"You should go see Doc Pete for these kinds of things."

Cap sipped whiskey from the jar before responding. "He asks too many questions. Too many hows and whys."

For the first time, Teddie looked Cap square in the eye. "Secrets don't stay hidden for long around here."

"I know."

Teddie finished his whiskey and poured more for both of them. "You always drink alone?"

"I'm not alone right now."

A sound came from Teddie's lips, and it took Cap a moment to realize it was a wry chuckle.

"Hold your head still." He lifted the kerosene lamp to the back of Cap's head and poked a dirty fingernail through hair clotted with blood.

"How's it look?"

"Like you'll need four or five stitches."

Cap didn't respond. Instead, he took another drink.

Teddie mumbled something and withdrew a pair of reading glasses with smudged lenses from his breast pocket.

"Try not to move. It's gonna hurt."

Cap heard the man exhale, smelled the sour mash on his breath, then felt the sting of the needle prick the flesh of his scalp.

Cap polished the leather with a horsehair brush in brisk, snapping motions. After setting the dress shoe down and buffing the second, his eyes stopped on the bottle of Wild Turkey on the bookshelf, and it struck Cap that he and old Teddie had more in common than he cared to admit.

He slipped on his shoes and laced them tight. Then he stood up straight, studied his reflection in the mirror, and fingered the gold tassels at the end of the stole. From all appearances, Cap presented himself as a devoted servant of God. After a few moments, he pulled his eyes away, unable to stare at himself a moment longer.

The call of the bottle was too strong.

He grabbed the bottle of bourbon and poured himself a two-finger shot. Before second-guessing his intent, Cap lifted the glass to his lips.

"To Teddie."

The moment he stepped out of his office, Cap heard the sound of two women bickering coming from the administrative office. One voice was much louder and more confrontational than the other, and he knew exactly who issued the condescending complaints. He considered slipping past the office and making a beeline for the sanctuary, but instead, he stopped at the threshold and observed. Everyone slows to witness a train wreck.

A full-figured woman stood in front of a desk with her hands perched on wide hips. She wore an expensive dress that clung to her body, and although somewhat revealing, it looked tasteful as well. Her hair was perfectly styled. Makeup precisely applied. Getting ready to be seen in public took her ample time. Her brow creased and her mouth drew straight as she let into another woman—younger, thinner, and ragged—who sat behind the desk and leafed through a stack of mail.

"How do you not have a list of kids that attend church? Isn't that part of your job?"

The other woman didn't bother looking up. Instead, she ripped open the envelopes one by one.

The heavier, better-dressed woman stomped her foot. "Robin, this is important. I need to know how many kids there are so that I have a basket for every child."

Robin opened her purse, withdrew a box of Newport cigarettes, and struck a match. "I dunno, Maggie. Probably fifteen. Maybe eighteen."

"Well? Which is it?"

Robin exhaled a cloud of smoke, which Maggie promptly waved away. "Do you have to smoke in here?"

"Too cold to smoke outside."

"Well, it's rude."

"To who? I'm the only one that works in the office."

Maggie marched across the room and heaved the window open with dramatic effort. "I'm not leaving until I get a headcount for the children."

Robin spotted Cap standing by the door and gave him an exasperated expression.

"Let me guess . . . the Easter parade," Cap offered.

Maggie turned, faced Cap, and her sour expression transformed into a coy smile at the sight of him.

"You giving Robin grief, Mags?"

"It's not easy organizing the Easter celebration, Cap."

"I know it's not."

"And unless you have someone else that wants to take over, I need some cooperation. I oversee the banquet dinner, the decorations, the parade, everything. I organize the volunteers and coordinate who's bringing casseroles, salads, drinks, and desserts. A thousand different things to keep track of. And all I ask of Robin is a count of the children, but she can't seem to get it through her head—"

"Eighteen kids total, Mags."

Robin tapped her cigarette into an ashtray. "Told you."

"No, you didn't." She returned her attention to Cap. "And why do you let her smoke in here?"

"Too cold to smoke outside." Cap grinned at Robin, then gestured toward the doors that led to the sanctuary. "Anyone?"

Robin shook her head.

"No big surprise, is it?" Maggie posed. "Did you really expect anyone to come to Teddie's funeral?"

Cap and Robin exchanged a look.

"What? He was nothing but a mean, old drunk. And I'm not saying anything that everyone doesn't already know."

"What about the two of you? Won't take long."

Robin stabbed out her cigarette. "Sorry, but I need to stop by the grocery store and get dinner ready for the kids. Chuck's no help."

Cap peered at Maggie, who promptly picked up her purse and straightened her dress across her hips. "And I have an errand list three miles long." She patted

Cap's arm on her way out. "Honestly, I don't know why you even bother, Cap. It's not like Teddie even believed in God."

Cap crossed the carpeted stage to the pulpit, deep in reflection, thinking about what the last moments of Teddie's life must have been like—had the man experienced a fleeting moment of fear, was his death painful, did he have any true regrets in his life—and didn't notice the older man sitting in the front pew with a wide brim felt hat clasped between knotted hands.

"Morning."

Cap jerked and his page of notes slipped from his fingers.

The older man stood up from the pew, fast and awkward, clapped on his sheriff's hat, then tugged it off again just as quick. "Christ, Cap. Didn't mean to scare the piss out of you."

It took Cap a moment to process Sheriff Lester standing there before him. The old man seemed a little more stooped and a little frailer than he remembered.

Cap painted on a slow grin to mask his surprise. "Lester. No. Just caught up in my thoughts, is all."

Lester extended a hand twisted by arthritis, and when Cap shook it, he held his breath for fear of the sheriff catching a whiff of his indulgence.

"Sit, sit," Cap offered.

Lester settled back onto the pew with a relieved grunt and motioned to the empty church behind him. "Wasn't exactly expecting standing room only, but I figured that a few of the old-timers might show up to pay their respects to Teddie this morning."

Cap bent down and collected his notes. "I guess people are busy."

"Busy doing what exactly? You're just being kind. Fact is folks don't give a God damn." He played with the brim of his hat. "Pardon the language."

Cap waved the apology away.

"I mean, hell, Cy Warner served with Teddie in the war, and the old goat can't be bothered to drive two miles from the farm?"

"Well, Teddie didn't exactly make it easy on people."

"Guess not, but still."

Both men gazed toward the raised platform where Teddie's casket stood, noticeably absent of flowers or a wreath, and were silent for a moment. Finally, Lester shook his head.

"A hit and run is a hell of a way to go, Cap. Hell of a way to go."

"Learn anything new about what happened?"

Lester tugged his cap onto his head. "Not a damn thing. No one saw it happen. If it was a local, I have my eyes on the lookout for a dented hood and smashed-up headlight. If it was someone passing through, they're long gone by now."

"I don't understand how someone could do that, then just drive off."

"Maybe they were scared. Or maybe they were drunk and didn't even know what happened."

Cap kept quiet.

"Well. You're doing a good thing here today, Cap. Maybe it doesn't mean anything to most folks, but it means something to me."

Cap acted as if he didn't hear the compliment. "How's your better half feeling?"

Lester inspected the inside of his hat like seeing it for the first time and his mouth drew straight.

"The doctors have anything new to say?"

Lester snorted out a small, hard laugh. "Nothing I want to hear."

"Bonnie's a fighter."

"Don't I know it. Helluva lot stronger than me. That's for damn sure."

"I'd like to stop by and pay her a visit if that would be okay."

"She'd like that, Cap. She could use the company. Might find it hard to believe, but she's just about sick and tired of looking at this old mug."

Cap grinned. Stared down at his handwritten notes. "How about you and I give Teddie a proper send-off?"

"That'd be just fine, Cap."

Cap stepped beside Teddie's casket, ran his hand atop the smooth wood, and then took his place behind the podium. When he peered down at his notes, he noticed that his hands trembled ever so slightly. Part of him wished he hadn't taken that drink, and the other wished he had taken a few more.

FOURTEEN DAYS BEFORE GOOD FRIDAY

2

The snow came down steadily, just as the weatherman had predicted it would. It wasn't yet noon and four inches had already fallen, and by the looks of the sky, a few more inches were on their way before the day was done.

Cap had the truck's wipers working at a frantic pace, rubber squeaking against the glass. Black Walnut's Main Street stood barely visible through the windshield. In the center of the village, snow covered the better part of a statue of Reverend Samuel Sturdevant, one of the town's first white settlers. Virgin snow pretty much concealed everything—sidewalks, fire hydrants, mailboxes, parked cars, and power lines.

He drove past stores and shops that had barely changed over the last thirty years—same brick facades, same hand-painted signage, same worn canvas canopies. Agway's parking lot was filled with rusted pickups, almost every one of them equipped with a gun rack. Lights glowed from inside Colgrove's Barber Shop—someone sitting in the chair getting their hair sheared. Bennett's Appliances, Lacey's Hardware, and the IGA Market were open for business, and a few farm trucks parked out in front of Red's Tavern, but everybody else had the good sense to stay inside and out of the nasty weather.

He rumbled up Old Route 6 and down Brown Hill, passing only a handful of cars on the straightaway through Terrytown. A gust of wind occasionally pulled at the truck, but Cap kept his hands tight on the wheel. The radio played what sounded like a Hank Williams' song through a tangle of static, so he shut that off and peered toward the Susquehanna River. A layer of fog churned atop the surface, but he could make out the flow of the fast-moving current carrying chunks of ice, both big and small.

The truck hit a patch of black ice and veered across the center lane until the treads found traction once again, and Cap regained control of the Ford. Part of him considered stopping at the next turnoff and doing the sensible thing—heading back home and making his visit on another day. This storm was only going to get worse. But he thought about Sheriff Lester and how compromised the man seemed, knowing that his wife was slowly dying right there in front of him.

He gazed out the window as one barren cornfield after another blurred past under the distorted vestige of the sun that crept its way west. Weeks ago, nothing more than brown rutted patches of dark earth, now covered with a foot of pristine snow. Despite the cold and wind, Cap was fond of what winter brought with it. Snow had a way of concealing all the nastiness left behind from the rainy days of fall.

His mind wandered back to Lester and Bonnie. People reacted a hundred different ways when forced to stare death in the face. Some grew sullen and angry, bitter that their last days were upon them. Others found themselves swallowed up by fear, afraid to close their eyes at night, not knowing if they'd be opening them one more time. Cap had held the hands of many awaiting the end, asking him all kinds of questions. *Why did they have to go so soon? Would they be able to see their loved ones again? Would God forgive all their sins?*

But Lester and Bonnie were of a different ilk. Private. Resilient. Hopeful.

Through the curtain of white in front of his truck, Cap noticed a pair of headlights weaving from one lane to the next. Moving quickly—too quickly.

He flashed his high beams, but the car seemed to pick up speed and barrel straight toward him. He pumped the brakes and rode along the shoulder of Route 6, the truck rattling and shaking like a carnival ride. He squinted out the windshield, and the approaching car—a green Pinto—drove faster, more erratically, crossing the centerline and into his lane. Only twenty yards away. He stomped on his brakes as the car bore down upon him, then pressed his eyes closed and waited for impact.

Through flashes of darkness and light, he heard the roar of the Pinto's engine. Felt the force of air shake his truck, the car missing him by mere inches. A split second of quiet, then a thunderous clap filled the countryside, followed by the sound of breaking glass and collapsing steel. Sharp and penetrating. These familiar sounds were visceral, triggering memories long buried but not forgotten: a Dodge Coronet station wagon losing control, skidding off the road, flipping and rolling end over end, the windshield shattering, tossing the passengers backward, forward and side to side, their screams finally silenced by the impact of steel colliding against the trunk of an oak tree, and after that, unsettling silence.

Cap's eyes flashed back open, and his heart hammered in his chest. His hands shook. Mouth went dry. He fumbled with the keys, and it took a moment to coordinate his fingers to cut the engine, then he swung open his door and stepped out into the cold.

Heavy gusts of wind greeted him, causing his eyes to water, numbing his nose and cheeks in an instant. Under the howl of wind, Cap heard a sound, high-pitched and constant, like a woman screaming.

Driving sheets of snow forced him to shield his eyes as he sprinted to the edge of the road and searched for the Pinto. He took a step into the ditch and his shoes disappeared under six inches of powder. Sidestepped his way down, his dress shoes slipping on wet snow until he arrived at the bottom of a gorge.

The Pinto was flipped on its roof, teetering halfway off an outcrop of rocks—the bottom of the ravine twenty-five feet below—and the sight of the drop-off caused Cap's heart to thud even faster.

The wheels of the car spun, emitting a shrill whine that mimicked a panicked scream of distress. The front tires rotated faster and faster, the gas pedal still engaged, as if the driver intended to drive their way out of this mess.

He approached the car, noticed liquid leaking from the well of the engine and pooling into the snow. The wind kicked up harder and the Pinto began to sway, slipping closer and closer to the edge of the rocks.

"You okay in there? The car is about to roll off." His voice echoed down the ravine before being swallowed up into nothingness.

Cap kneeled next to the driver's door and peered through the window. A young woman was strapped into the driver's side by her seatbelt, hanging upside down. She didn't appear to be bleeding or hurt. She clutched the steering wheel with both hands and stared straight forward like she thought she was still driving the car. When she spotted Cap outside her window, she jerked back at the sight of him.

"Are you hurt?"

The young woman stared at his lips. Seemed unsure. Maybe in shock.

Cap felt the car shift, tilting forward, slipping a few more inches off the outcrop of rocks. "Got to get you out of there right now."

The young woman tilted her head and kept staring at him as if she wasn't sure what to do. She appeared young—late twenties, maybe thirty.

The Pinto shifted a little more, pulling Cap from his scrutiny of the woman. He grabbed the door handle and gave it a good yank, but it didn't budge. "Can you open the window?"

The woman shook her head and stared forward once again.

Cap banged on the glass. "Miss, open the window."

The woman's left hand finally went to the window crank and fought the awkward angle at first, but then the glass panel jerked open a few inches at a time.

Cap extended his hand toward hers. "Grab a hold of me."

The young woman stared at his hand but declined to accept it.

"Please," Cap urged. "The car is about to slip over the edge."

Her dark eyes studied him for a moment. Her lips moved—praying maybe. Then she shook her head, deliberate with a touch of defiance, snatched her purse from the ceiling of the car, and clutched the bag to her chest like an infant.

Cap reached inside the car and seized her by the wrist. "You need to release your seatbelt."

Her head snapped back and forth once again.

"Well, then we're both gonna go over because I'm not letting you go."

Her eyes hardened with a flash of anger, but Cap maintained his grip on her arm.

The wind rocked the Pinto and Cap thought they were both about to slip off the edge when he heard a *click*, and she collapsed to the ceiling of the car, nearly pulling him down inside with her. He regained his balance and tugged hard, slowly easing her out the window.

The woman was breathing hard, and Cap could smell both the bitter and sweet on her breath—cigarettes and chocolate. They crouched next to one another beside the driver's door when the Pinto finally tipped over the edge. He snatched the woman's hand and they scrambled backward as the car toppled off the rocks.

There was a moment of silence before the sound of metal smashing against rocks boomed from below and echoed across the Susquehanna.

Cap stared at the spot where the Pinto had rested. He stood. Brushed the snow off his pant legs, then offered his hand to her.

The young woman stood up on her own accord and walked to the edge of the outcrop. It was then that Cap got a good look at her. She had an exotic appearance, like she was from someplace far away, maybe even another country. Dark hair the color of molasses, with a dark set of green eyes to match, and Cap had a hard time reading her.

"Anybody else in there?"

She looked back at Cap but didn't respond.

"You were the only one in the car?"

She nodded.

"Well, let's get out of the cold and figure out what to do next."

The young woman nodded again, and as Cap worked his way out of the ravine, she pulled her purse tight against her shoulder and followed him.

3

Maggie stood in front of the bedroom's full-length mirror not wearing a stitch of clothing and hated what stared back at her. Only forty-three and this was what she'd become? What would she look like when she turned fifty? Or sixty?

She rotated her body and scrutinized her profile. Her belly pulled toward the floor, exposing the traces of fourteen-year-old stretch marks. Breasts that were once the envy of classmates and the obsession of most boys, now reduced to two shapeless mounds. She lifted her arms and pinched the flab between her fingers. Depressing. So damn depressing.

Stripped of her clothing as well as layers of eye shadow, mascara, and foundation, Maggie felt naked in more ways than one.

She ran manicured fingernails through brown, flat morning hair and noticed a few strands of gray peeking through.

How had this happened?

How could she let herself become so middle-aged?

She slid open the closet door and traced her finger along dozens of expensive dresses, suits, and skirts, searching for the outfit that would make her feel better. She selected a pleated sleeveless dress and held it up for a moment. She had only worn it a handful of times because it exposed her arm fat. She dropped it to the floor and selected another dress. Maybe. But then she turned it around, inspected the back and remembered—it made her ass look a mile wide. That dress fell to the floor and she selected another. This one accentuated her side-rolls and down it went. She picked another and another, dismissing and dropping each one at her feet, everything too revealing, too tight, too ordinary.

Maggie finally backed away from the closet and sank onto the edge of the bed. Crossed her legs and sat in the quiet—so quiet that she could hear a shrill ringing in her ears. She stared at her wedding band and tried to spin it around her finger, but even that proved to be tight. She'd probably have to get it resized.

Her heart started to race, and the walls closed in on her as that familiar tug of anxiety pulled at her from the inside out.

Not now.

Garnet-colored fingernails dug into her thighs to try and force away the approaching storm. Mornings were the worst. When it was quiet. When the house was empty with Wade at work and Butch off to school, and she was all alone. Even after all these years, she still couldn't get used to the daylight quiet, no matter how hard she tried. The morning silence proved deafening, and the absence of conversation became suffocating, like massive hands grabbing at her, squeezing her tight, forcing out her breath to the point where she could barely take in air.

There had been a time when the thought of a quiet house made her giddy. Raising a child had not been what she imagined it to be. She hadn't been prepared for the constant chaos—the tantrums, mood swings, and general fussiness. Butch had been such a sweet, happy baby, but once he turned six, he became quiet and sullen, off in his own world. She could never figure out what the boy might be thinking.

In the days and weeks leading up to when Butch started kindergarten, all Maggie could do was daydream about having the house entirely to herself. She'd be able to clean without Butch making a mess right behind her and sip a mug of tea in front of *The Family Feud* if she wanted. With Wade working at the store and Butch confined to a classroom, there'd be no one to tend to, nobody whining or crying or asking for something to eat or something to do. She would finally have *me time.*

But after nearly a decade of *me time*, she had come to hate the empty, meaningless hours of waiting for Butch to come tromping inside the house so she could hear about his day. It was all that she had to look forward to. *How did you do on your social studies test? Did you eat your lunch? Were you warm enough in that jacket?* And then there was the last question. Asked every day. *Did you get picked on at the playground?*

Butch was her life. Her entirety. In the time between him leaving and returning from school, all she did was vacuum and dust and putter around the house, checking the clock every few minutes to see if it was almost time for Butch to come home.

The walls pushed in tighter. Faster. Harder.

Take your pill. You'll feel better.

If she skipped a single day, Maggie could feel the consequences almost immediately. Like somebody took a knife, carved out part of her brain, and let darkness seep inside.

She yanked her nightstand drawer open. A half-dozen prescription bottles sat next to a hairbrush, a jar of face cream, and a few romance novels. She shook out a pill and dry-swallowed the white capsule, then sat up straight and crossed her legs like it was perfectly natural to sit naked on the edge of the bed in the middle of the morning.

Time flew by so fast. Before she'd know it, Butch would graduate high school and go off into the world, and she wouldn't even have her son to distract her from her hollow existence.

She picked up a bottle of Dexatrim and swallowed two pills.

Her heart hammered in her chest and a wave of dizziness drifted across her like a gust of cold air. The room started to spin. Splotches of black crept across the walls and beads of sweat formed at her hairline. The high-pitched ringing in her ears grew louder.

What happens after Butch leaves?

She knew the simple answer to that question: she'd be all alone with Wade. Waiting for him to come home after work, enclosed in that bubble of his. Just the two of them sitting at the dinner table, eating in awkward silence. Watching mediocre sitcoms together in the evening, but not exchanging a single word or laugh between the tracks of canned laughter. Taking turns in the bathroom, putting the seat down because he never remembered, brushing their teeth, washing their faces, then pulling on their pajamas, precisely in that order. After the lights went out, both rolling in the opposite direction. Lying next to her husband in an empty house, wondering if he was awake or, like her, pretending to be asleep, then rising at the same time every morning to fix poached eggs and English muffins and watch him drink his coffee and read his newspaper. Finally, after Wade shut the door behind him on his way to work, she'd clean the kitchen, go up the stairs and sit naked on the edge of the bed.

A pathetic moan escaped her lips, the sound making her sick to her stomach. She fell back on the bed, closed her eyes, and tried to will the panic attack away. But with her eyes closed, the silence only became louder. So loud that it hurt.

Her eyes snapped open and she stared up at the ceiling fan. The blades spun and whooshed, blowing air upon her bare skin, and it triggered a memory that she thought to be long buried. She and Cap on the Wyalusing Rocks, basking under the summer sun, a sweet breeze on their cheeks. Sitting on a musty blanket. Drinking a six-pack of Genesee Cream Ale. More drunk from one another's presence than the beer. The hum of semis rolling down Route 6 safely behind them. Nobody else in the world.

As the memories washed over her, Maggie wondered about what could have been. She also wondered, not for the first time, whether Cap still had thoughts about her and whether he, too, experienced any regrets.

The phone rang from downstairs. Once, twice, three times. She stood back up. Noticed that she was still naked. As she pulled on a plain blue housedress, her mind drifted from thoughts of Cap to what she would make for dinner. Maybe she'd make pork chops—Butch loved her fried pork chops.

4

The woman had not spoken.

Not a single word.

The snow continued to fall, slow and easy, making for poor visibility, so Cap kept his attention focused on the road. Route 6 was coated with frozen patches of black ice, and his wheels occasionally spun, causing the truck to drift before he managed to right its course.

He glanced over at the woman. She sat rigid and upright, like she might be thinking about flinging open the door and jumping out of the truck at any moment. He gave her a smile and she tried smiling back, but it was evident that the accident still had her rattled. That, or maybe riding in a truck with a complete stranger put her on edge.

"We'll drive up here a couple of miles and talk to Scott and Skeeter and see if they can tow that car of yours out of there."

The young woman stared at Cap's lips as he spoke. It seemed as if she was trying to figure him out or considering how she should answer, but she said nothing and merely nodded instead.

They rode for another minute and Cap shifted in his seat. Although he was accustomed to living in quiet, her peculiar silence was unsettling. Not that she was being rude or disrespectful, but the extended lulls of utter silence were unnerving.

"What happened back there, anyway?"

The woman clutched her purse tighter in her lap.

"Well, these roads are a mess right now. Must have hit a patch of ice or something."

She tilted her head—*maybe*.

They drove for another mile before Cap spoke again.

"You're not from around here, are you?"

She shook her head.

"Yeah, well, you don't look like you would be."

For the first time, a trace of a smile creased her lips, and she gave him a curious look.

"I mean you just don't look like other women in the area." Cap knew he was rambling. "That doesn't sound right, either."

Now the woman smiled, and it transformed her entire face. Gone was the wall of distrust and an air of innocence replaced all of that.

"My name is Cap. What's yours?"

The woman stared out the windshield and let out some air that sounded like a sigh. Her mouth drew straight, and her brow furrowed like she might be thinking about what to say, then she looked back at Cap, touched her lips, then ears, and shook her head.

Cap watched her for a moment, processing what she meant. "Oh. I see. You don't speak?"

She shook her head, then touched her ears again.

"Okay. I understand."

The truck rolled to a stop at the turnoff to Vandervort Road and Cap watched the woman unzip her purse and dig inside. She pulled out a small, black spiral-bound notebook and pencil, put the tip of lead to a sheet of paper and wrote something down, then held it up for him to see.

My name is Tess.

"Nice to meet you, Tess."

She nodded.

"So, you can read lips?"

If you talk slow.

He cranked up the heater a little bit. "Not that it makes any difference, but I'm a pastor, not some kind of nutcase."

She flipped her notebook to a new page and scribbled on the paper.

Thank you for helping me.

"You bet. Sorry about the accident. Could've been worse, though."

She didn't seem convinced.

"Well, once we get someplace with a phone, you want me to call someone for you? Your family? Husband, maybe?"

She shook her head and the walls went back up.

Cap waited for her to face him again before speaking.

"Where you from? If you don't mind me asking?"

She stared down at her notebook and thought about what she wanted to write. Then she scribbled a single word.

Nowhere.

Up ahead of the truck, flashes of brown streaked across the road—a couple of does followed by a ten-point buck.

"Well, as you might imagine, this area doesn't exactly have its pick of hotels, but there's a little motel and diner up the way that's supposed to be pretty clean, and they serve a nice breakfast."

He noticed a slight tremor in her hands.

"Someplace for you to sleep tonight."

She peered out the windshield for a moment before looking back at him. "You got money to pay for something like that?"

She didn't answer the question.

Cap's hand went to his mustache, and he tugged at the whiskers. "You sure there's no one I can call for you? Any family at all?"

No.

Tess closed her notebook, slipped it inside her purse, and turned away from Cap so that he couldn't look her directly in the eye.

5

Wade tried his damnedest to keep his thoughts focused on the spreadsheet before him—Agway's year-end inventory for feed, fertilizer, insecticides, and gardening supplies. He knew his father was waiting for the report so that he could, in turn, lecture Wade on the importance of not over-ordering supplies with a limited shelf life. His old man had been pestering him for the report since January, and here it was mid-March, and the damn thing still hadn't been completed.

All the columns and rows of codes and long numbers blurred together into one big splat of black ink. Wade rubbed at weary eyes, stood from his seat behind the desk, the top of his head a few inches from touching the seven-foot ceiling. Standing six-foot-five, with his long legs and arms, he had been one of the best high school basketball players Black Walnut had ever produced. But now, after twenty years of spending most of his days perched behind his desk or sitting in the truck hauling equipment and feed because his old man was too cheap to hire a regular driver, the beginning of a paunch formed above his beltline.

He paced his office like a caged tiger, restless and antsy. He could feel the nervous energy start down in his feet and work its way north. Walking it off didn't offer any relief, but he continued to pace anyway.

He stared down at his ledger, then at the handful of framed photos of Maggie and Butch arranged on his desk. A couple of school pictures of Butch in kindergarten, third grade, and sixth, the boy sprouting up and looking skinny and awkward, and so very different from Wade when he was the same age. There was one of Maggie back when she was thin and still wore her hair long and wild, the way he liked it. And then there was the picture Wade couldn't stand having on his desk—the three of them wearing matching bright red and green holiday sweaters. They looked ridiculous. Like a bunch of circus clowns. Each one of them wore broad, phony smiles. The picture looked like one of those obnoxious photos that come in a picture frame with the perfect family—the perfect, *happy, happy, happy* family.

Maggie had insisted on posing for this family portrait. She wanted to create a special holiday memory. When they arrived at the photo studio at the Sears up in Binghamton, and Maggie took those sweaters out of a box, Wade wanted to crawl under a rock and die. Then, to make matters worse, she handed the two of them elf caps.

He put his foot down and said, *Hell no,* but Maggie wouldn't hear it. She went through all the time to order the hats and thought it might be fun. *Fun? Over my dead body.* And for once in his life, Butch took Wade's side, making two against one. Maggie pouted and stewed but finally gave in and settled on just the Christmas sweaters.

Wade couldn't bear the sight of his family when the restlessness took hold of him, gripping him by the throat. It was as if his wife and son were watching him, waiting for him to make his next inevitable mistake.

This feeling of agitation came over him more and more frequently recently. What started as once a year soon became once every other month. Now, it seemed like the need reared its head every few weeks. It generally manifested with bouts of irritability and impatience. If Wade didn't do something to nip it in the bud, it evolved into sheer nastiness, all his thoughts jumbled and irrational. Fortunately, or unfortunately—depending on how you looked at it—Wade was self-aware enough to see all the signs.

He had tried turning to Maggie for help—he really had—but she was nothing more than a homemaker now, living in her own private bubble. The woman he married—feisty, funny, and unpredictable—had morphed into someone uptight and moody, and they barely shared anything in common anymore. She didn't like to talk about his work. Didn't approve of him drinking beers down at Red's. Certainly wouldn't watch Steelers games with him. They ate dinner together and slept in the same room—that was about it.

There proved to be only one sure way to shake him out of his funk. One means to cleanse himself of the damn affliction, but it left him bearing an overwhelming weight of guilt. And, of course, he felt shame for his actions. If the tables were turned and Maggie were the one burdened with the condition and alleviated it by the means he resorted to, he could not, would not allow it.

Back and forth he paced across his second-story office, from one wall to the next. He finally stopped and stared through the pane of glass that looked down at the store below. Harry Lane stood in the middle of the fertilizer aisle, giving poor, dumb Glenn an earful of what Wade figured to be about the increase in prices. It happened every year at this time. Harry was like all the other farmers in the area—putting up a fuss about price increases without even trying to understand that when the distributors upped their prices, so must Agway. It wasn't that complicated, but folks like Harry never saw it that way.

Wade watched Glenn straighten his apron, remove the pencil from behind an enormous ear, and slowly attempt a subtle retreat from Harry's rant. But as

Glenn backpedaled his way toward the safety of the storage room, Harry kept pace with the man, foot by foot, tile by tile.

He rubbed at his eyes and thought about getting a cup of coffee and a slice of rhubarb pie over at the Friedenshutten. He needed to get out of the office for a while, away from the ledger and reports and invoices that covered the better part of his desk.

He grabbed his wool coat on the hook by the window when his eyes happened upon the two registers at the front of the store. Carol operated register one, the same register she'd been working behind for the last thirty-some years. Carol might not be much to look at, but she was dependable and honest.

Then there was register two with Amy Fitzgerald, barely out of her teens. Amy bent down and picked some trash off the floor. Her jeans fit snug and left very little to the imagination. As she stood back up, he noticed how tight Amy's apron squeezed across her breasts.

Wade pressed his eyes closed, replaced his wool jacket on the hook, then returned his gaze toward Amy. His jaw tightened and his tongue slipped from between his lips out of sheer reflex.

He didn't try to fight the growing compulsion. He simply went back to his desk, flipped the picture of Maggie and Butch facedown, picked up the phone, dialed extension two, and waited for Amy to answer.

6

Ending the pain should've been easy, but it wasn't. She should've driven faster but didn't. At the last moment, Tess hit the brakes instead of the gas pedal. Human instinct kicking in, against her will.

Now she was stuck in the middle of nowhere and her car was in the bottom of a ravine.

She pressed her eyes closed and forced herself to breathe easy—to take small, deep breaths to keep the mounting panic at bay. She needed to keep it together. Stay calm. Think.

Tess opened her eyes and stared through the windshield toward the man who called himself Cap—a funny name for a grown man. Especially a pastor. He seemed nice enough, but something about him felt a little off—like he might be hiding something. At least he didn't speak slow and exaggerated like most people did after learning that she was deaf. Most people either tried to ignore her or spoke to her like she was a small child or mentally disabled.

Cap talked with two men who looked exactly the same, standing in front of an auto shop. Same height. Same weight and build. Same nose and cheekbones and color of hair. Both covered with grease. They smoked cigarettes, faces void of expression as they listened to what Cap was telling them. The only difference between the two men was that one sported a close-cropped beard, and the other did not.

Tess couldn't read Cap's lips from the truck, but he'd occasionally point in her direction, explaining the situation.

The truck engine idled. The vents blew a steady flow of warm air against her face. She felt sleepy even though she wasn't tired. Her eyes fell on the keys dangling in the ignition and she considered her options.

Her hands still shook a little as she replayed the final moments before her Pinto slid off the road and into the ditch. That moment—maybe two or three seconds—moved so slowly. Snow slapping against the windshield, the rumbling sensation of the car as it skidded off the road, the row of trees racing toward her, then closing her eyes and waiting for everything to be over in a split second.

She looked at Cap again. The first thing she had really noticed about the man was his harelip. Maybe he thought that his mustache concealed the flaw, but it did not. She knew why he tried to hide the crease in his lip—people could be so cruel. A defect was a defect. Didn't matter whether it was visible or not.

Tess found her eyes going back to the keys and she resisted the growing impulse that coursed through her—to slip behind the wheel and drive and keep driving until she woke from this nightmare. Then she felt the heaviness in her purse and that gave her some kind of comfort.

Cap dug into his pant pockets and extended some money toward the twins. The one with the beard accepted the cash and stuffed it in the front pocket of his overalls without saying a word.

Cap kept talking to the men about something. Both mechanics flicked their cigarettes to the ground in unison, then tapped out fresh cigarettes from their respective packs—even their brand of cigarettes was the same. They appeared to mimic one another without thinking about it. They would nod at the same time, in the same manner. When one shifted their leg or scratched at their face, so did the other. When one brother gazed at her sitting in the truck, the other followed suit.

Tess watched the mechanics smoke their cigarettes for a minute, dipped her hand inside her purse, and pulled out her own pack of cigarettes, but it was empty as she knew it would be. She crumpled the box and watched the twins smoke. Now all she could think about was a cigarette. Not the accident, nor her car, nor what she was going to do, nor where she'd go.

A cigarette. She needed a cigarette.

She swung open the door. Stepped out into a few inches of snow, pulled the strap of her purse tight across her shoulder and walked toward the three strangers.

Cap smiled and tilted his head. "Boys, this is Tess."

The two mechanics looked at her with mud-colored eyes. Their expressions weren't malicious or unkind, merely blank.

"Tess, this is Scott and Skeeter. They're going to try and get your car out of the ravine."

The one with the beard nodded.

"But I guess because of this storm, it'll have to wait a day or two." Cap looked to the twins. "You'll be able to tow it out, right?"

The one with the beard nodded again.

The four of them stood in the snow, not a word spoken between them for twenty seconds, but it felt like twenty minutes.

Tess waited for something to happen, but nothing did. Finally, Cap turned to her so that she could read his lips.

"You left your keys in the car, Tess?"

She nodded.

Cap blew on his hands and said, "Well."

Tess opened her purse and took out her notebook and flipped it to a page that had already been filled out, then held it up to the mechanics.

Thank you.

Scott and Skeeter looked at the notebook, then to Tess. Their eyes shifted to Cap for a moment before settling back on Tess. They sucked on their cigarettes and nodded in unison.

Tess stuck her notebook back in her purse, then motioned to their cigarettes and touched her mouth.

The mechanics weren't sure how to respond, so they gazed at Cap instead.

"I think Tess would like a cigarette."

Tess nodded that she did.

The one without the beard offered his box of Marlboros. Tess tapped one out, and when she tried to hand the pack back, he waved it off and spoke for the first time. "Keep it."

The other twin dug in his pocket for his Zippo and cupped the flame for her. Tess pulled hard on the cigarette, and when she exhaled, a sigh of relief escaped her lungs as well as a cloud of smoke.

The three of them smoked in silence, side by side with Cap, until their cigarettes burned down to the filters.

7

It wasn't as if Robin hated Chuck, but she sure wasn't in love with him anymore. It had been years since she felt any kind of love for her husband. She was more afraid of him than anything else. And if she was being honest with herself, the feelings that she experienced for Chuck when they married ten years ago were more than likely fueled by the desire to get away from her father and the awful things he forced Robin to do.

Besides, what did she really know back then? She had been barely eighteen and Chuck had been her one and only boyfriend in high school.

But the man lying on top of her now wasn't even close to the kind of man she had dreamed of growing old with.

When Chuck returned home after drinking at Red's, the moment he walked through the door, she caught that look of his—that dull expression he wore like a Halloween mask after a dozen beers. The outcome was inevitable, one plus one equaled two, and she preferred to get it over with. She put the kids to bed early even though they pitched a fit and acted like it was the end of the world.

Chuck thrust in and out of her with little grace—merely a race to finish. He was drunk and time moved differently for him. For Robin, it felt like it was taking him an eternity.

Robin stared up at the ceiling and noticed that the water stains were getting worse. There was a leak in the roof that wouldn't get fixed anytime soon. Probably never. It was just one more item on a growing list of house repairs—a broken hot water heater, the septic tank that desperately needed to be pumped, and the furnace that blew nothing but cold air. They lived in a house that was falling apart quicker than their marriage.

She forced her eyes shut, sweeping herself from the present to the past, returning to a time right after high school when she and Alex had experimented for the very first time. This was her safe place—just she and Alex, and where the rest of the world didn't exist. Robin had revisited memories of Alex more and more the last few years, replaying their adolescent explorations to mask her disgust at making love with Chuck. Although she never actually considered what Chuck did *making love*—he merely fucked her.

As Chuck grunted atop her, she could smell the beer on his breath, and she wanted to scream out for him to stop, to finish, to climb off her. Instead, Robin pushed away reality and imagined Alex's sweet kisses, envisioned Alex's tongue exploring her breasts. She kept thinking about Alex's tender hands and blue eyes, and those private moments that Robin kept stored away brought her to a powerful finish like they always did.

Chuck's body tensed up and she knew he was close. She tried to keep her mind focused on Alex, but thoughts of money and bills and her marriage proved too much. She pressed her head into the pillow and fought the urge to scream out.

Chuck finally rolled off her without fanfare, no final kiss. She lay rigid, listened to her husband draw breath, felt the rise and fall of his chest. Chuck didn't say anything. Didn't ask how her day had been or mention that he forgot to pick up milk and cereal for the kids' breakfast but had remembered to stop and buy himself a carton of cigarettes.

Robin knew she should let him pass out, that now wasn't the time to speak up, but she couldn't help herself. "Did you look for some work today?"

His body stiffened next to her.

"Shit. That the first thing you got to say?"

Robin stared at the ceiling once again. "We're in trouble—"

Chuck bolted upright. "Not right now."

"We barely have enough money to buy groceries, Chuck."

"Bullshit. We got enough."

"No, we don't. The kids need new winter clothes. Darla's growing fast."

"They got what they need." Chuck pulled on his jeans and T-shirt.

"We can't keep going on like this."

He spun toward Robin, his face smeared by the dusk light peeking in through the window. "Ain't my goddamn fault I got let go."

But, in fact, it *was* Chuck's fault. Over the years, he had been issued multiple warnings at Taylor's meatpacking plant for his negative attitude and unprofessional behavior. Showing up late to work repeatedly, giving his supervisor lip, and then the final straw—drinking during his lunch break and cold-cocking Del Benscooter for eating his meatloaf sandwich. Del received nine stitches on his eyebrow, and Chuck received his walking papers.

Robin sat up in bed, and when she tucked her dirty blonde hair behind her ears, she looked so young. She barely looked old enough to drink, let alone old enough to have three young kids. She was neither pretty nor unattractive. Merely plain and unremarkable, with a face that most people easily overlooked.

"What about Sylvania? Or the Charmin plant? Aren't they hiring?"

Chuck searched the floor for his boots. "We've already been through this."

"Dale works up at Sylvania, doesn't he? Maybe if you ask him—"

"They ain't hiring."

"You sure? Can't hurt to ask."

Chuck dropped back on the bed and laced up his boots.

"I heard that the high school needs a janitor."

"Fuck that."

"What? Work is work."

"I ain't a fucking janitor."

"We need to do something, Chuck. I only work at the church two days a week and with you drinking down at Red's every day—"

Robin didn't see the back of his hand coming. Didn't see the sneer spread across his face. Instead, she felt the dull impact on her cheek. A flash of white blossomed in front of her. Her head snapped back and banged against the wall. Her vision blurred and she could feel her heart thudding in her ears.

"Shut-the-fuck-up. You hear me?"

She watched as Chuck's face transformed into her father's. They were the same kind of man. Taking what they wanted, when they wanted. The shock from the slap was quickly replaced by anger—dull, raging anger. She sprang off the bed and clawed at his face, but Chuck grabbed her by the neck and heaved her to the floor.

He glared down at her. Waiting to see if she might come at him again. "I'm sick and tired of hearing you run your mouth every goddamn day. All you do is bitch, bitch, bitch, and I ain't gonna put up with it no more."

Robin kicked him in the shin, which prompted Chuck to kick her back. Once in the leg. Another to the ribs.

"You done, woman?"

She grunted.

"That's about what I thought." He grabbed his wallet off the dresser and thudded out of the bedroom, cussing as he went.

Robin heard the front door slam. The truck fire up. Gravel peppered the side of the house. Robin waited as the night grew quiet. She sat on the floor, sucking in air, fingers touching at the tenderness on her cheek. It hurt to swallow, and she hoped that she wouldn't bruise. She tried not to cry, but her eyes burned hot, and the tears began to flow.

The patter of tiny feet approached.

"Mama?"

Robin peered up at Darla, who clung to the doorframe, looking so small and scared.

"Mama?"

"Go back to bed, baby. I'll be there in a sec."

Darla lingered at the doorway for a moment, then slinked away, silent as a shadow.

Robin wiped at her eyes. Grabbed a robe hanging off the bedpost, then found some Kleenex to clean the sex from between her legs. She made her way down the darkened hallway and poked her head into the kids' room. The overhead light still burned white in the tiny space that could barely fit the bunk beds and a third mattress down on the floor—her sweet babies stuffed into their bedroom like sardines in a tin can.

She checked on the boys first—Mikey and Chuck Junior, six and seven, curled up under the covers on the bunk bed, sound asleep. She kissed Chuck Junior on the cheek and brushed the hair from Mikey's eyes. The poor kid needed a haircut, but she'd have to do it herself since they couldn't afford to take him to Colgrove's for a proper cut.

Darla's big eyes tracked her every movement from under the blankets.

"Hey, sweet thing. You having trouble sleeping?"

Darla nodded.

Robin stroked her cheek.

"Is Papa mad again?"

"No, baby."

"Where'd he go?"

Robin felt her eyes burn once again. "He went out for a while. He'll be back."

"My tummy feels funny."

"It's okay. Mama's here." She stared down at her four-year-old daughter, hoping and praying that Darla wouldn't end up like her, marrying young and settling for someone less than she deserved. Robin hoped that Darla might get the chance at a better life, maybe go off to college and escape this town that had nothing left to offer.

She kept stroking Darla's cheek and hummed *Hush Little Baby* until the girl's eyes grew heavy and eventually fluttered shut. She shushed away all the bad thoughts from her daughter's mind until her breath drew steady and relaxed, and Darla fell into a fitful slumber.

Robin kept humming, smelling the oil and sweat in her daughter's hair, and wishing that life was different. She tucked the blankets around her youngest child, snapped off the light, and made her way downstairs to the kitchen. She ran a sponge under the faucet, then wiped down the counters and kitchen table. The sink sat full of dirty dinner dishes, but she didn't have it in her to tackle them in her current state. Instead, she poured a glass of Diet Coke, opened a drawer, pulled out a few old telephone books, and finally found what she was looking for: the 1978 yearbook from Black Walnut High School. She sat down at the kitchen table, lit a cigarette, and flipped through the pages.

She recognized all the familiar faces of the kids, most of whom still lived in the area, then came to the page she had been searching for. Black and white photos of her classmates. Girls with big, poofy hair parted down the middle, and boys with either shaggy bangs hanging over their eyes or a country buzz-cut.

Her finger traced the glossy page, pausing on the photo of Alexandra

Anderson smiling her gap-toothed grin. Even though the picture was in black and white, Robin remembered Alex's sparkling blue eyes. She wondered where Alex might be now, and if the girl—a woman now—ever thought about their intimate encounters. She figured that she probably didn't.

She stared down at the photo and continued to drink her soda while smoking a cigarette. Her heart felt that familiar ache, and she didn't move a muscle when one of the boys cried out upstairs with a nightmare.

8

Even though his mother blabbed on and on while barely taking a breath, all Butch could hear was the sound of his father chewing. He chewed louder than anybody he knew. The constant slurping, smacking, and crunching triggered a growing spike of anger. It hadn't always been this bad. Started as mild annoyance when Butch was around twelve years old. The sound of chewing made him uncomfortable and anxious. But over time, his response had developed into a simmering rage.

"This is the last year I'm planning the Easter parade," Maggie announced. "It's too much work. And not only that, nobody ever bothers to show a little gratitude. Not even a single thank-you."

"You say this every year," Wade mumbled mid-chew.

Butch stared at his father, who methodically chomped on an ear of corn, from one end to the next, completely unaware that two kernels clung to his chin.

"I mean it this year," Maggie sniffed. "Jed Belcher said he can't be the bunny this year, and I don't know who I'll get to replace him."

"Well, don't look at me," Wade declared.

Butch swirled his mashed potatoes around with a fork, watched his father shake more salt on his corn, and tried blocking out what his mother jabbered on about. That was another thing that drove him nuts—when his parents talked with their mouths full.

Wade caught Butch staring. Set his ear of corn down and took a sip of milk. "What?"

Butch gazed down at his plate. "Nothing."

"Your homework done?"

"Not all of it."

"No TV after dinner until it's done."

"Okay."

"I mean it. I don't want you falling behind."

"Leave him alone, Wade. He always finishes his homework," Maggie interjected.

"I didn't say that he doesn't. Just stated that he can't watch television until his homework is finished."

"You sound like a broken record. I think he understands the rules by now."

Wade sighed, rolled his eyes, and slumped in his chair all in one exaggerated motion. "Can I have a conversation with my son? Would that be possible?"

"Please. By all means. We're all ears."

Wade cut her a look before continuing. "Baseball season starts up here pretty soon."

"Uh-huh."

"Thought any more about trying out for the team?"

Butch shook his head. He hoped the subject to be closed but didn't get off that easily.

"Why not?"

"I dunno."

"That isn't much of an answer."

His father had a point, but it was the same answer he'd given last year and the year before that.

Maggie passed Wade a platter stacked with corn on the cob. "Have another ear."

Wade set one on his plate and proceeded to smother it with butter and salt. "I think once you're in high school, you should try out for the team. It'll be good for you."

Butch shrugged. "Maybe."

"What's the matter? You don't like baseball?"

"You know that he doesn't like baseball, Wade. Or football. Or basketball. None of that silly stuff." She patted Butch on the knee. "Isn't that right?"

Butch glared at his mother and wished that she would shut up for one single second. "I like them. What are you talking about?"

"No, you don't, Butch. And that's okay."

Wade rolled his eyes and sighed once again. "I think the boy is capable of deciding for himself."

Maggie ignored the remark and held the platter of corn in front of Butch. "Have some more corn, Butch."

"No, thanks."

"You always have two ears. Want me to cut it off the cob the way you like it?"

"Christ, Mags. You want to chew it for him, too?"

"Oh, stop it, Wade. Just because you had a bad day at work, that's no reason to be all moody and bossy."

"You stop it. He's fourteen. Not four."

Maggie proceeded to cut the corn off a cob and onto Butch's plate.

"It would be good for you to get out there," Wade announced. "Make some friends, maybe."

Butch knew it was a waste of time to argue. "Fine."

"He doesn't want to, Wade."

"Well, I think he should. Young boys are supposed to play sports."

"And who died and made you king?"

Butch felt like standing up and screaming at his parents to *Shut the hell up and leave me the fuck alone.* But he didn't and probably never would. "I said *fine.*"

Maggie acted as if Butch wasn't even there. "He's not like you, Wade. He doesn't like sports. He's more the artist type. Writing stories and using his imagination and whatnot."

"Writing stories and using his imagination? And where exactly is that going to get him in life?"

"The same place playing sports got you, probably." She stared at Wade and dared him to challenge her.

Wade took a calming breath, leaned forward, and spoke emphatically. "Playing sports teaches you how to be part of a team. How the only way to win is by working together. Every person out there has to contribute and sacrifice and do whatever they need to do in order to help their team win. *That's* what playing sports does for a person."

Maggie tilted her head, a patronizing smile settling upon her face. "You have corn stuck on your chin."

Butch slid his chair back and stood up.

"Where are you going?" his mother asked.

"Homework."

"You want some peach cobbler?"

"Maybe later."

Butch walked out of the kitchen but could feel his father's eyes tracking him the entire way. He held his breath and marched down the hallway. When he reached the staircase, he heard the words start to fly. *Goddamn this* and *Goddamn that.*

He stomped upstairs to his bedroom. Shut and locked the door behind him. He heard the scrape of chairs on the floor as his parents bickered and yelled over one another.

He slumped behind his desk and pushed his schoolbooks off to the side. Slipped on a pair of headphones and stuck a new cassette into his boom box.

I was born to run. I was born to dream. The craziest boy you ever seen. I gotta do it my way.

He opened his desk drawer and took out his notebook and a handful of pens. He flipped to a blank page and stared out his window as snow tumbled down.

Well, I've had all I can take. I can't take it no more. I'm gonna pack all my bags and fly, baby. Or no way at all.

He looked down at the blank page and put the tip of a black pen to the paper.

So why don't you turn me loose? Turn me loose. Turn me loose. I gotta do it my way, or no way at all.

Butch tried blocking out all the noise in his head—his parents, baseball, homework, getting picked on at school every single day—but he couldn't. Tried to think of something to write, something to create that was his and only his, but he couldn't come up with one single thing.

9

"Can I fix you a drink of some kind?"

Tess sat at the kitchen table, her purse on her lap, appearing neither comfortable nor relaxed. *Yes, please.*

Cap took two glasses from the cabinet and set them down on the counter. "I've got bourbon and vodka. Might even have a few bottles of beer in the refrigerator." He opened the liquor cabinet and poked around. He pointed to the bottle of Wild Turkey, but Tess shook her head. When he held up a fifth of vodka, she nodded.

"Mixed with a little orange juice okay with you?"

Yes.

Cap filled their glasses with ice, poured a few fingers of vodka in one topped with orange juice, then a bourbon on the rocks for himself. He settled into the seat across from her, sipped at his drink, and let out a long sigh.

"Sorry about all this. Probably not exactly what you were hoping for when you woke up this morning."

She tasted her drink. *No.*

They drank in the quiet for a minute. When Cap looked at her, she would hold his gaze, but he had a hard time knowing what might be going on inside that head of hers.

"You hungry?"

No.

"Good. I like to relax a little with a drink or two before I eat something."

Both stared out the window above the kitchen sink. White flakes of snow kissed the glass and melted on contact, turning clear before running down the window. Cap glanced at Tess, who seemed to be watching the snow, but maybe she was looking past it, toward something out there he didn't know about.

Before he knew it, they both finished their drinks, and when he offered her a refill, she accepted.

"I thought you could stay the night down in the old rectory inside the church. It's nothing fancy, but the bed's comfortable and you'll have your privacy. And if you need anything, just run up here to the house. Door will be open."

Thank you.

Tess took out the pack of cigarettes that Scott and Skeeter had given her, packed it against her palm, and lit one up.

Cap grabbed an ashtray from under the sink and watched her smoke for a moment. He wasn't sure what to say or what to do. Having a stranger in his house—especially a woman—felt odd.

She removed her notebook from her purse and wrote something down. *How did you get the name Cap?*

He sipped at his drink before answering. "Well, my given name is Evan, but when I was a little kid, around five or six, I wouldn't go anywhere without wearing a baseball cap. School, the store, inside, outside. Even to bed at night. So, my parents started calling me Cap and the name kinda stuck."

Tess smiled briefly before writing down another question. *Do you live alone?*

"I do."

She looked away. Played with her cigarette a little.

"Look. I'm sure all of this is strange. The accident. Sitting in a strange house with someone that you don't even know."

Yes.

"If you like, I can take you to the motel and get you a room."

Cap watched as she considered the offer but couldn't tell what she was thinking.

It's okay. I'll stay here.

They sipped their drinks in silence, and Cap could feel the slow tug of alcohol wash over him. "If you don't mind me asking, have you always been deaf?"

Since I was six. Meningitis.

"Oh. I see. Has to be difficult."

No. She scribbled something else on the paper. *I prefer the quiet.*

Cap read her words. Took another drink, then read them again. "I can understand that."

Most people don't.

He tugged at his mustache. "That doesn't surprise me."

I can't read your lips when you cover your mouth.

He moved his hand away. "Sorry. I was just saying that I wasn't surprised. About the quiet. People are afraid of what they don't understand."

You like the quiet, too?

"Yeah. Guess I do."

Is that why you're not married?

He smiled. Looked down at his fingers. "The answer to that might require another drink or two."

She tried to smile back, but Cap saw something broken in her eyes.

"Look, I know that it's none of my business, but I get the feeling that you're running away from something. Or someone."

She stubbed out her cigarette and studied him for a moment.

"Sorry if I'm being too forward. Part of my job is reading people."

Ever wrong?

"More times than not."

She gave him a look that made him a little uneasy—as if she compensated for being deaf with the ability to see deeper into people. It was clear she was not going to answer his question. At least not tonight.

"Well, I hope that wherever you end up, you find what you're looking for."

Tess closed her notebook, slipped it into her purse, and finished the last of her vodka and orange juice.

"I'll get dinner started. Help yourself to another drink if you want."

But she was staring out the window again and didn't see his lips move.

10

The rectory bedroom smelled like an elderly person's home—the odor of mothballs and musty linens enveloped Tess like a blanket. The room was small with a low ceiling. It felt empty and lifeless as if it hadn't been used in many years. An oil painting of Christ hung above the queen-sized bed, his eyes pressed closed, hands clasped in prayer. Next to the bed stood a large dresser with an arched mirror eaten up by black age spots along its edges. A white ceramic bowl containing dried rose petals, bottles of perfume with old-fashioned atomizers, and a dog-eared Bible sat atop the dresser.

Tess felt the vibration of Cap's footsteps walking down the church hallway outside the bedroom. She waited until they faded away before she turned the lock on the door.

She stood at the threshold and could feel the presence of the former occupants—cold and impersonal. Something about the room felt wrong. It was a nagging feeling, like she was someplace she shouldn't be. A trespasser. An unwanted guest. Or maybe she was just feeling nervous and jumpy. Her life had flipped upside down in the last twenty-four hours. The life she knew—or thought she knew—was no more. What she thought was truth had only been lies. Normalcy had morphed into the unimaginable. Thinking about how quickly she had lost everything caused her eyes to burn.

She peered up at the painting of Christ again, then set her purse on the bed and went about doing what she needed to do. Took one of the feather pillows and shook it loose from its case, then climbed up on the bed and draped the material across the painting.

Once finished with that task, she removed the Bible from the dresser. Pulled open a drawer. Then another and another. The odor of mothballs pulled at her eyes. Each drawer filled with folded women's sweaters and nightgowns. She placed the Bible under a shirt in the bottom drawer and shoved them all closed with her hip.

Next, she switched off the overhead light, felt her way through the darkness, and sat down on a chair next to a window. The absence of light made her wish she could stay in the dark forever.

As her eyes adjusted to the dark, she noticed a closet door in the corner of the room. The door appeared closed, but part of her wanted—*needed*—to make sure that the door was latched. Another part urged her to fling open the door and check to see if the Man in Blue were hiding inside.

She pressed her eyes shut and waited for the darkness to put her in the place where she needed to be, and then repeated to herself: *The closet is empty. You are safe. The closet is empty. You are safe.*

One final breath and her eyes reopened. She peeled back the curtain and stared out through the window. The night was black and still, and she felt a draft of cold air sneaking in from a crack in the windowpane. She wondered what Aaron was doing. Would he be searching for her yet? She knew that he probably was. She wondered whether he would eventually find her, and she knew the answer to that as well.

The weight of her purse sat heavy upon her lap and that gave her a strange sense of comfort. Her hand found its way inside the bag, and she felt the cold steel press against her palm.

THIRTEEN DAYS BEFORE GOOD FRIDAY

11

Robin hated driving Chuck's old Chevy—the truck was falling apart faster than they could keep up with the repairs. Rusted out from sixteen hard years of traveling on salted roads, the shocks were shot, the clutch kept slipping and would need to be replaced sooner than later, and the entire cab reeked of exhaust from a leak in the muffler system.

Until four months ago, Robin used the Pontiac Firebird, which wasn't in much better shape. At least it didn't stink of exhaust, but soon after Chuck got himself fired from Taylor's, they'd had to sell one of their vehicles. And Chuck being Chuck said it was a no-brainer—sell the damn Firebird. Robin didn't argue or put up a fuss. There was no use in complaining. It was either Chuck's way or the highway.

She turned off Heller Hill Road and onto Marbaker Road, which wound its way down a few miles toward the Black Walnut Presbyterian Church. She'd been working at the church every Wednesday for the last few years, helping Cap with the bookkeeping and some light administration duties like mailing get-well cards to folks that were ill, and keeping the parish roster updated with members' addresses, telephone numbers, and birthdays. Robin initially took the job to earn a little pocket money since Chuck was so tight when it came to giving her a dime to spend on herself. But after Chuck's dismissal, that pocket money became essential for household expenses.

When Cap found out about Robin's financial situation, he asked if she'd be willing to come in on Fridays as well. Cap was good that way. Even gave her a twenty-five cent an hour raise. He never made a big deal of it, presenting the opportunity like she'd be filling a dire need and doing him a favor in the process.

Robin didn't notice the one-hundred-and-sixty-pound buck standing alongside the road until it was too late. The truck's barking muffler spooked the stag, and instead of bounding into the woods, it sprang across the road. She jammed down hard on the brake pedal, skidded on a patch of ice, and clipped the buck in the hindquarters. Metal buckled and glass shattered. The deer flipped into the ditch, flailing and twisting something awful. The truck continued its slide across the ice, skidding off the road before jerking to a stop a few feet from an old maple tree blackened by a strike of lightning.

Robin's hands clutched the steering wheel with ten white knuckles. Her heart thudded in her chest so fast that she didn't know if it would ever slow down. A hissing sound broke the quiet and a wisp of smoke drifted from under the hood. Then she heard an awful grunting sound from the ditch.

She shoved the door open with her shoulder and stepped out onto the snow-packed road, where the bawling sound got louder and more urgent. She walked to the front of the truck, ran her hand across the crumpled hood, and noticed that the driver's side headlight was busted out.

Weeds thrashed in front of her, and the bleating of the injured buck filled the still country air. Every part of her wanted to climb back into the truck, drive away and forget about what just happened. But she knew she couldn't. Couldn't leave the animal behind without knowing its condition. She checked the road, hoping to spot another car, but nobody was coming, nor would they, since the only time Marbaker Road saw much activity was on Sunday as folks headed to church.

The wail of the buck turned wet and ragged as the animal retched up fluid. She forced her feet forward across patches of ice and clods of frozen dirt. A few stalks of brown pussy willow flashed in front of her as she stepped into the ditch and peered at the sight before her.

The stag's black eyes stared right back at her, tongue protruding from its mouth, panting fast, specks of red mixed in with the white foam oozing from its throat. The deer's back legs splayed at one hundred and eighty degrees, shattered and useless.

Robin's hand slapped over her mouth but couldn't suppress a horrified gasp. The buck kept staring at her, eyes wet and bulging in terror, and tried to scramble away.

With her hand still clutching at her face, Robin backed away from the deer, pressed her eyes closed until she bumped up against the truck fender. She fumbled with the door handle. Climbed inside and discovered that the truck was still idling. She threw the Chevy into reverse and the wheels spun in slush, kicking slop every which way before rocking back onto the road. She avoided looking in the rearview mirror as she jammed the gear into drive and pulled away. She only drove a few yards before slamming on the brakes and pressing her forehead against the steering wheel.

Robin closed her eyes once again and considered her options. She could go back home and ask Chuck for help, but she knew he either wouldn't care or would be out drinking somewhere.

The other option hung right behind her head.

She sat for a minute, forced to listen to the buck grunt and discharge blood from its lungs, then climbed out of the truck. Took a breath, reached inside the cab, and removed the .30-.06 from the gun rack. She figured Chuck would have a box of shells in the glove compartment and she was right.

She loaded a shell into the chamber like Chuck had shown her once years ago, then switched off the safety and climbed back into the ditch.

12

The storm had passed sometime during the night, leaving behind powder blue skies with barely any wind to speak of. A murder of crows fluttered overhead, soaring from one bare alder tree to the next, cawing as they flapped and swooped through the crisp winter air, their chatter pricking holes in the country quiet.

Cap and Tess walked down the steps of the house and made their way toward the church at the bottom of the hill, each carrying a mug of coffee. Tess stared up at the church steeple, piled with a few inches of snow. Inside the open spire hung a large brass bell with a thick rope that kids got a kick out of tugging on before church services.

Cap scrutinized her profile and had a hard time telling exactly how old she might be. In broad daylight, with the snow illuminating her face, there didn't appear to be a single wrinkle or flaw. She looked like she could be as young as twenty-five.

She caught him staring, then gestured toward the steeple.

"They don't make churches like this anymore."

Tess kept looking up at the bell like she was waiting for it to ring out.

Inside, Cap sat in the front pew, a perspective he wasn't accustomed to, while Tess wandered around the church, her fingers tracing the stained-glass windows and the wooden armrests. She climbed the three steps to the pulpit and peered up at the vaulted ceiling thirty feet above her.

She took in every inch of the sanctuary like it might be her first time in a church. The windows and chandeliers and the dais and altar and hymn books. But when her eyes fell upon the ten-foot carving of Christ hanging from a cross, something shifted and changed inside her. Something visible. She looked away from the crucifix and gazed around the church like she was searching for something in particular.

She finally sat next to Cap and they stared up at the pulpit like they were waiting for a sermon to begin. Cap sipped his coffee as she put pencil to paper.

Have you always lived in this town?

"Born and raised. I escaped for a few years when I went off to college."

Escaped?

"Maybe that's too strong of a word. I like being in a small town. I do, but sometimes it feels a little bit like living under a microscope."

No anonymity?

He let out a wry chuckle. "None whatsoever. Especially in a profession like mine. Can't even go to the market without someone bending my ear about something that's weighing on them."

Did you always want to be a pastor?

"Definitely not. Probably the *last* thing I wanted to be."

What do you really want to do?

Cap rubbed at his jaw and gave that some thought before answering. "I don't know exactly. But being a pastor isn't all that bad. Worse things to be, I guess."

But if you don't like it, why do you do it?

"You're pretty direct, aren't you?"

Yes.

"And you ask lots of questions."

Yes.

"Well, I guess the honest answer is that I did it because I had to."

Why?

"That's a long story."

Silence fell between them once again, neither one of them feeling the need to speak. They sat that way for a minute. Maybe two.

I've always been afraid of churches.

"Really? What's to be afraid of?"

Her right hand gestured toward the entirety of the church before writing in her notebook.

The quiet in a church is different.

"I suppose you're right, but most people take some kind of comfort in that." She shook her head.

This kind of quiet feels wrong.

Cap caught himself playing with his mustache and pulled his hand away before responding. "Well. For some, it's a time to get away from all the noise and distractions in their day. No bosses. No responsibilities. None of that."

I feel like I'm being judged in here.

"You're not supposed to be. That's not what it's about."

And if you don't believe in God?

Cap shifted on the bench before answering. "I take it that you're not a believer?"

No.

"I see."

Tess gave him a bemused look before writing in her notebook.

Aren't you supposed to try and convince me to believe?

Cap stared into her eyes for a moment. Her expression so serious, like she was challenging him, daring him to try. He looked down at his feet and noticed the water leaking from the soles of his boots, pooling on the hardwood floors.

"I'm not that kind of pastor, Tess."

What kind are you?

Cap let out a laugh. "Still trying to figure that out, I guess."

Maybe it was the quiet of the church or being comfortable in Tess's presence, but whatever the reason, he began to utter words that had only been unspoken thoughts buried deep inside him for the last fourteen years—questions and doubts all scrambled together.

"I guess I don't know what I believe, to be honest with you."

Tess's eyes went from his lips to his eyes, watching and waiting.

"Faith is . . . well, it's tough. Grasping at something that isn't really real—not like you and I sitting here right now. Flesh and bone. Or this church. Wood and stone. Those things are real. You don't have to believe in them because you can reach out and touch them."

He stared down at his hands, searching for something he knew he might never find.

"But with God or any kind of religion, you've just got to take that leap of faith. Like jumping off a cliff in the dark. You just don't know what's really out there. And you don't know how far the bottom might be."

Are you this honest with your congregation?

"No, Tess, I'm not. But sitting here with you right now, I feel like I'm in some kind of confessional."

They sat in the quiet for a moment, with only the wind rattling the windowpanes.

Cap noticed that her hand shook a little as she scribbled in her notebook.

Why are you being so kind?

"Well, I might not be good at much, but I like helping where I can. Why? You're not used to people wanting to help?"

Tess's fingers went to the hem of her jeans, worn thin at the knees, and Cap couldn't help but notice that her hands didn't match the rest of her—fingernails chewed down, the tips red and raw. They had seen hard days.

Tess noticed his scrutiny of her hands and quickly tucked them back into the pockets of her jacket.

"You don't have to answer this because you don't owe me a thing, but was the situation you left bad?"

Yes.

"Somebody hurting you, maybe?"

Yes.

"If that's the case, and I believe that it is, shouldn't you notify the police?"

When Tess laughed, it was the first sound he had heard her make since meeting her. It seemed foreign and odd, and it made him wonder what her voice might sound like.

The police won't do anything.

"Why not? Have you gone to them before?"

She simply held up the same words to him and stared at him with an intensity that made his stomach uneasy. He rubbed his palms against his knees and straightened his back, searching for something—for the right thing—to say.

"I'd like to help you, Tess. Any way I can. If you'd tell me a little more about where you come from and who's hurting you, I think I could help you."

She smiled at his words, at the kindness he offered, but Cap had seen that look of hopelessness before. It was the expression of futility, thinking that he didn't know the half of it.

She closed her notebook and placed it inside her purse, then grabbed her pack of cigarettes and motioned toward the door. She didn't wait for his response. She simply stood up and walked down the center aisle of the church and pushed open the doors.

Cap remained seated and watched her step out into the glare of sunlight reflecting off the snow, then the doors thudded closed, leaving him all alone inside his sanctuary.

13

The report of the gunshot still reverberated in her ears, but Robin wasn't sure whether the sound was real or her imagination. What she did know was real was the smell of gunpowder on the sleeve of her jacket and that her hands rattled against the steering wheel.

Chuck would give her all kinds of grief for not being more careful. They could live with a broken headlight and dented hood, but if the truck suffered mechanical problems, she didn't know where they would find the money to have it fixed. Maybe if she told Chuck about the buck, he could end up selling some of the meat. That might be her only way out of this mess. The last thing she needed right now was to give him any reason to be nastier to her and the kids.

As the truck rounded the final switchback on the way to the church, the last moment of the stag watching her with its big, black eyes, waiting for her to pull the trigger, flashed in her mind. She couldn't shake the image. One second the buck stared at her, chest heaving and steam billowing from its snout, the next, after that awful crack of the rifle, the deer lay lifeless on the cold ground. Blood pumping through the hole in its neck, its hooves still twitching against the ice as if it was getting a running start toward the hands of death.

The truck crested the hill that led down toward the church and Robin spotted Cap tromping across the snow with a woman she had never seen before. The stranger wore a pair of blue jeans that were a little too tight, and her dark hair was cut and styled differently than anyone else's in the area. In fact, she looked like she might be a foreigner. From Greece or Italy, maybe.

When Cap noticed her truck, he flashed that disconcerting grin of his and waved.

Robin pulled the truck back behind the church and parked where she always parked. Quickly checked her reflection in the rearview mirror and noticed a speck of deer blood on her cheek. When she wiped off the blood, it caused her to wince. The side of her face was still red and tender from where Chuck had left his mark. She brushed her hair over the welt, then stepped out to greet Cap and the stranger.

Cap examined the front end of Robin's truck and leaned away from the smoke that continued to leak out from under the hood. "By the looks of things, I'd say that you had a run-in with a deer or a very large mailbox."

Robin glanced at the woman at Cap's side and was taken aback by her stunning eyes—big and green, with long, exotic eyelashes. Something about the way the stranger looked at her made Robin feel like her eyes burrowed into a place deep inside her that she thought to be hidden.

She tore her gaze away from the stranger and forced a smile at Cap. "The poor thing jumped out right in front of me."

"It's a wonder that I've never hit one before. Had plenty of close calls."

Robin noticed a few clumps of fur stuck in the grill of the truck. "Didn't kill it, though. Just broke its hind legs. I had to put him down."

The woman beside Cap cocked her head at the mention of killing the deer, and her eyes seemed to be judging Robin.

Robin held the stranger's gaze and she felt butterflies flutter inside her belly. "I didn't have a choice." She forced her eyes away from the woman—looking at her made Robin nervous somehow. "Chuck carries a rifle in his truck. It was in pain. I had to do it."

The stranger dug in her purse and scribbled in a notebook. Then she held the page up to Robin.

You shot it?

Robin stared at the page. Read the words. Looked at the woman for a moment before turning to Cap.

"This is Tess. She's deaf, but she can read lips." Then, catching himself, Cap looked at both women with an apologetic smile. "Robin's my right hand in the church. Takes care of everything above and beyond my very limited capabilities."

Tess extended her hand to Robin to introduce herself.

Robin hesitated before grasping Tess's hand in hers. "I didn't want to kill it. I really didn't." She held onto Tess's hand for a few moments longer than necessary, then flushed red when Tess finally pulled away and shoved her hand in her jacket pocket.

The three of them stood there beside the truck, stuck in awkward silence until Cap motioned toward Robin's cheek. "Got yourself a pretty nasty welt there."

Robin's hand went to her face and covered the lump that Chuck had left behind. "Must have bumped it on the steering wheel when I hit the deer."

"Want me to grab some ice?"

"I'll be fine. Thank you, though."

When Robin looked back at Tess, she noticed the way the woman stared at her cheek and could tell that Tess knew she was lying.

"Well, I should be getting to work. Lots to do. Nice to meet you, Tess." Robin turned her back to Cap and Tess and had to resist the urge to run.

ELEVEN DAYS BEFORE GOOD FRIDAY

14

Tess was alone in the house for the first time. Cap said he'd be gone for a few hours and to make herself at home, but as she gazed around the living room, she couldn't put herself at ease. Something felt off. It was clean and organized, but no photographs adorned the walls or shelves. No knick-knacks or clutter or souvenirs from vacations or trips. It seemed stripped of personality, and she wondered what kind of person could live in a house like that. It was as if the rooms were preserved, like a museum exhibit—something to be observed rather than lived in.

She found herself wandering from one room to the next, not knowing what to do with herself. She didn't belong in this house or in this town, but she didn't have anywhere else to go or anyone to turn to. She couldn't go back home. Not now. Probably never. Couldn't face her mother because she knew that her mom would uncover the truth. Tess wouldn't be able to hide it. And once her mother discovered what Tess had done, it would destroy her.

She was all alone now, but maybe she was better off that way. No one to hurt. No one to hurt her in return.

She poured herself a cup of coffee, but it tasted old and bitter. Dumped it into the sink, swung open the refrigerator door and stared inside. A loaf of bread, a jug of milk, a carton of juice, eggs, an unopened block of Velveeta cheese, and a few bottles of condiments. She didn't feel hungry, but she needed something.

A cigarette.

She grabbed an ashtray and walked back into the living room. Her eyes fell upon a small crucifix mounted to the wall and the immensity of her situation flared before her, and she felt like crying. She had no money. No job. No place to call home. She had nothing. She stared at the wooden crucifix and wished she had something to believe in. Anything. A god. Herself.

She sat down on the couch, took out her pack of cigarettes and shook out the last one. Her hands rattled and it took her three strikes of a match to finally light the tip. She smoked for a minute and considered her options.

She stubbed out her cigarette and removed the pistol from her purse. Opened the cylinder. Six bullets. She had never fired the gun before but had been instructed in how to do so.

Six bullets.

One was all it would take.

It would be easier on everyone this way. Especially on herself. No more fear. No more heartache. No more betrayal.

She stared down at the pistol through burning eyes. Closed the cylinder and traced her thumb along the edge of the hammer. One squeeze of the trigger would put a stop to the pain. Her eyes pressed closed, and her mind raced.

Please. Please. Please.

She placed her finger around the trigger and waited for the inner fortitude to present itself and end the hurt.

Please.

But instead of pulling the trigger, her eyes flickered open, and she was looking at a bookshelf filled with hardbound books. One caught her attention. She recognized the spine. Of course, it had to be the same book that started her nightmare in the first place.

Tess knew most of the patrons that frequented the Beauchamp Branch Library. She knew all the regulars' names and what kind of books they liked to read. She also knew their routines. People had their particular habits. They liked to sit at the same table at a specific time of day or on a certain day of the week. Some people came to the library to be alone with their thoughts. Others came to seek companionship or because they didn't have anywhere else to go.

All the regulars knew Tess as well. Hers was the first face they greeted. They'd ask her for recommendations of books and her opinion of new authors.

The library was a place that revered silence, so it was the perfect environment for Tess. She loved the order of a library. Everything had its place. And the smell of books made her feel alive.

She had noticed the man as soon as he crossed the threshold and could tell that he was new to the library. His head pivoted to the left and right, getting his bearings and taking it all in.

He was tall and slender, graying a little bit around the temples, and he wore dark slacks and a jacket that looked expensive. When he walked across the library floor, he moved with grace and confidence. He appeared comfortable in his own skin.

He stepped up to the reference desk and placed his hands on the counter, and Tess surprised herself by looking to see whether he wore a wedding band. His finger was bare. He smiled at Tess and said hello, and although she couldn't hear the word itself, she could feel the warmth in his voice.

Tess returned his smile and slid a laminated card across the desk she used when meeting patrons for the first time. *Hello, I'm Tess. How can I help you?*

The man maintained his kind smile, and unlike most people that discovered her affliction, he didn't appear uncomfortable or unsure of what to do next. Not only did he take the knowledge in stride, but he was also the first person to remove a pen and slip of paper from her desk and begin to write.

Hello, Tess. My name is Aaron. I'm hoping you can help me find a book today.

Tess read his note and wrote her own in response. *I'd be happy to.*

She wasn't generally attracted to older men—he appeared to be in his late forties or early fifties—but something was charming and genuine about the man. His blue eyes sparkled, and she felt a sense of ease around him as if she had known him for a long time.

"Great," he said. He wrote on another slip of paper. *I'm looking for the book McTeague by Frank Norris.*

Tess stood from behind the desk and guided Aaron to a row of bookshelves in the back of the library. She felt him watching her, but it didn't make her uncomfortable. In fact, she enjoyed the feeling it gave her.

When she checked out his book and slid *McTeague* across the counter, Aaron smiled and said thank you and wrote her one final note.

It was nice to meet you. I'll be back soon for another book.

Aaron returned three days later.

15

Cap knew better. He needed to stop playing with fire. The best thing to do was drive home before the school bus arrived in town. He cranked the ignition, put the truck into gear, and told himself to drive away. But instead, he cut the engine and waited.

He knew the boy's routines and habits. He knew the boy walked home from where the bus dropped him off in town. Cap knew all the boy's shortcuts. Knew that he liked to stop on the bridge across the Tuscarora Creek to watch frozen chunks of ice float past, occasionally slinging rocks at them like they were enemy warships.

Every few weeks, Cap would feel the itch to head into town right before 3:15. He might tell himself that the trip was to run a quick errand—a stop at the market or to fill his tank with gas—but he always ended up parking next to the bank so that he could watch Butch traipse his way home from the bus stop.

He knew Wade worked in the Agway store until closing and that Maggie would be home fixing dinner, so Butch would be alone.

And as hard as it proved to be, Cap resisted the urge to reach out to the boy and make eye contact, let alone talk with him. He never left his truck. He'd simply sit in the cab and watch Butch from afar.

Right on cue, bus number eighteen pulled into the bank parking lot, and out spilled a dozen kids from the middle and high school. But Cap didn't notice or care about the rest of them—only Butch mattered.

Some of the kids walked in packs of three, a couple in pairs, and then, like always, Butch walked alone, his narrow shoulders slumped under some unseen sadness that was too much for a fourteen-year-old boy to bear. The boy tugged a wool cap over a thicket of red hair and made his way alone without talking or saying goodbye to any of the other kids.

Cap watched the boy and felt the dull ache in his chest like he always did. All he wanted to do was sit next to Butch, talk to him a little, find out how he was doing in school and ask him why he didn't have any friends. Was it because he felt different than everybody else, or was there trouble at home?

Even though it began to snow a little harder, and the wind blew stronger, Butch shuffled along the sidewalk down Main Street, not seeming to notice the wind nipping at his cheeks.

Cap put the truck into gear, flipped on the windshield wipers, and pulled away when he noticed two other boys around Butch's age begin to follow him. Cap recognized both boys, Monte Canfield and Brian Schorr, and knew their reputations as well. Like their fathers, both boys were bullies, preying on those who were quiet and different.

They trailed after Butch and Cap could hear the names they were calling him: *pussy* and *freak*. But if Butch heard their taunts, he ignored them. Cap noticed the body language of both Monte and Brian and knew that nothing good was brewing.

Monte scooped up a handful of snow and packed it good and tight. The ball of ice flew from his hand and thudded against the back of Butch's head. Monte and Brian howled with laughter as Butch's feet went out from under him, and he sprawled face-first to the sidewalk.

As Butch staggered to his feet and muttered something at the two boys, Monte and Brian immediately lost their triumphant smiles and pounced. They snatched Butch's backpack and ripped the hat from his head, slung them onto the road, and then proceeded to shove and poke at him and spew more names.

Cap's heart thudded in his chest at the sight of Butch's face. The boy tried to fight back tears and attempted to scramble away, but the bullies weren't done yet. They slammed Butch to the pavement and pressed his face into the snow.

Cap couldn't stop himself. He threw the truck into park and flung his door open.

"Enough."

Monte and Brian looked up as Cap approached, shit-eating grins still planted on their faces.

"Get off him. I mean it. Right now."

Both boys stood slowly but didn't seem intimated by Cap's presence.

"We were just messing around," Monte claimed.

Cap peered down at Butch, the boy's cheeks red and wet from the snow. "You okay, Butch?"

Butch didn't respond. He stood, tears and snot leaking down his face. He wiped his eyes, looking embarrassed and ashamed, like he wanted to crawl under a rock.

"I know your parents," Cap said to the bullies. "How would you like me telling them what you two were doing?"

Brian shrugged. Spat on the ground and smirked. "Go ahead. I don't care."

"You think this is funny?"

Brian shrugged again. "We weren't doing nothin' wrong."

"Looks to me like Butch might think differently."

Butch still wouldn't look Cap in the eye. "It's fine."

Cap watched Brian and Monte exchange a shit-eating grin. "Why don't you boys head on home?"

Brian stood his ground. Shook his head. "We don't have to listen to you."

"No, Brian, you don't. But if you want to end up like your father, then you're right on track."

Brian glared at him. "What's that supposed to mean?"

"I think you know what I mean."

Brian's face transformed, shifting from belligerence to uncertainty in an instant. "Whatever." He pointed at Butch. "We'll see you at school, *bitch*."

Cap listened to their laughter and felt sick to his stomach. He watched Butch gather his backpack and hat and tried to help.

"I got it," Butch snapped.

"You want a ride home? I can drop you off."

"No."

"You sure? I don't mind."

Butch slung his backpack onto his shoulder. Didn't say a word. Just walked away.

Cap wanted to say something but didn't. Instead, he climbed back into his truck and felt his entire body shake. He stared at the thermos in the passenger seat that contained a blend of bourbon and water. As he gave the desire for a drink serious consideration, he noticed Butch cross the road and make his way toward the creek. Without taking his eyes off the boy, Cap picked up the thermos.

He prayed to the God he'd grown to question so much recently to make things different but knew his prayers would fall on deaf ears.

He poured a cup full of bourbon and drank it straight down without hesitating. He poured another and drank that one down, too. He recapped the thermos, put the truck into gear, and drove away from Butch like he'd done a hundred times before.

TEN DAYS BEFORE GOOD FRIDAY

16

Maggie certainly hadn't intended to sneak up on Wade to catch him in his latest act of infidelity. She merely wanted to drop off the lunch pail that he had forgotten on the kitchen counter. It wasn't as if she woke up that morning hoping to find her husband up to no good.

In hindsight, Maggie should have suspected something when she noticed Carol's deer-in-the-headlights expression as she marched through the store's front doors. Carol stared at her like she had a banana stuck in her ear. Had even tried to strike up small talk but ended up merely stammering without being able to look her in the eye.

Now Maggie knew why.

"Hey, Mags . . . whatcha doing here?" Wade chirped in an unusually high-pitched voice. He sprang up from a leather couch in the corner of his office—a leather couch he claimed to never use but kept because his old man liked to have a place to sit when he made one of his grand visits to scrutinize the business he handed down to his only son.

Maggie held up Wade's black lunch pail as to answer his question.

Amy Fitzgerald, who might as well have been sitting on Wade's lap, stood up like a shot, her face blossoming as red as a Macintosh apple.

"Forgot your lunch," Maggie managed through a faux smile. "I guess something must have been on your mind this morning. Only one thing I can think of that you like better than food, though."

Amy straightened her apron, inched her way toward the door, desperate to vacate the office as quickly as possible, but Maggie blocked the girl's escape route.

"I hope I'm not interrupting important business."

Wade painted on a harmless grin. "Heck, no. Amy here is new, and I'm just giving her the lay of the land, is all."

Maggie never took her eyes off Wade, acting as if Amy wasn't standing two feet away. "That right? I suppose you gave Glen and Fred and Mark and all the other men the same *lay of the land*?"

Wade nodded earnestly. "When they first started, you bet. It's a big operation with a thousand different things to remember. It can be overwhelming."

Amy edged her way toward the door, but Maggie kept rooted to her spot.

"Well, I certainly didn't mean to interfere with your *big operation*." She extended the lunch pail to Wade. "Your soup might be cold. Seems like everything goes cold around here."

"That's fine. Thank you, Mags."

Maggie finally turned her attention on Amy and stared at her for a moment, scanning the girl from head to toe. "You're Sarah Fitzgerald's girl, aren't you?"

Amy managed a barely audible, "Yes."

"And you just graduated high school a couple of years ago, didn't you?"

Another mumbled yes.

"My, my. And look at you now. You must have all sorts of boys lining up to ask you out."

"No, ma'am. Not really."

"Oh? And why's that?"

Amy glanced at Wade for help, but Maggie didn't give him the chance to intercede.

"Pretty little thing like you. The boys must want to just eat you right up."

"Mags—"

She snapped her head toward her husband. "What? You mean to tell me that you don't find her attractive? You never noticed?"

"That's enough. You're making something out of nothing."

"Am I?"

"Look here, Mags—"

"No. You look, *Wade*. You really think that your daddy would like you dipping your quill in the company ink? And with a nineteen-year-old to boot?"

"I'm twenty," Amy announced.

Both Maggie and Wade seemed utterly shocked by Amy's abrupt participation in the conversation.

"What?" Maggie asked, not even pretending to mask her patronizing tone.

"I'm twenty years old. Not nineteen. Almost twenty-one," Amy stated.

"Oh. Almost twenty-one. Well, excuse me. That makes all the difference in the world then, doesn't it?"

"Stop it, Maggie," Wade blurted.

Maggie ignored him. Didn't take her eyes off Amy. "You think you have it all figured out, don't you? So young and pretty. The world at your fingertips."

Amy stood her ground and barely flinched from Maggie's condescending manner. "Just because I'm young doesn't mean that I'm stupid."

"Did I say that you were stupid?"

Wade could only watch on in disbelief.

"I think that you're just jealous of what I have. What you *used* to have."

"Pardon me?" Maggie stammered.

Wade stepped between the two women. "Go back to work, Amy."

Amy gave Maggie one final look, one final smirk, then marched out of the office.

It was silent for a few moments. Awkward as well.

Maggie returned her gaze to Wade and shook her head. "Really, Wade? Is that what you want out of life?"

Wade hemmed and hawed.

"Word got out about something like that, and it could hurt business, don't you think?"

Wade's mouth opened to say something, but he snapped it back shut instead.

"Not at work, Wade. Not at work."

"It's nothing like that, Mags."

"What *is* it like, Wade? You really think I'm blind to what you do?"

Wade attempted to bite his tongue but failed miserably. "No. But maybe you're blind as to *why* I do it."

Maggie stood her ground, and Wade did the same. The office grew quiet, with only the clanking of chains coming from somewhere out in the store.

Maggie finally broke their face-off as she opened the office door. "Destroying our marriage is one thing. Ruining our livelihood is another."

17

Cap felt the weight of guilt pressing down on his shoulders, knowing that he should tell Tess the truth. She deserved nothing less. He'd gotten a call from Skeeter before leaving the house, letting him know about Tess's car—it had a smashed hood, cracked windshield, dents and scratches from fender to fender, and a broken front axle that might take a few days to repair. The Pinto wouldn't be pretty, but it would be driveable. When Skeeter asked him if they should start working on the Pinto, Cap surprised himself with his answer—*Hold off on any repairs for right now.*

He knew it to be a selfish act and tried convincing himself that a few more nights wouldn't hurt and that he'd tell her eventually, but the truth of the matter was that he simply wasn't ready to say goodbye to this woman he barely knew.

He glanced at Tess and she stared back at him with a look that made him wonder if she was reading his mind. Maybe she could see that he was holding something back.

"You hungry?"

No.

"Want a cup of coffee or hot chocolate or something?"

No, thank you.

"Well, let me know if you want anything."

Tess kept staring at him with that look of hers and merely nodded.

Cap guided the truck into the Agway parking lot and pulled beside a set of gas pumps. "Going to fill up the tank, then we'll head over to the IGA and pick up something for dinner."

He stepped out into the cold, relieved to remove himself from her prying eyes. Gray clouds loomed overhead, blocking the efforts of the sun, and by the looks of things, another snowstorm wasn't far off.

It struck him odd that he was out running errands with the woman. In fact, it felt strange to have a companion for the last few days, eating meals together, drinking coffee at the kitchen table, sleeping in the rectory, and now, taking her shopping.

He spun the gas cap off and filled the tank.

The woman had a right to know about her car. She had the right to get on with her life. What was he really expecting from keeping her in his home for another few days? It was nothing less than dishonest.

He watched Tess tuck the hair behind her ears and couldn't help but think how vulnerable she seemed when she told him that she was in a bad situation. Just jumped in her car and drove off from wherever she was living, not knowing where she was headed, and barely had a dime to her name.

Maybe he was doing the right thing by not telling her about her car. She might be in some kind of danger but was too proud to ask for help. Maybe it was his duty as a pastor to help.

Cap rubbed at his jaw and wrestled with right and wrong, grappling with the fact that he was trying his damnedest to justify a reason for not telling Tess the truth when he spotted Maggie flinging open the glass doors of the Agway store. She looked madder than hell and marched right toward him.

Cap's first reaction to the sight of Maggie was wondering if he'd done something wrong. He racked his brain for something he may have said to her—people in this town sure could take something the wrong way and hold a grudge for the longest time. Then Wade hustled out of the store like a five-year-old caught flushing his hamster down the toilet. The big man looked flustered, face red and knotted together, and he was busy tucking in his shirt over his paunch.

"Mags! Hold up a second, now."

Cap took one glance at Maggie's sour expression and could tell that she didn't intend to *hold up* for even a half-second. He tried to look away, but Maggie caught him staring. He gave her a small smile and felt like a fool immediately—as if he was mocking her.

She stomped past him, not uttering a word, opened her car door and flung in her purse like it was about to burst into flames. Her door slammed, the engine barked to life, and gravel flew as her tires spun in reverse.

Cap watched her cut a hard U-turn and barrel right toward Wade, who stood in the middle of the parking lot with both arms dangling at his sides. Maggie gunned the gas pedal harder, leaving Wade little choice—he dove out of the way.

The station wagon thumped onto the road, the muffler eating up a chunk of asphalt and kicking a fury of sparks every which way. She cut off a delivery truck, blared her horn at the driver for good measure, and fishtailed down Main Street.

And just like that, it was over.

Cap and Wade made eye contact, the latter of the two still sprawled in the gravel. Wade pulled himself off the ground and brushed off the dirt and snow that coated his shirt and pants with as much dignity as he could muster.

Cap nodded in the direction of Maggie's abrupt getaway. "Guess your wife must have a pie in the oven?"

Wade hawked and spat onto the ground. "No, but she's got a few damn screws loose."

"Don't we all?"

Wade failed to see the humor in the situation and went about re-tucking his shirt. He glanced at the store, then turned back to Cap. "And don't act like this isn't funny as hell to you."

Cap recapped the gas tank and snapped the cover shut. "Not sure what you mean by that."

"Cut the horseshit, Cap. It's just you and me out here."

Cap's eyes went to the cab of his truck, where Tess watched the entire encounter. Wade followed his gaze and seemed surprised at the sight of a woman in Cap's truck.

Cap knew that Wade was curious but offered no explanation. He zipped up his jacket tight around his neck. "I'm sure every marriage has its struggles."

"I'm sure they do, but I'm talking about me and Maggie."

"Well, I don't know what happens behind closed doors, but if either one of you want to talk to me, together or separately, I'd be more than happy to listen."

Wade walked up a little closer to Cap, towering over him by a good five or six inches. "I wouldn't tell you what happens in my home and you damn well know it."

Cap averted his eyes for a moment before returning them to Wade's. "Why does it have to be like this, Wade? We're both doing all right. You've got a family and a thriving business."

"Yeah, I've got a thriving business that was handed to me. But you and I both know that's not what I wanted."

Cap stared up at Wade, really staring at him, but not with contempt or judgment, but rather, with mild disappointment. "All that was a long time ago."

"Doesn't make a difference if it was two damn days ago as far as I'm concerned."

"Come on, Wade. Most people in town happen to be envious of everything you have."

Wade spat again. "Including you?"

Gray clouds overhead finally released a light curtain of snow that tumbled down slow and easy as if in no particular hurry to meet the ground.

"I chose my calling."

"Bullshit. Choices were made for us."

"Not all of them."

Wade didn't argue the point, and Cap stood quiet as well, neither man choosing to leave quite yet.

"Maggie and I will be just fine. So, you can save your charity for someone else."

Cap gazed down at his boots and toed the gravel. "I feel sorry for you sometimes, Wade. I really do. You just don't know the half of it."

Wade's jaw tightened and his fingers clenched into fists. He grabbed Cap by the jacket collar and shoved him against the truck. "I know more than you might think."

Cap started to say something when Tess stepped out of the truck.

Wade looked at Tess, and then his eyes traveled south along her body. His face immediately softened, and it appeared that he wanted to say something to her—an introduction, something, anything—but Cap wasn't about to let that happen.

"Sorry to keep you waiting, Tess. We were just finishing up, weren't we, Wade?"

Wade stared at Tess for another moment before releasing Cap from his grip. "Yeah. We're about done, all right."

NINE DAYS BEFORE GOOD FRIDAY

18

The woodshop felt like the one place that was truly Cap's—not the house and certainly not the church. Those places would always be his father's domains. Cap merely occupied them, and despite his ownership, they'd never really be his.

But the woodshop was different. He had built the structure with his own two hands. Pouring the foundation, framing the building, running the electrical and installing the wood-shingled roof. It was a place to retreat from the responsibilities of the church, away from the house with all its rooms furnished and decorated by his parents, removed from the demands and expectations of the community. It was a place that was his and no one else's.

He hunched over a workbench along the back wall, sanding the shelves of a small bookshelf. He wasn't wearing goggles or a mask, and his face and hands were coated with a fine layer of yellow sawdust.

The door to the shop opened and Tess stepped inside, clutching two mugs of hot coffee.

"Must have read my mind."

He grabbed a rag from his back pocket and went about cleaning off his hands. He wasn't accustomed to visitors entering his workspace. In fact, Tess was the first woman to step across the threshold, and Cap felt a strange tug of nervousness like she might glimpse a part of him that he wasn't prepared to share. He didn't seem quite sure what to do with himself, so he paced the floor and kept wiping his hands with the rag.

"Welcome to my little hideaway."

Tess roamed the shop, studying the hand tools hanging from hooks, every one of them meticulously cleaned with not a trace of dust or grease. Her eyes stopped on a small table tucked in the corner of the room, and she ran her hand across the polished surface, admiring the detailed craftsmanship.

"I finished that piece a few weeks ago. Didn't turn out quite the way I wanted."

She took out her notebook and pencil.

It's beautiful.

"It's okay. I keep making these things but don't have a place to put them."

Why do you make them then?

"I don't know. Guess the same reason a writer writes and a painter paints."

Tess continued to walk around the shop, inspecting all his work—a set of chairs, a nightstand, and an end table.

This place feels like you.

"Yeah? How so?"

The house and church feel like someone else's.

Cap pulled out two chairs for them to sit on, then drank some of his coffee and looked around his shop before responding. "I guess they do to me, too."

She gave him a quizzical look.

"You have a way of making people talk about themselves, don't you?"

Some people.

"Well, I guess you've got my number." He stared into his mug of coffee until he heard the sound of Tess's pencil pressing onto paper.

Why did you become a pastor?

Cap read her question. Took another sip of coffee before answering. "I took over the church after my father passed away. More out of obligation than desire."

Why?

He sighed long and hard, his face shifting and changing. "Well, the short answer is that I had to."

Tess stared at him for a long time before holding up the same question. *Why?*

Cap pulled a bottle of bourbon from a shelf and topped off his coffee. When he held up the bottle to Tess, she shook her head.

He tasted his drink again before continuing.

"I never wanted to be a minister. Not really. But growing up as a pastor's son, I always felt a sense of obligation. Ever since I was seven or eight, my father informed me that I'd be entering the seminary. I never once questioned or objected. Simply did as I was told." He sipped some more of his spiked coffee. "My old man was pretty no-nonsense. Super strict. High expectations. Scared the hell out of me and my brother."

You have a brother?

It took him a moment to answer. "I did."

Tess's pencil hovered over the notebook, but Cap responded before she could ask her question.

"He was only eighteen years old when he died."

I'm sorry.

"Me, too. Me, too." He drank again. "After getting my bachelor's degree, I went off to seminary at Roberts Wesleyan College in Rochester. I studied hard and kept my nose to the grindstone."

Did you like it?

He stared into her eyes before answering. "No. I didn't. Had too much doubt. Could never give myself over to blind faith. There were too many holes in religion. Holes big enough to drive a truck right through them."

He took another drink from his mug.

"When I finally graduated, if I knew one thing, it was that I would never become a minister. Especially not in my father's church. I left that to my brother. My father was grooming Max to take over one day. He would've been a great pastor."

Tess watched him finish his drink, then refill his mug with a few fingers of straight bourbon.

"Anyway. I stayed in Rochester, got myself a job in a paper factory adding bleach and water to batches of pulp slurry. And, boy, did I ever love that job. I didn't have to *believe* in anything. It was a straightforward task. Nothing to question or grapple with. Every time my parents called, I'd tell them that I was looking for a position in a church somewhere. That bought me some time, but my old man was pretty smart and grew wise to my charade after about a year of the same old story."

You worked in a paper factory?

Cap shrugged. A trace of a smile. "Best job I ever had."

He sipped his drink and his grin slowly dulled until his expression became unreadable. "One night I got a call from my old man. And he never called me. Hated using the phone, in fact. He got straight to the point. Asked me about my relationship with God. I led him to believe my relationship with God was fine, but then he asked me why I wasn't trying to secure a position within the church." Another sip of bourbon. "Maybe I could keep lying to myself, but I couldn't keep lying to the old man. So, I told him point-blank that I didn't want to preach. That I questioned my faith. Well, he hung up on me as soon as those words were out of my mouth."

Cap fingered the lip of his mug before taking another swallow. "We didn't talk for about three months after that. I chatted with my mother, of course. She might have been disappointed, but she'd call me every week or so. And she tried her best to get my old man on the phone, but he wouldn't budge. Just plain stubborn."

He swirled his drink and seemed to struggle with if he should keep going on with his story or stop right there. He decided on the former.

"One morning, I got a call from her, saying that they were coming to see me the next day. Max, too."

Tess lit a cigarette. *Were you close to your brother?*

"Yeah, I was. And even though there was a six-year gap between us, we got along really well. He was a good kid. Max was everything I wasn't. Extroverted. Wise beyond his years. Everyone was drawn to him, and I think I looked up to him more than he did to me." He picked up Tess's cigarettes. Played with the pack for a moment, then tapped one out.

"I barely slept a wink that night. The next morning, it started snowing something awful. One of the worst storms I had ever seen. I was supposed to go to work that day, but I called in sick and waited for my parents and brother to show up. Longest day of my life."

He smoked for a few moments, and the whole time Tess stared at him but didn't push for anything more.

"I waited and waited for their Dodge station wagon to pull up outside my apartment. I was climbing the walls. I called their house a half-dozen times, figuring they turned around because of the snow and went back home, but nobody answered the phone. Then, about ten o'clock that night, I received a call from the hospital up in Towanda. The doctor informed me that they had been in a car accident on Route 6. Mom was in the ICU with a broken back, a collapsed lung, her face and chest torn up pretty bad. She ended up losing her left eye."

He worked on his cigarette while staring into his mug. "My father and Max died in the accident. Pronounced dead before they even arrived at the hospital."

That's awful.

"It was. Still is."

And you think it was your fault?

Cap stabbed out his cigarette in an empty coffee can. "The first thing my mother tells me when she sees me at the hospital was that it was God's will. Can you imagine? The poor woman just lost her husband and youngest child. Her life would never be the same. And *that's* God's will?"

Tess reached over and squeezed his hand. It was a fleeting moment of flesh pressed against flesh.

"I came back home to Black Walnut to take care of her after she got out of the hospital. She refused to sleep in her bedroom without my father. So, she stayed in the old rectory inside the church. Pretty much bedridden. Needed help with everything. Going to the bathroom, getting dressed, eating. Everything."

And you stayed here?

"One thing led to another, and I found myself taking over the church."

Tess drew on her cigarette and shook her head. *It's hard letting go of the past.*

"It sure the hell is."

He finished the bourbon in his mug and reached for the bottle once again.

"What are you trying to let go of?"

She cut him a look.

"From your past."

I'm not ready to share that. Not yet.

"Okay. But whenever you're ready."

Thank you.

They sat in the quiet for a few moments.

Can I ask you for a favor?

"You bet."

Tess wrote in her notebook, then clutched it to her chest, struggling with whether she should share her words with Cap. She finally handed him the notebook and watched him read her words.

Cap peered back at her and nodded. "You can stay here as long as you want, Tess. As long as you want."

19

Tess inspected her jeans and black sweater. Noticed the grime and spots where she had spilled coffee. She'd been wearing the same clothes since arriving in Black Walnut.

She walked into the kitchen, then into the laundry room beside it, and like the rest of Cap's house, the room was neat and organized. Boxes of detergent and fabric softener lined up on a shelf with folded towels and linens.

When she opened the lid to the washer, her eyes cut to the back of the room and spotted a utility closet. The door stood partially opened—a foot, maybe two. Couldn't see inside. Nothing but darkness. Her heart rattled and her stomach tightened at the sight of a closet with the door slightly ajar. Her first impulse was to scream. To turn and run away. But she did neither. Instead, she stared into the mouth of darkness and waited for the Man in Blue to emerge.

After their fifth date, Tess was certain that she and Aaron belonged together. She knew that to be silly—probably merely fleeting infatuation—but all she could think about was Aaron. At work, at home, in the grocery store. Everywhere and all the time.

Aaron swung open the door to the suite—it was the biggest hotel room she had ever seen, and everything about it seemed perfect. A fireplace crackled blue and orange in the corner of a living room decorated with a modern sofa and loveseat. A king-sized bed perfectly made with chocolates arranged on the pillows. One wall constructed entirely of glass offered a view of the Syracuse skyline.

"Well? What do you think?"

Tess had yet to cross the threshold.

She felt Aaron's hand on her lower back. "You okay?"

Yes.

"We don't have to do this yet. We can wait."

She smiled. Took his hand in hers and pulled Aaron inside the room.

While she sat on the edge of the bed and soaked in all the amenities, Aaron crossed to the wet bar and held up a bottle of red wine.

"Nightcap?"

Yes, please.

She studied his profile as he uncorked the wine, and even though she was attracted to Aaron, it struck her how little she knew of the man. He didn't like to talk about himself. No mention of where he grew up, previous relationships, his past, or anything about his family. The only personal information he shared was that he worked as a physician in a hospital, but she didn't even know which one. He would simply show up at the library every few days and make arrangements for another date. Tess never questioned this pattern.

Aaron handed her a glass of wine, and they sipped the merlot and peered out the window, admiring the glittering view of the city.

He moved them to the sofa, where they drank wine in comfortable silence. He refilled their glasses as Tess grabbed her cigarettes from her purse and struck a match.

"You should quit smoking."

Tess smiled. Smoked her cigarette and wrote in her notebook. *I know.*

"I don't have to be a doctor to know that it's bad for you."

Don't you have any bad habits?

Aaron pretended to think about this. "No."

So, you're perfect?

"Far from it."

She gave him a playful shove with her shoulder. They drank in silence for a few moments.

You don't like to talk about yourself, do you?

Aaron shrugged. "Not much to tell."

I know nothing about you.

"What would you like to know?"

Tell me about your friends.

"I don't really have any friends. Too many hours at the hospital. All I have are *co-workers*."

That's sad.

He grinned. "I'm okay with it. Besides, I have you now."

Would you like to meet my friends?

He stiffened at the question and was slow in answering. "Let's wait on that."

I don't want to keep you all to myself.

"Not yet, Tess." His words were clipped. "I'm a private person and I'd like to keep it that way. At least for now."

Sounds mysterious.

Tess took a final draw on her cigarette and stubbed out the butt.

If you don't want to meet my friends, I guess you're not ready to meet my mother.

She meant this as a joke, but Aaron's mouth drew straight, and he stared down at his hands.

Tess wondered if she said something wrong, but then he kissed her on the lips. Once. Twice. She kissed him back. Her heart fluttered, knowing, wanting what was about to happen—she was ready.

When Aaron pulled away, his warm smile had returned. "I need to get out of this suit and tie."

All she could think was *Hurry. Please hurry.*

He picked up his overnight bag and stepped into the walk-in closet. The light clicked on, and Aaron closed the doors behind him.

Tess waited, uncertain whether she should undress and climb into bed. Would that be too presumptuous? She began to unbutton her blouse but stopped herself—maybe she should let Aaron undress her.

She drank some more wine and felt the warm glow of alcohol in her head and stomach. Nervous and excited, she didn't want to get ahead of herself.

She finished her glass of wine and poured another.

The closet light snapped off and the doors opened. She saw Aaron's silhouette. Tall, lean, and nothing but a shadow. He stepped out of the closet wearing a pair of blue pajamas, and Tess's heart rattled at the sight of him. Something about the way he stood at the threshold and how he was dressed.

A tiny voice whispered inside her head. *The Man in Blue.*

Her wine glass trembled in her hand as Aaron walked across the room. He wasn't smiling and his face seemed different—like a mask had been stripped away.

Tess stared into his eyes and a surge of inexplicable fear coursed through her.

Aaron didn't speak. Instead, he removed the wine glass from her hand and kissed her. Tess froze. Allowed him to kiss her mouth, her neck, but unlike before, the feeling of his lips repulsed her.

She pushed him away, but he grabbed her by the arm and pulled her against his chest. He kissed her again. Harder. More passionate.

The Man in Blue from the closet.

She felt one of his hands cup her breast.

Tess's mind swirled with visceral disgust. Everything about his touch felt familiar. The smell of his skin—sweat mixed with aftershave. The roughness of his whiskers upon her face. His soft, probing hands.

Her chest tightened and she suddenly found it difficult to breathe.

Aaron's other hand slipped below her waist.

The Man in Blue.

She shoved him away. Stared at him with wide eyes.

No, she signed.

"What is it?"

She kept signing, *No. No. No.* She backed away slowly. Small desperate steps.

"What's the matter?"

A burst of white dots blossomed in front of her. Blood rushed to her head, and her legs threatened to buckle beneath her. Aaron was speaking, but her blurred vision prevented her from being able to read his lips.

He reached for her hand, but Tess yanked away.

She grabbed her purse from the bed and kept backing toward the door. Her palm found the door handle and she fought the urge to scream. She flung open the door and stumbled down the hallway, and under the beating of her own heart, she heard a tiny voice call out once again.

The Man in Blue from the closet.

EIGHT DAYS BEFORE GOOD FRIDAY

20

Maggie guided her shopping cart down the baking aisle of the IGA and simply browsed. The cart was empty and she had no intention of buying a single thing. Maggie had been feeling cooped up for the last twenty-four hours and hadn't known what to do with herself at the house. She was tired of cooking and cleaning, and all she could think about was that stupid look on Wade's face when she walked into his office and caught him with Amy Fitzgerald—that naive, fucking Barbie doll. She should have scratched the girl's eyes right out of her pretty, blonde head. How could someone sleep with a married man?

Maggie had always known about Wade's affairs. She wasn't stupid. Tolerant, yes. Stupid, no. Most of them one-night stands. A few of his flings lasting for a few weeks until the novelty wore off. She knew all the women, of course. Wade never strayed far from home. All his women were young, pretty, and dumb as dirt. The affairs were all harmless enough. Nothing but conquests. Some of the women probably dreamed of falling in love, thinking that Wade would walk out of his marriage and sweep them off their feet. But Maggie knew better. None of them stood a chance. Wade wasn't looking for love and affection. A man like Wade needed stability in a woman. Someone sensible and practical.

What surprised her about Amy was that the girl actually stood up for herself. With that shitty smirk on her face. Maggie couldn't get that snotty expression of Amy's out of her mind.

I think that you're just jealous of what I have. What you used *to have.*

Maggie's blood boiled. She wished that she had slapped that look right off the girl's perfect little face.

She went down another aisle and the wheel on her cart kept sticking and squeaking like a rat caught in a trap. Seemed like she always picked the wrong thing. Wrong cart. Wrong husband. Wrong life. She guided the squawking cart to the next aisle and perused the hair care supplies. Shampoo, conditioner, hair spray, and a selection of hair color kits. She'd been noticing a few gray hairs sprouting up here and there and didn't particularly like the idea of turning prematurely gray.

She picked up a box of brown hair dye, looked at the price, and nearly did a backflip—$3.99 for hair color. That was way too much to spend on something as frivolous as a hair dye.

Cap and a woman she had never seen before pushed a cart down the aisle and headed straight for her. That was one thing about living in a small town—she couldn't even go to the grocery store without bumping into half the community. She felt irritable and ugly, and even though she wasn't prepared to chat with Cap, she was certainly curious about his female companion. Seeing Cap in the company of a woman caused a spike of not only inquisitiveness but something bordering on jealousy. She liked to think that Cap would be permanently single.

The woman looked her in the eye, then so did Cap. Maggie painted on a pleasant smile in an instant and gave a perky little wave of the hand.

"Good morning, Cap," she practically sang.

"Morning to you, Mags. How's your day going?"

"Glorious. Just glorious."

Maggie's eyes wandered to the young woman, who stared back at her with big, green eyes, and Maggie couldn't help but notice that the woman was nothing short of stunning. "Well, who's your pretty friend here?"

Cap's fingers went automatically to his mustache. "This is Tess."

Maggie scanned Tess from head to toe before responding. "Are you new to the area?"

Tess nodded.

"And what brings you to Black Walnut?"

"Tess is kind of in-between places right now."

Maggie's grin didn't falter one bit and she gave Cap a curious expression. "I see. And isn't Tess capable of answering her own questions? Or has the cat got her tongue?"

Cap rocked on the balls of his feet. "Well. Tess is deaf, Mags."

Maggie's smile went flat in an instant. "Oh."

After a moment of awkwardness, Tess extended her hand, and Maggie glanced quickly to Cap before accepting the gesture.

"Tess can read lips."

Maggie's face reddened. "I'm sorry. I didn't mean to be rude or anything."

Tess smiled and shook her head.

"So, you're new to Black Walnut? Isn't that nice. Whereabouts are you living?"

"Tess is staying with me right now."

Maggie did a poor job of concealing her shock. "Really? At your house?"

"Down in the old rectory, actually."

"I see. Well, that sure is kind of you, Cap. Always willing to help others in their time of need."

"I do what I can."

Maggie addressed Tess, speaking loudly and painfully slow. "Do you like it here? In Black Walnut?"

Tess nodded.

"Wonderful. It's a good place. Most people are nice enough."

Cap gave one final tug on his mustache. "Well, we'll let you get on with your day. Nice bumping into you, Maggie."

Maggie felt Tess's eyes on her, and something about that look of hers made her feel uneasy. She nodded, then once again, spoke slowly and a little too loudly. "Nice-meeting-you, Tess."

Cap pushed his cart down the aisle, and Maggie watched Tess's perfectly firm backside and thought for a moment. "Cap?"

He stopped. Gave her a curious look.

"You haven't forgotten about Sunday afternoon, have you? I'm throwing your birthday party at the house after your sermon."

"Is that this Sunday?"

"Yes. It is *your* birthday, isn't it?"

Cap rubbed his jaw. "You sure you want to go through all the bother?"

"It's already planned. Besides, it will give us the chance to talk about the Easter parade. It's going to be our best one yet."

"I don't doubt that."

Maggie smiled at Tess. "And, of course, you've got to bring Tess. Introduce her to folks. You can't keep her all to yourself now, can you?"

"All right, Mags. Looking forward to it."

She smiled and watched as they turned the corner, and her smile slipped straight away. It struck her very odd that Cap would take some stranger into his home. What would people think? A pastor and a single woman—a stranger—essentially living together.

Honestly. What is Cap getting himself into?

She noticed that she still clutched the box of brown hair dye. The young model on the cover of the box smiled back at Maggie with a broad, gleeful grin, looking so carefree and gorgeous with perfect white teeth. The model ran manicured fingernails through her long mane, showing off a head full of luxurious hair without a single trace of gray. The woman couldn't have been older than twenty-five. Of course, she didn't have gray hair. She was young and free of responsibility, making a living by simply smiling for the camera.

As she was about to return the box back on the shelf, a thought came over her like someone standing behind her, shouting through a megaphone. *Put it in your purse.*

She cut her eyes around the store, checking for other shoppers, or to see if Cap and Tess might be coming back down the aisle, but she was all alone. She glanced down at the box of hair color, staring at the model's cheerful smile and flawless hair, and it struck Maggie how much she resembled Tess.

Put it in your purse.

She deserved to be pampered a little bit. Spend more time on her appearance. It had been six or seven months since she had gone to the hairdresser and got a proper cut and style. What were four measly dollars in the grand scheme of things?

Put it in your purse.

Maggie had never stolen anything before in her entire life, and before she could talk herself out of it, she slipped the box of hair dye into her purse, zipped it up tight, and proceeded to push her cart back down the aisle.

Joe, the owner of the IGA, worked at the register and Maggie's heart raced so hard she thought that she might faint right there on the linoleum floor.

She grabbed a package of toilet paper and some paper towels from a shelf and nudged her cart up to the register. She exchanged pleasantries with Joe and noticed how her fingers shook when she opened her wallet, but the man was so busy gabbing, he never glanced at her hands.

It seemed like it took forever for him to count out her change. He wanted to know how Butch was doing and asked about Wade, then checked around the store before whispering some gossip about the new principal of the high school: *Seen sharing a bag of popcorn with another man at the drive-in theater up in Wysox.* Maggie had never felt so nervous and antsy. Part of her wanted to blurt out that she just stole a box of hair color.

When she finally walked out of the market with her grocery bags, Maggie felt so alive—so free. Her heart soared in her chest, and she couldn't stop shaking. She wanted to sing out and dance right there on Main Street.

She climbed into her car and dared a quick peek at the contraband in her purse. When she peered back out the windshield, Tess stood on the sidewalk, staring right at her.

Did the young woman know what she did? Had she seen Maggie steal the box of hair dye?

No. She was just being silly.

Maggie lifted her hand and gave Tess a little flick of the wrist.

21

Wind rattled barren limbs of black walnut and birch trees as a light snow tumbled and floated, appearing to be suspended in mid-air before kissing down on the forest floor.

Tess wore a red plaid winter jacket that Cap had purchased at Dottie's Closet over in Wyalusing. She refused at first but finally accepted after insisting that Cap let her pay him back. The coat was nothing fancy, but it was made of wool and went past her waist and had a thick collar to help block the wind.

They'd been hiking in the woods for about twenty minutes. Across frozen creeks and through thickets of pussy willow and blackberry briars that snagged at their jackets and tugged at their hair.

Cap gazed at Tess, and she gave him an inquiring look. "Just a little farther. I promise."

She raised her eyebrows.

"It'll be worth it. Trust me."

They crested a slope of shale rock and walked for a few more minutes. From somewhere out in front of them, an Eastern Screech-Owl softly hooted six or seven times before going quiet.

Ten yards ahead of them, twisted vines and scarred earth encircled a gaping mouth of rock that exposed an entrance into an underground cavern. The opening stood barely four feet high, narrow, and dark as a moonless night.

When Tess stared at Cap, he didn't even have to ask her what she was thinking.

"It's an abandoned black bear den. Leads to a whole system of underground caverns."

He took a seat on a log covered with a thick layer of carpet moss and Tess sat next to him. "Used to play down there when I was a kid."

Tess had taught Cap a few different words in sign language, and she presented one that he understood: *Why?*

Cap laughed. Rubbed at his jaw. "Well, when you're a ten-year-old boy and you live near an old bear cave, what better place to explore?"

Tess took her notebook out of her coat pocket. *I can think of a thousand different places.*

"I guess you're right." He peered down into the black mouth of the cave. "A little scary down there, but me and Wade sure had some fun down in those tunnels."

The man at the gas station?

Cap cocked his head. Nodded. "Wade and I used to be best friends in grade school and through most of high school. Glued to each other's side most of the time. And we loved exploring in that old tunnel, searching for arrowheads and animal bones."

Tess lit a cigarette and exhaled a cloud of smoke into the air. *Sounds dangerous.*

"It was. There are dozens of tunnels down there. Every one of them as scary as the next, but we didn't know any better. Thought we were invincible at the time." Rubbed his hands together to warm them from the cold. "I can still remember the day that I discovered a new tunnel and I crawled deeper and deeper, not really noticing that the tunnel was getting smaller and smaller. I heard Wade yelling for me, but I kept going, wanting to spook him, but I was the one that ended up getting spooked instead."

Cap listened to the faint trickle of water running down the sides of rock and he could smell the dampness and decay.

"Before I knew it, I got myself wedged in there good and tight. Couldn't move forward. Couldn't push backward. Then my flashlight started to die and that scared me the most. Being trapped in the dark. My mind thinking the worst. A few feet in front of me, I spotted the remains of a possum. The jawbone, a few ribs, and a dried-up leathery tail. That was the last thing I saw when my batteries finally gave out completely. I panicked and screamed bloody murder, and my chest expanded, wedging me in even tighter. I couldn't see behind me, and up ahead was nothing but a dark hole that seemed to go on forever. I kept yelling for Wade until my voice went hoarse. I figured that he went home for dinner and left me there to die."

He tucked his hands into his pockets. "Seemed like hours went by. And when something tugged on my ankle, I was convinced that a bear had crawled from the darkness and was going to drag me away. Then I was pulled backward, and there was Wade, laughing and pointing at me, and calling me all kinds of names."

Little boys sure are different than little girls.

"Sure are."

You're not still friends with Wade?

"No. Not really."

What happened?

Cap's grin grew distant, and it took him a moment to answer. "The oldest story in the book is what happened—a girl came between us."

Maggie?

Cap gave her a look. "How'd you know that?"

Tess merely shrugged.

Cap kept staring at her, baffled by the woman's intuition. "Yeah, it was Maggie that tore me and Wade apart. Or at least we allowed her to come between us."

She doesn't seem like your type.

"Well, Maggie used to be different. Funny and spontaneous. You'd never know what she was going to do next. But I guess we all change the older we get."

Do you still have feelings for her?

Cap didn't answer right away. "No, not like that. It's . . . just a little complicated with me and Maggie."

They peered at the woods, watching the snow fall faster and thicker, covering up patches of brown.

"Do you have any family?"

Tess stared at him for a moment before writing in her notebook.

My mother.

"Do you get along with her okay?"

Yes.

"Maybe you should let her know that you're all right. She's probably worried sick about you."

Tess didn't respond.

"Do you want me to call her?"

I don't know what to say to her.

"What about your father?"

Tess's entire body grew tense. She flicked her cigarette into the snow. *I don't have a father.*

"That has to be rough. Not knowing your own father."

Tess lit another cigarette with trembling hands.

"You never met him?"

She pointed at the same words written in her notebook: *I don't have a father.*

Cap nodded but wouldn't let it go. "I wish I had the chance to speak to my old man one last time. Coping with regret is no way to live."

I can live with regret. And with that, she snapped her notebook closed and stood abruptly.

Cap reached for her hand, but she pulled away. He watched the snow tumble down around her, the woods turning whiter and whiter until she disappeared into a grove of alder trees.

22

The hot water felt too good to get out of the shower just yet. A few more minutes—only a few more.

Tess turned and faced the stream of water. Closed her eyes and tried to block out all the doubts trying to creep in. But it was hard. Every time she closed her eyes, Aaron was there. If her mind drifted even for a second, it was Aaron's face she'd see. Right before she went to sleep; making something to eat; getting dressed. All of it the same—Aaron found his way in.

Hello, mom.

Tess's mother signed in return. *Thanks for stopping by, sweetheart.*

In one hand, June held a glass of white wine even though it was only three o'clock in the afternoon. In the other, a Virginia Slim smoldered between her fingers. Somehow, the woman managed to sign with both a wine glass and cigarette in hand—or at least Tess could understand her, anyway. Another deaf person probably wouldn't understand her mother's modified sign language.

Tess crossed the threshold and walked into the house that she had lived in for the last two years of high school, and the sight of all the moving boxes caused her stomach to tighten. She had slowly come to accept her mother's decision to move halfway across the country—*I need warm, dry weather, Tess. I can't take Syracuse anymore*—but seeing all those boxes and pictures removed from their hooks made it all too real.

Tess thought she would have gotten used to helping her mother move by now. They had packed and unpacked so many times over the years. Right when Tess thought they had finally settled into the right town and into the right home, June would suddenly announce that they were moving once again. From one city to the next—Baltimore, Allentown, Trenton, Charlotte.

June set her glass down. Stubbed out her cigarette. Lit another.

I hate moving.

Tess gave her mother a forced smile, then looked around the living room. The same couch she used to hang out on with her friends. Same coffee table. Same bookshelf. The only update was the television, which like always, was tuned to a game show, the sound muted. For some reason, her mother never watched TV with the volume up. Maybe she did it because of her. Maybe she wanted to share her daughter's experience of a world without sound.

When does the moving truck come?

Tuesday.

You have a lot to do.

June sucked on her cigarette. *I know. I know.*

Her mother's auburn hair was pulled back into a ponytail. Aside from the smoker's lines around her mouth, they could almost pass for sisters. June gave birth to Tess when she was only nineteen, and due to the proximity of their ages, their relationship had always been more of a friendship than that of mother-daughter. June was not exactly the maternal type. A single mother raising an only child proved hard on her. She did her best, but Tess learned to take care of herself at an early age. She didn't have a choice—June worked as a flight attendant and would be gone for a day or two at a time. By the age of twelve, Tess cooked, cleaned, got herself off to school every day, and even learned to pay the bills.

You want some wine?

Tess's first impulse was to say*, No, it's the middle of the day.* But then, as she prepared to help her mother pack up her past, she thought a glass of wine sure wouldn't hurt.

Yes, please.

June couldn't mask her surprise and appeared slightly giddy that she wouldn't be drinking alone. She filled a glass with some white wine, handed it to Tess, and raised hers in a toast.

Instead of signing, June spoke out loud. "If we have to pack, we might as well get good and drunk."

Tess tried not to, but she smiled at her mother. Shook her head and sipped some wine.

They wrapped glasses in sheets of newspaper and packed them in cardboard boxes. June smoked cigarettes the entire time and opened another bottle of wine. She refilled her glass a few times, and after Tess's second glass, Tess waved away June's attempt to keep her drinking.

Her mother signed something, but Tess couldn't understand.

You're getting drunk. Just speak.

June appeared hurt for a moment, then quickly shrugged it off. "Why don't you come with me? To Arizona."

Tess finished wrapping another glass before responding. *Because I have a job.*

"There are libraries in Scottsdale."

I have friends here.

"No, you don't."

Tess looked hurt.

"You've always been such a loner. Besides, you can make new friends there."

Tess ignored her mother's comment and gestured toward the bookshelf. *Are you taking the books or donating them?*

"I don't know. Taking them, I guess."

Tess felt her mother's hand on her shoulder, and when she looked at June's face, she could tell that her mother was on the verge of crying.

"Please come with me, Tess. *Please.*"

Tess felt the overwhelming urge to start crying as well.

"Maybe I shouldn't move. Maybe this is a horrible idea."

It'll be good for you. And I'll come visit.

"You promise? For all the holidays?"

Cross my heart.

June made her do a pinkie promise and promptly broke down into tears, which caused Tess to do the same. They hugged one another, burying their faces onto each other's shoulders, releasing their sadness and anxiety like air from a balloon.

"We're being silly, aren't we?"

June wiped her face clean, drank some more wine, and lit a fresh cigarette. "I need a change. I deserve it. I've spent too much of my life here, Tess. Almost ten years. In this town. In this house."

I know.

"And you don't hate me?"

No, mom. You know how much I love you.

"I love you, too, baby."

They both blew their noses.

And just like that, June moved on to a new topic. "Are you seeing anyone right now?"

Tess finished the rest of her wine and shook her head. *No. Not really.*

"What's that supposed to mean?"

Nothing.

"Don't *nothing* me. Who is he? Where'd you meet him?"

Mom. Stop.

"You're no fun." She pointed toward the bookshelf. "And just for that, you get to pack up my books."

Tess tapped out one of her mother's cigarettes and struck a match under the tip.

"Do you want to drive to Scottsdale with me? Take a little road trip?"

Maybe. I'll have to see if I can get some days off from work.

"Really? You would do that? Oh, Tess, that would be so much fun. Just me and you and the open road."

I said maybe.

June squealed, already imagining the two of them driving across the country. "We'll be just like Thelma and Louise."

They died in the end, Mom.

June waved her off. "Not that part. Only the fun stuff."

Tess smiled and pulled books off the shelf, stacking them in a box one by one. She cleared off one bookshelf, then continued to the next. So many books. Then she spotted an old, tattered photograph stuck in between two novels, lost and forgotten. She picked up the picture and stared at the image. Her hands began to tremble, but she couldn't take her eyes off the photo.

Her mother's twenty-year-old face grinned big and wide, and in her arms, she cradled baby Tess, maybe six months old. Beside her mother stood the man she didn't remember—the man she had never been permitted to see.

Tess held the photo up to her mother. June's eyes went to the picture and her face drained of color.

Is this him?

Her mother didn't answer. Then she looked away from the picture.

Is this him?

June finally looked into her daughter's eyes and her voice trembled. "Yes. That's your father."

Tess stared at the photo, her eyes burning hot. She stared at her father's face. Unlike June, he wore no smile for the camera. He appeared uncomfortable. Out of place. Tess's vision blurred with tears, but it didn't matter. She knew it was his face. Her father's face.

Aaron's face.

SEVEN DAYS BEFORE GOOD FRIDAY

23

Wade couldn't wait to loosen his damn shirt collar and yank off his tie. He hated wearing a stupid monkey suit, but Maggie insisted and always seemed to get her way. So, every Sunday, the entire family had to put on their fanciest clothes and shoes. Every Sunday, he and Butch were forced to slick back their hair with Brylcreem. And every Sunday, they would sit wedged together on a church pew like a bunch of sardines just like a normal family.

Strutting around like a damn rooster, Wade thought to himself as he watched Cap pace behind the podium, stroking that mustache of his that the man thought concealed his harelip. It didn't. Not one damn bit.

He squirmed and fidgeted and held back the sigh that wanted to explode from his lungs. Then his eyes drifted once again to the young woman sitting up in the front pew, right in front of Cap. It was the same woman that he had met briefly at Agway. She was attractive in a sullen, unpredictable kind of way, and Wade was immediately drawn to that air of recklessness about her. She was different. All the other women in town were the same—the way they dressed, their hairstyles, even the way they talked was the same. He knew all the women in the area, and he was bored with every single one of them.

The stranger had been sitting in the front pew when he and Maggie entered the church and took their usual spots with Butch. The woman kept to herself like she was uncomfortable—a church service seemed to be the last thing she wanted to attend. And through Cap's sermon, she kept her eyes locked on the man, watching him closely like she was afraid of missing a single word he said.

Wade stared at the woman's profile and watched the way she licked her lips every so often. She craned her neck from side to side and their eyes connected for a moment. Wade smiled and nodded, and the woman did the same before returning her attention to Cap. And although their exchange was fleeting—only two or three seconds—Wade felt the familiar tug in his loins.

Then he sensed Maggie's probing eyes on him. She placed a hand on his knee and whispered in his ear. "She's living with Cap. Can you believe that?"

Wade didn't respond to his wife's snarky comment.

"She's deaf, too."

"So?"

Maggie gave him a sour look and withdrew her hand from atop his knee.

Wade sat motionless for a minute before sneaking another look at Tess and those hazel green eyes.

24

Maggie's stomach lurched at the sight of Robin entering the house—she not only brought her three little monsters to Cap's birthday party, but Chuck as well. She could tolerate her sister and her kids in small doses, but why did she have to bring that husband of hers? Robin always had the worst taste in men. Always went after the *bad boys.* She knew the moment she met Chuck that he was no good and wouldn't amount to a damn thing. He was one of those men that wouldn't look you in the eye and carried a sour smile like they just drank a spoonful of vinegar. Maggie told her sister she shouldn't marry Chuck, but Robin didn't listen—Robin never listened to anybody.

She watched her kids head straight for the dining room table and tear into the food like they hadn't eaten in weeks.

They better not break anything.

Chuck gazed around the house, looking for something when his eyes locked on Maggie's for a moment, and she could tell in a second that he was already drunk. He gave her a big, stupid grin, and he immediately reminded Maggie of her father. That drunken look in his eyes when he was in the house with her and Robin. He'd sit on the couch, watching them but saying nothing. Maggie could still remember the smell of whiskey on his breath. Could still hear him breathe through his nose. Poor Robin endured the worst of it. For whatever reason, Maggie had escaped the wrath of their father. Robin would try to hide from him, but he always managed to find her—the outcome always the same.

The oven timer pinged behind her. Maggie slipped on a pair of oven mitts and forgot about Robin and Chuck, and most of all, her long-dead father. She had hosting duties to attend to.

Everyone stared at Tess or pretended not to. Pretended that they weren't talking about her. She knew that she was the talk of the town—a deaf stranger staying at the local pastor's house. Both mysterious and scandalous.

Never before had she attended a pastor's birthday party, but it proved to be what she imagined: primarily elderly men and women dressed in polyester gathered around the dining room table, scooping green bean casserole, potato salad, meatloaf, Jell-O with floating chunks of fruit, and salted chips onto paper plates. What she hadn't expected was beer and wine being consumed like water.

A handful of kids ran around unchecked. Screaming and pushing. Either eating food or throwing it.

Cap had been whisked away by a gaggle of elderly women who *Needed to talk to him about the matter of Shelley Cole's low-cut dress that she wore to last week's sermon.* Cap complied, giving Tess a conspiratorial look as he was escorted away in a flurry of overlapping chatter.

From across the living room, Tess sensed that Wade was still staring at her—he had been for the last few minutes. She also knew it was only a matter of time before he would head in her direction.

She didn't have to wait long.

He made his approach slowly, pretending to be casual, smiling and nodding at folks as he snaked his way toward her.

"We meet again."

Tess forced a smile.

He held out his hand. "I'm Wade."

She shook his hand, then flipped her notebook to a prewritten page. *I'm Tess. Nice to meet you.*

"I'm not a big fan of these kinds of parties, but Maggie is pretty much the boss around here."

Beautiful home.

"Thank you." He pulled on his beer bottle before continuing. "I heard through the grapevine that you're staying over at Cap's place."

Yes.

"That must be a little strange."

Tess tilted her head, unsure what he meant by that.

"I've known Cap a long time. He's a bit of an odd duck."

She didn't respond. Lit a cigarette instead.

"I mean, no offense to Cap or anything, but the man is in his mid-forties, never been married, lives alone. Sometimes you have to wonder."

Tess smoked her cigarette and simply stared at him.

"Sorry. Are you and Cap—well, you know?"

Tess knew what Wade was fishing for but waited for more.

"The two of you. Just friends, then?"

Tess noticed that Maggie was watching them quite carefully.

Your wife is keeping an eye on you.

Wade shrugged. "Let her watch."

I don't want you getting in trouble.

"Hell. I'm always in trouble. According to Maggie, it's my middle name." He laughed and guzzled more beer.

Tess searched the room for Cap, but he was nowhere to be seen.

"Well, I can't imagine that living with Cap is much fun, so if you ever want to get out and do something different, let me know. It can be boring as hell around here."

Tess could smell the food before she saw it—a platter of stuffed mushrooms appeared before her, and then Maggie's painted-on smile.

"Would you care for a mushroom?"

Tess took one, even though she didn't care for mushrooms.

"There's plenty, so help yourself."

Tess could feel the tension between Wade and Maggie.

"I hope I'm not interrupting anything," Maggie chirped.

Wade drained the rest of his bottle. "No, Maggie. You're not interrupting anything."

Maggie's smile didn't falter as she glanced back to Tess. "And would you mind smoking outside? I don't care for the smell in my home."

The plates had been cleared. Everyone was done eating, but not done drinking. Bottles of wine and beer dotted the table—most of them empty. The kids were all long gone, playing upstairs, leaving the adults to their own devices. Everyone's dulled eyes betrayed various levels of intoxication.

Wade sat across from Tess and cocked his head toward Cap. "I could tell you some stories about Cap here, all right."

"We should probably start cleaning up here pretty soon. It's getting late," Maggie interjected.

Wade acted as if he didn't hear a word his wife uttered and cracked open a fresh beer. "Cap and I used to be the best of friends, didn't we, Cap?"

"Yeah. I guess we were."

"But now I think we put up with one another more than anything else. Isn't that right?"

"We've just gone our separate ways, I suppose."

Wade leaned across the table and addressed Tess directly. "Bet you didn't know that Cap here is the reason I got stuck here in Black Walnut."

Maggie stiffened. "Let's not get into all that, Wade."

"What? Tess here probably wants to know a little bit about the man she's staying with." Wade grinned at Cap. "You don't mind, now do you, Cap?"

"Would it matter if I did?"

"Hell, you and Maggie are about as much fun as a bag full of sticks." He waved them both off and returned his attention to Tess. "It was during Christmas break our senior year and we had pretty much run out of things to do around here, so we were looking to find some booze. Thought we'd throw a little party on the Wyalusing Rocks, invite some girls, the whole nine yards. So, we came up with a plan."

"*You* came up with the plan," Cap corrected.

"Whatever. Anyway, there was this little old woman that lived down on Church Street next to the river. Old Lady Shoemaker. She lived alone, and everyone in town knew she was into the sauce about half the time, so Cap and I decided to sneak into her kitchen and swipe a bottle." Sipped his beer before continuing. "Well, we waited until sundown, then snuck in through her back porch, quiet as a pair of mice, but as it turned out, it wouldn't have mattered if we marched in, beating on two sets of drums. We got inside and there was Old Lady Shoemaker, lying in the middle of the kitchen floor, stiff as a board and about as purple as an eggplant. You remember that, Cap?"

"Kind of hard to forget."

"We took one look at Old Lady Shoemaker and hightailed it out of there. We couldn't find the door fast enough." Wade jabbed his thumb toward Cap. "But Honest Abe here decided that we should tell our folks about what we discovered."

"As he should have," Maggie added.

"Hell. Dead is dead. Besides, I knew for a fact that if we told our folks what we found, they'd ask why we broke into the old lady's house, why we were snooping around her house, and there'd be hell to pay."

"It was the right thing to do," Cap insisted.

Wade ignored the comment. "So, after Cap went squawking to mommy and daddy, they called the sheriff, and pretty soon half the town was racing over to Old Lady Shoemaker's, and we had a full-on circus on our hands." Drained the rest of his beer.

"And when my old man found out what I did, he yanked me off the basketball team, forcing me to miss the rest of my senior year. And just like that, I lost my shot at going off to play college ball and make something of myself."

Maggie rolled her eyes. "But who knows if you would have been any good anyway?"

"I know," Wade snapped. "I know for a fact that I could've played at Division I—"

"And made it into the pros," Maggie interrupted. "I've heard it a million times."

"It's true, goddamnit." He pounded on the table with both fists.

All conversation grew quiet for a moment, and then Wade felt Maggie tugging on his arm. "Maybe you should start taking out the trash."

"The night is young." He popped open a fresh beer and leaned closer to Tess. "Besides, I want to learn more about Tess here."

Robin didn't understand why Chuck wanted to come with her and the kids. He hated birthday parties. Hated socializing. He especially hated being around Cap and Maggie. But she put two and two together pretty quick: free beer.

She watched him stand in the corner of the kitchen, drinking one bottle of beer after another. He didn't talk with anyone. Merely rocked on the balls of his feet and stared at the crowd with disdain, internally mocking them. That always made him feel better about himself, somehow. She knew he was way past drunk and that she should get him out of the house before he caused the kind of scene that would embarrass or frighten the kids. It wasn't a matter of if, it was a matter of *when.*

She watched him twist off the cap from a fresh bottle of beer and wondered how she could convince him to leave. It could go one of two ways. The first way would find him itching to get the hell out of the house and away from what he called *Bible-thumpers.* Or the second would involve belligerence, cursing, and someone getting physically hurt.

Robin knew it probably wouldn't go the first way.

Maggie's legs bounced under the table, her hands clenching and unclenching in her lap. She tried breathing in and out slowly to prevent the growing anxiety attack, but her entire body vibrated, and it felt like her scalp might catch on fire.

She glanced around the dinner table, watched Wade staring at Tess and knew that he was undressing her with his eyes. Then she looked at Robin and other folks from church, their mouths opening and closing, everyone drinking and talking at the same time, but all she heard was nonsensical jibber-jabber. It seemed to get louder and louder, and she felt the walls close in around her, threatening to crush her if she didn't get some fresh air.

Maggie noticed that Tess stared at her with a quizzical expression. Why was she staring at her? Did Tess know what kind of man Wade was? Would she sleep with him, too? She forced her eyes from Tess and stood up as slowly and naturally as she could manage.

"Excuse me."

Maggie willed herself not to race out of the room. Willed herself not to screech like an owl. She painted a pleasant smile upon her face, pushed her chair in, and made her way out of the dining room like a normal, grounded woman, not like someone on the verge of a complete meltdown. She hurried down the hallway and could still hear the chatter from the dining room. Stopped and placed both hands against the walls to steady her quivering knees. Took a deep breath, telling herself to snap out of it.

The bathroom door was ten feet away—only ten feet away—and Maggie thought if she could make it into the restroom, then she would be able to find a way to compose herself. She inched her way forward, past jackets hanging from the wall, when she noticed a purse dangling from a hook as well. She knew in an instant that it must be Tess's.

Maggie didn't hesitate. She snatched the purse and hustled into the bathroom. Closed the door behind her, leaned against the sink and ran cold water on shaking hands. As she splashed water upon her face, she caught her reflection in the mirror—her cheeks red and splotchy. She kept rubbing at her skin like she could wipe away this awful feeling inside her, but it didn't help. Her hands rattled and her heart raced, and her legs felt unsteady below her. She knew that she couldn't go back out there and face everyone—especially Tess. The woman seemed to be silently judging her.

She swung open the medicine cabinet door and searched through bottles of pills until she found the one she wanted. Shook out a Valium and swallowed the tablet. Cupped her hand under the faucet and drank some water. Wiped her face and hands with a towel and gazed around the bathroom. Then her eyes fell on Tess's purse.

She glanced toward the door before sitting down on the toilet and placing the purse on her lap. She opened the bag and stared at the contents. A hairbrush, wallet, pack of cigarettes, handful of pens, and loose change. Then she felt something else. Something hard and cold and unnatural in a woman's purse. She pulled out the object and stared at a pistol.

Maggie turned the pistol over in her hands, surprised by the weight of the gun. She had never held a revolver before, but there was something strangely appealing about feeling the cold steel pressing against her palm. She raised the gun and pointed it at her reflection in the mirror. Her index finger wrapped around the trigger and her hand was remarkably steady.

"*Bang*," she whispered. "*Bang, bang, bang.*"

She returned the gun to the purse and her eyes fell on an object partially hidden on the bottom—something she missed before. Shiny and gold-colored. She reached in the bag with trembling fingers and grabbed a tube of lipstick. Slipped off the cap and inspected the shade of makeup. Dark plum. Not a color she'd wear in a million years.

But the mere act of holding the lipstick made her feel better—a calm washing over her entire body. She pocketed the tube without another thought, adjusted her hair in the mirror, and right as she stepped out of the bathroom and replaced the purse back onto the hook, a high-pitched scream erupted from the living room.

Cap felt like the entire sequence played out in slow motion. He watched Chuck's lips pull back, revealing teeth the color of mustard. Saw the unchecked rage in the man's eyes. Heard the five words uttered: "The fuck you staring at?"

Chuck's hand snapped forward, knocking the wine glass from Tess's fingers. Glass shattered against the floor and exploded into tiny, jagged pieces, red wine splattering like a gunshot wound. He shoved Tess against the kitchen wall and reared his hand back.

"ENOUGH," Cap shouted. He seized Chuck's wrist and twisted his arm behind him.

Chuck resisted, flailing in Cap's grasp, spittle spewing. "Lemme go, goddamnit."

"You need to calm down."

Chuck continued to thrash but Cap held tight. Then, slowly, Chuck lost his fight, and his body went limp. Cap released his arm and Chuck stumbled forward on unsteady feet. Felt all the eyes on him.

Robin was still screaming while Chuck stared down at Tess sprawled by his feet. It was almost as if he didn't know where he was or what exactly was happening.

Cap helped Tess to her feet. Her eyes were wide, and she had a hard time catching her breath.

"What the hell are you thinking?" Cap snapped.

Chuck stared back at him with crimson-streaked eyes. "She wouldn't stop staring at me, Cap." Speech thick and slurred.

"Staring?"

"I told her to stop, but she wouldn't. Just kept staring at me."

"All right."

"I warned her. I warned her a bunch of times."

"Okay. Let's step outside for a minute."

Chuck didn't resist as Cap guided him toward the front door.

"You can't stare at people and not say nothing."

"I know, Chuck. I know."

As Cap ushered Chuck into the cold, all he could hear was Robin crying and repeating the same thing over and over again: "Why does he always have to do this?"

SIX DAYS BEFORE GOOD FRIDAY

25

Cap never quite knew when the phone might ring with calls of an urgent nature. There was no predicting it. Sometimes weeks went by with the phone never ringing—not once.

So, typically, the moment the bells clanked on his black, rotary dial phone, Cap knew the caller to be someone that had lost a family member or needed someone to confide in—or both. The sound of his phone making that dull clanging had Cap programmed to think the worst: someone in the area had passed from this world to the next.

Cap picked up the phone and discovered that he was right on both accounts. Someone had lost someone and needed to talk to him urgently.

Alice Hunsinger weighed nearly five hundred pounds. She'd always been a big girl even back in her school days—taller and wider than all her classmates, and even heavier than some of her teachers. Then, as adulthood kicked in, so did the diabetes. When Alice turned thirty, she tipped the scales at three hundred pounds. When she celebrated her fortieth birthday, Alice crossed the four-hundred-pound threshold. As her age increased, so did her weight gain. By the time she was in her mid-forties, Alice never left the house—her body literally couldn't fit through the front door of her trailer.

Her husband, Benny, told Cap over the phone that when Alice's cat, Tulip, ran away and didn't return, Alice decided that she'd finally had enough—life had lost all meaning.

Benny returned home from his mail route to find Alice lying in a heap in the center of the living room floor, stiff and cold as a mound of rocks. Benny removed the plastic bag from around his wife's head and covered her with a flannel sheet before calling his pastor.

Benny propped open the door and waved Cap inside. He was not a tall man, nor was he short. A thick neck and short-clipped hair made his enormous ears appear even larger. The most remarkable aspect of the man's appearance was his massive hands—they looked as if they could crush a tin can with a single squeeze.

Benny spoke with a prominent stutter, and it took him a few moments to form the first words he directed at Cap. "Do you want a *co-co-co* cold beer or a *cu-cu-cu* cup of coffee?"

Cap declined both, then gazed at Alice's concealed mass. "The sheriff hasn't shown up yet?"

"No." Benny took out a handkerchief and cleared out his nose before continuing. "Haven't *ca-ca-ca* called him yet."

Cap returned his attention back to Benny, but Benny offered no explanation.

"I'm sure this is extremely difficult, Benny, but we really need to call Sheriff Lester."

Benny took a seat on a sofa dotted with cigarette burns and motioned for Cap to take a seat as well. Benny didn't appear all that uncomfortable with his wife of twenty-eight years lying dead on the living room floor only a few feet away. "I *n-n-n* needed to talk to you first."

"Okay. I'm here for you, Benny. I'm listening."

Benny stood and fetched two beers from the refrigerator. He cracked open both cans, handed one to Cap, and then sat back down on the sofa. Drank down half of his beer before speaking. "I'm worried about Alice, you see. She *g-g-g* gonna go to hell, Cap?"

Cap hesitated before sipping his beer. Then he drank again. "Why would you ask that?"

Benny rolled the can of beer in between massive palms. "Because she *t-t-t* took her own life. Ain't that a *m-m-m* mortal sin? The Bible says . . ." Benny finally broke down. His shoulders shook, and his chest heaved, and tears rolled down the man's rutted face.

"She's *g-g-g* gonna go to hell, ain't she, Cap?" He stared at Cap with desperate eyes and waited for an answer. Waited for guidance. Waited for some comforting words.

Instead, Cap drank more beer.

"Alice *h-h-h* hasn't been happy in a *l-l-l* long time, Cap. You know that, don't you?"

"I guess I do."

She's *h-h-h* had it hard. Her whole life."

Cap cleared his throat, but before he could offer any consolation, Benny continued.

"She didn't *m-m-m* mean to get in the way she did. She didn't mean to become *w-w-w* what she become."

"There wasn't anything wrong with who Alice was, Benny."

Benny nodded. Wiped his nose with the back of his hand. He attempted to compose himself, then looked back to Cap with a stronger set of eyes. "You know what I mean, Cap. I ain't saying anything that everybody in town doesn't know."

Cap sipped from his beer can. Searched for a way to make the man feel better but came up with nothing.

"I know what folks thought of my wife. I know what they were saying."

"People talk. They're only words. It doesn't mean anything."

Benny shook his head at Cap. "Maybe they are just words, but there's meaning behind them. They're full of judgment. Full of judgment even when the words aren't spoken out loud."

Cap realized that the man had stopped stuttering.

"Alice hasn't had a visitor here in a long time, Cap. You know how long?"

"No. I don't."

Benny leaned forward. Rested thick forearms on his legs. He motioned toward his wife and his eyes reddened once again. "Ten years, Cap. Ten goddamn years have gone by since Alice has seen or talked to someone besides me. Do you know what that does to a person?"

Cap didn't have an answer.

"Did Alice deserve that?"

"No. Don't even think that for a second."

"All my wife had in her life was me and Tulip. She loved that damned cat. When Tulip ran away and left her, it was too much. Alice couldn't take it no more."

"I'm sorry for all this, Benny."

"Tell me the truth, Cap. Do you think that God is gonna punish her? Is she gonna go to *h-h-h* hell for taking her own life?"

Cap finished the rest of his beer. He stood up and grabbed two fresh cans from the refrigerator. Like Benny did before him, Cap cracked both cans, then sat back down next to the man.

Both men drank in silence. Both staring at the sheet that concealed Alice Hunsinger.

Cap cleared his throat before speaking. "I didn't know Alice that well. Only met her twice, in fact. Once in church right when I started serving as the pastor. The other time, maybe eleven, twelve years ago, over at the carnival in Wyalusing." He finished half his beer. "I'll be honest with you, Benny. I don't really care what the Bible has to say on this matter. A woman like Alice belongs in heaven and heaven will be lucky to have her."

Tears streamed down Benny's face as he processed Cap's words.

"I believe that Alice is in a place where she belongs, Benny. I do. I really do."

Benny smiled and set his can of beer on the floor. "Would you say a prayer for her, Cap? Before I call the sheriff?"

"You know I will."

Benny knelt next to his wife and pulled back the flannel sheet.

Alice Hunsinger lay on the trailer floor, face-up, eyes still open. And there, cradled in the nook of her massive right arm, Tulip the cat slept next to her mama.

Benny's voice jarred Cap from his silent scrutiny. "Tulip finally came home. Guess she snuck in through the hole in the bathroom floor."

Cap gazed at Benny and the man wore a bittersweet smile.

"Alice would've been happy that Tulip finally came home, Cap. I know that she would."

"I bet she would, Benny. I sure bet she would."

Cap knelt down beside Alice Hunsinger and began to pray.

26

Tess peered at all the items on Cap's meticulously organized desk—a leather-bound daily planner, a coffee mug filled with sharpened pencils, an inbox with letters and bills, and a dog-eared Bible.

The church study smelled of Cap—cologne, leather, and bourbon. She thought about how she had only known him for a little over a week, but she liked his company, and she wished he'd hurry back from wherever he was.

Every time Cap left the house, his absence felt unbearable. It was when she was all alone that the doubts and fears crept forward and reared their ugly heads.

Why did Aaron have to show up at the library?

What would he do if he found her?

How could she not have known who he really was?

The house was quiet and off-putting. Hallways felt darker. Closed doors seemed suspicious, as if someone was waiting on the other side.

But in Cap's presence, Tess felt what a normal life might possibly be like. Maybe he drank too much. Maybe he was damaged by something from his past. And maybe he was numbing himself, but something about him made her feel grounded. Normal.

A flash of movement outside the window caught her eye. Her heart rattled as she peered out the pane of glass, and her first thought was that Aaron had finally found her. She half-expected to see her father standing outside the church, staring at her with those cold, unreadable eyes. But it wasn't Aaron. Of course, it wasn't. A handful of crows swooped from tree to tree, beaks opening wide and letting out a sound that Tess would never be able to hear again. She watched the flock of crows cawing at one another, and she couldn't remember what the call of a bird sounded like.

She lit a cigarette and smoked in the silence. She opened the top desk drawer, then the side drawers, looking for something, but she didn't know exactly what. One drawer contained stacks and stacks of yellow legal pads with Cap's tiny handwriting filling the pages. She tried reading his cursive writing but could barely make out a single word.

She closed all the drawers. Crushed out her cigarette and lit another. Her eyes wandered to the bookshelf and stopped on a photo of Cap wearing a graduation cap and gown, standing next to a gray-haired man and a woman, short and squat. The woman was the only one in the picture with a smile on her face.

Even though the woman didn't resemble her own mother one bit, Tess couldn't help but think of June. She thought about her mother, how sick with worry she must be. They saw each other almost every day and here it was a week without a word from her. She had just disappeared. How could her mom be able to move to Arizona without knowing where her daughter was or whether she was even alive?

She opened the top drawer of the desk. Found some stationery and a box of envelopes. Selected a pencil from the coffee mug and thought about what to write. What to say. How many details to give.

Her cigarette burned down to the filter before she began to compose a few simple sentences—that she was all right, that she was safe, that she wasn't coming home for a while, that she'd write again soon, to please not worry, but most importantly of all, that she loved her.

Tess folded the stationery and slipped the paper into an envelope. Her hands trembled as she licked and sealed the envelope. She found a stamp and wrote her mother's address in the middle.

She lit another cigarette and waited for Cap to come back home.

27

The scream of the steel blade cutting into the trailer's aluminum siding bore a hole in one temple and right through the other. Orange sparks flared from the doorframe, mixing with a gentle snowfall that accumulated on the gravel driveway.

Cap leaned against his truck and watched as Benny and three volunteer firemen from Black Walnut and Wyalusing cut a section around the trailer door in order to remove Alice Hunsinger's body from a place she had not left in a decade. Cap knew all the men well. They attended church most Sundays unless the Steelers game was on TV. Warren Abrams and Eddie Updegraff owned an insurance company in Wyalusing. They bickered like brothers almost all the time and had been known to come to blows on occasion. Maurice Slabicki worked the register at Bluhm's Mini Market. He always had his nose stuck in a book while puffing on a cigar even though he wasn't supposed to smoke inside the store.

Cap watched as Warren and Eddie stripped away a jagged piece of the siding, and he wondered how the trailer could be repaired. It most likely couldn't. Not fully. Benny's trailer would be forever scarred. The burnt and twisted aluminum siding would be a constant reminder of how his wife had left this earth, every time he entered and exited his home.

Sheriff Lester walked down the trailer steps, drew on his cigarette, and toed the butt into the snow. He shuffled up the driveway and leaned against Cap's truck as well. "Thanks for being here. I know Benny appreciates it."

Both men stood in silence, watching as another strip of siding was removed and tossed into the yard.

"A helluva thing. Sad day for sure." Lester tapped out a fresh cigarette and struck a match under the tip.

Cap couldn't tear his eyes away from the grim operation playing out before him. Benny pried away the door threshold with a crowbar, while behind him, his wife sprawled on the floor, covered with a sheet. Maurice chomped on a cigar as he backed a flatbed truck next to the trailer to haul Alice away since an ambulance couldn't do the job. And crouched in the crook of a mighty elm tree, Tulip the cat watched with restless eyes, tail twitching.

"Cap? You with me?"

Lester's question shook Cap from his fixation, and he rubbed at the stubble on his chin before responding.

"It's hard, Lester. You and I know what people in this town go through. We're privy to how bad their lives have become before their loved ones do. We know their dark secrets. Shameful acts. But we have to keep it to ourselves. Just . . . bottle it up." He watched Benny struggle with the doorframe. "It's hard to let these things go. Hard to go back home and go about your day as if other people's pain and loss didn't even happen."

"Well, I suppose you're right, but what choice do we have?"

Cap didn't have an answer to that.

"You did what you needed to do, Cap. You gave Benny some peace. That's important. Don't overlook that fact."

"I hope you're right."

"Why don't you head back home? I'll take it from here."

The howl of the circular saw cutting through aluminum started up again.

"You sure there's nothing more that I can do?"

The sheriff pinched off his cigarette and pocketed the butt. "Matter of fact, there is one thing you can do for me."

Lester and Bonnie's house hadn't changed much over the years. Constructed with red sandstone and a wood shingle roof, the home looked to be from a different time, when horses were the primary mode of travel. Board and batten shutters painted midnight blue were mounted on both sides of all the windows. Smoke coiled from the chimney. Rose bushes neatly trimmed and awaiting their spring bloom filled raised garden beds that lined the front porch. The walkway had been recently shoveled and salted.

The moment Cap stepped out of his truck, the chatter of birdsong filled the country air. The yard resembled a bird sanctuary. Dozens upon dozens of tufted titmice, white-breasted nuthatches, fox sparrows, mourning doves, robins, chickadees, and a northern cardinal swooped from the limbs of birch trees and hopped along the snow.

Birdfeeders dotted the yard. Hanging from the trees, mounted outside windows, installed atop metal poles. Every feeder filled with seeds and millet.

Cap climbed the steps to the porch, and before he could rap his knuckles against the door, the sound of a woman's voice got his attention. Coming from somewhere outside the house. He walked to the edge of the porch and spotted Bonnie tossing handfuls of feed onto the snow. And even though the old woman was bundled up in a wool jacket, Cap could see how skinny she had become. A strong gust of wind could probably send her head over heels.

Her hands resembled claws, nothing but skin and bone, yet she scattered seeds from a bucket at a fast clip while chatting with the birds like she was gathered with a group of childhood friends. She smiled from one ear to the next and didn't seem bothered one bit by the bitter cold.

Two cats perched on a window ledge inside the house, watching the activity in their yard—their hunting ground—with great interest.

"You *trying* to catch a cold out here?"

Bonnie peered at him from under a knit cap. Cheekbones protruded beneath dark, sunken eyes, but despite the disease that was eating her up from the inside, her blue eyes had a twinkle about them. "Catching a cold is the least of my worries." She tossed another scoop of seed onto the ground. "Besides, you don't think Lester actually feeds these hungry rascals, do you?"

Cap hopped off the porch and trudged through the snow. "Guess not. I imagine Lester has a hard enough time feeding himself."

"And tying his shoelaces. Finding his truck keys. Putting the toilet seat down. The list goes on and on."

Cap gave her arm a light squeeze. "How are you faring, Bonnie?"

"I'm still standing upright, so that's something." She hobbled across the yard, tossing seeds as she went. "And to what do I owe the pleasure?"

"Lester's been trying to call you. Wanted me to check on you."

Bonnie pointed to a bird feeder hanging from the limb of a birch tree just out of her reach. "Will you take that down for me? Lester hung it too high."

As Cap untied the string, he cut her a serious look. "You want to tell me how you're really feeling?"

"Nope."

"All right. But let me know when you do." He moved the birdfeeder to a lower branch. "Lester is going to be a while."

"Alice?"

"Afraid so."

"Poor Benny. God bless his heart."

"Not a pretty scene. Lester has a lot to sort out." He tugged at his mustache. "You want me to stay and make you some dinner?"

"I'd be lying if I said yes."

"Don't trust my cooking?"

"Not one damn bit."

Cap laughed and Bonnie joined him. Then Bonnie's laugh turned into a coughing fit. A sharp, violent attack. Cap could hear the rattle of phlegm inside her lungs. He waited for the episode to subside. Watched a cardinal land on one of the feeders and scare off all the other birds. After establishing his territory, the cardinal commenced pecking at some seeds.

"Oh, dear," Bonnie wheezed. She took a Kleenex to her leaking eyes. "Sounds worse than it feels."

"That's good."

"I count my blessings where I can."

She filled the last of the birdfeeders and made her way to the porch. Cap couldn't help but notice how gingerly she moved. Favored her right leg a bit. Breathed hard through her nose.

He held her by the elbow and Bonnie allowed it. She gestured to a cushioned seat by the porch railing. "Let me rest a minute."

Bonnie let out a heavy sigh once settled in.

"Get you something?"

"My youth back maybe."

"I was thinking more along the lines of a cup of tea or glass of water."

Bonnie delivered a playful swat to his arm. "Shoot. And I was hoping for some kind of miracle."

"Well, I'm praying for one, Bonnie. You know I am."

She forced a smile before staring across her yard, where a dozen or so birds flitted about. "So peaceful. I savor these small moments."

They watched the birds in silence for a few beats of time.

"I'll tell you something. Even though cardinals and blue jays sure are a sight to see, the birds I'm most drawn to are the tufted titmouse, the nuthatch, and chickadees. Maybe they're not as colorful or flashy, but those birds don't mind sharing what they've got. They're not bullies. They're not aggressive or out to prove anything. They get along with one another just fine, and to me, that is a beautiful thing."

Bonnie squeezed Cap's hand and gave him a wink. "Ramblings of an old woman."

"Old maybe, but wise as well."

She waved off the compliment like a bothersome fly. "Say, when exactly are you planning to bring that girlfriend of yours for a visit?"

"Well, she's not exactly my girlfriend, Bonnie."

"*Lady* friend or whatever they call it nowadays. She is the talk of the town."

"Talk is cheap."

"You're no fun."

"Not the first time I've heard that. Probably not the last."

Bonnie clucked her tongue. "Don't be so hard on yourself."

"I'm kidding."

"I know you are, but I'm not. You have always carried such weight on your shoulders. Behind that smile of yours, I see the sadness."

Cap did not argue the point. He watched the birds instead.

"You're a good man, Cap, whether you know it or not." She patted his knee and stood slowly, wincing as she went. "I better get out of this cold. Lester will read me the riot act."

"You sure there's not anything I can do for you?"

Bonnie pressed her palms on both of his cheeks. "Yeah. There is, actually."

"You name it."

"Savor the little moments. And if something good comes your way, take it. Big or small. You deserve it, Cap."

She opened the front door and shooed the cats from escaping. Pointed a finger at him. "Don't be a stranger. And next time, bring that *lady* friend of yours with you."

Cap sat in the cab of his truck and listened to the howl of wind. Rubbed at his jaw, thought about what Bonnie said, and opened the glove compartment for his thermos. Twisted off the cap, but thought twice. He watched the snow fall for a minute. Then he replaced the lid and nestled the thermos between his thighs.

He took the long way back to the house. Drove along Crow Valley Road before turning onto Spring Hill Lane. Snow blanketed the roads, a few inches deep and unmarred by other tire tracks. Cap took it slow and easy. He wanted to get back home and see Tess, but he needed to clear his head a little.

Try as he might, he couldn't shake the image of Benny breaking down and crying in front of him.

She's gonna go to hell, ain't she, Cap?

Cap glanced down at the thermos, there for the taking.

He had told Benny what the man wanted, *needed* to hear. But he had lied to the man, too. He promised Benny something that he couldn't possibly deliver.

What was he supposed to say? That Alice's actions would send the woman straight to hell?

He didn't know what to think anymore.

His foot pressed harder against the gas pedal.

Death was all around him. Everywhere he turned.

Teddie.

Alice.

Max and his parents well before their time.

And now, Bonnie's courage in facing her own mortality made him feel foolish and selfish. What kind of pastor was he?

The more Cap realized that he preached words he didn't believe himself anymore—or at the very least, doubted—the faster he drove. He had spent the last fifteen years listening to the sins of others and passing judgment whether he intended to or not.

How much longer could he keep traveling down this road? His congregation deserved better. *He* deserved better than living this lie.

The tree line blurred past. Snowflakes attacked the windshield with a fury. Tires roared below.

Take the good in your life, Cap. Big or small. You deserve it.

The truck began to drift. Wheels spinning on ice. The back end of the truck fishtailed. But he kept his foot planted on the pedal.

Take the good in your life, Cap. Big or small. You deserve it.

He took in a deep take of air. Eased his boot off the gas. Gripped the steering tightly as the truck floated toward the ditch. He steered into the skid, and it took a couple of seconds before he managed to regain control of the Ford. The wheels straightened. The treads found traction.

Cap replayed Bonnie's words over and over again, until his heart rate steadied.

He slowed the truck and pulled off to the side of the road. Cut the engine and stared out the windshield, watching flakes of snow kiss the glass before melting in an instant. He listened to the perfect quiet all around him, put the thermos back in the glove compartment, then restarted the Ford.

Tess was waiting. He wanted to get back home and see her. He wanted that in the worst way.

28

Like a guest in his own home, Cap stood in the foyer and watched Tess for a minute. She sat on the couch, drinking a glass of wine. Her notebook rested on her lap, and she gazed at the fireplace, lost in thought, her mind a million miles away. Her brow was creased and her mouth drawn straight.

He couldn't stop staring at her and wondered what she might be thinking. He didn't know much about her, and, in fact, it occurred to him that he didn't even know her last name. But all of that didn't matter right now. And maybe it never would. Fate or destiny had brought her to this town, to his home, and he knew better than to question the reason.

He hung up his jacket on a hook and stepped into the living room. Tess's face transformed at the sight of him. She smiled, exposing a dimple on her right cheek, and stared back at him with those dark green eyes of hers.

Hello, she signed.

"Sorry I took so long."

That's okay.

Cap stood in the middle of the room like he didn't know what to do with himself.

Tess's eyebrows pinched together, and her smile faded away. *What's wrong?*

Cap didn't realize he was crying until he felt the tears roll down his cheeks. It had been so long since he last cried that he forgot what it felt like. It was not a loud cry, but rather, a slow release of sadness years in the making.

Tess set her glass of wine on the coffee table and approached him.

"Tess . . ."

She embraced Cap and held him tight.

He wasn't sure how long he wept, or whether he was crying for Alice Hunsinger or Bonnie or even himself—or maybe for all three. But the release felt good and long overdue. He pulled away from her and wiped his face with the back of his hand.

You okay?

"I am now."

She touched her lips with her fingertips, then gestured to his. *You want to talk about it?*

Cap didn't answer her question. Instead, he stared into her eyes as if searching for something.

Tess maintained his gaze and waited for a response.

He brushed the hair away from her face and she allowed it. When Cap leaned forward and pressed his lips against hers, she allowed that, too. He took her hand in his and guided her up the stairs. When he opened the door to his bedroom, Tess was the first to cross the threshold.

29

The boys had been a handful ever since they returned home from school. Chuck Jr. pitched a fit about doing his homework, not wanting to tear himself away from watching some awful war movie on television that was nothing but loud explosions and soldiers screaming at one another. Then, after Robin finally switched off the TV set and got him sitting at the kitchen table in front of his math worksheets, he squirmed and belly-ached like enduring a form of parental torture.

Twenty minutes later, after pulling teeth to keep him in his chair and do the best he could, it was bath time, and an all-out meltdown broke out between the boys. Chuck Jr. refused to take a bath with Mikey, and Mikey refused to bathe alone. Robin finally threw her hands up and instructed both boys to just clean up with a hot washcloth, which set off Darla, who claimed if her brothers didn't have to take a bath, then neither did she. By that point, Robin only wanted to get them all off to bed and made them promise to take baths tomorrow.

The wind howled outside, rattling the living room windowpanes. Robin sat at the kitchen table, drinking a Diet Coke, smoking a cigarette, and staring down at a pile of unopened bills. Most of them were past due and would remain that way until Chuck found a job or some other miracle happened. She glanced at the clock on the microwave. It was almost eleven. Chuck would be home soon because Red's closed at eleven on weekdays.

She picked up a JCPenney catalog from under the stack of bills and leafed through the pages of women's clothing, eyeing items she couldn't afford. Cute dresses and skirts and blouses looking so nice on all the models. When she came to the section of bras and panties, her eyes stopped on one model in particular. The model reminded her of Tess. Same color hair and wild hairstyle, similar facial structure, and the exact green-colored, almond eyes with heavy lids. Robin's gaze lingered on the model's cleavage and flat stomach, and she imagined Tess looked the same. The model's face was frozen in a playful bedroom smirk, the tip of her pink tongue peeking out between her straight, white teeth.

Robin closed her eyes and imagined Tess in the same pose, standing in front of her, caressing the delicate skin above the elastic band of her panties. She thought of how Tess stared at her with those penetrating green eyes, seeming to know who and what kind of person she really was.

Robin kept her eyes pressed closed and touched herself through her sweatpants. Her fingers pushed against the cotton material and the inside of her thighs quivered, wanting and anticipating more.

She kept thinking about Tess and her fingers found their way inside, probing deeper. Then the garage door banged open, followed by the laboring sound of Chuck's truck pulling inside. Her eyes snapped open, and she yanked her hand away from her sex, feeling a flash of panic at the thought of Chuck catching her in the act of pleasuring herself.

She waited for the sound of the truck to shut off, followed by Chuck's drunken footsteps, but she heard the engine continue to idle and labor. When she lifted her glass to her lips, she noticed that her hands trembled, and she thought about sneaking off to bed and pretending to be asleep, but something kept her at the kitchen table instead.

After a minute of waiting for Chuck to come staggering into the house, Robin crushed out her cigarette, walked to the garage door, and listened. All quiet except the sound of the truck engine rumbling. Maybe Chuck was sitting in the cab, smoking, and finishing up another beer. She didn't really feel like facing him and looking into those drunken, hateful eyes, but before she could stop herself, she cracked open the door and peeked inside.

Gray exhaust filled the garage, smelling so toxic and foul, and Robin waved away the smoke. Chuck hunched over the steering wheel, not moving or seeming to do anything.

"Chuck?" she called, her throat and eyes burning from the smoke.

She stepped down into the garage in her bare feet, the cold of the concrete sending a shock throughout her body. She peeked inside the cab—Chuck's head drooped forward, an unlit cigarette dangling from his lips.

It was a wonder that he had managed to make it back home alive, and a part of her—almost all of her—wished that he had plowed off the road and driven straight into a tree.

She stared at her husband's face, so transformed from too much selfish living. He looked much older than his thirty-eight years. Deep smoker's lines etched around his eyes and at the corners of his mouth, his skin blotchy and red, his hair thinning. As exhaust continued to billow out from the leaking muffler, Robin kept searching Chuck's face for something redeemable, something good and worth loving, but she couldn't find a single thing.

The boys feared more than loved him. And the thought of Chuck Jr. and Mikey turning into their father scared the hell out of her, but that's all they knew. And poor Darla—would she end up marrying someone just like her daddy?

She opened the truck door and reached inside to cut the ignition. Her face a few inches away from Chuck's, she could smell the whiskey and beer and cigarettes on his breath. At one time long ago, she thought that to be nothing less than manly. He mumbled, and his crimson-streaked eyes opened for a moment and glared at Robin with absolute ugliness. He muttered something nasty before closing his eyes once again.

A dull, throbbing headache began to crawl up Robin's neck. Her fingertips touched the keys dangling from the ignition. She hesitated. And as if she'd been planning for this opportunity for a lifetime, Robin pulled her hand away and closed the door to the truck. She didn't second-guess her decision as she walked to the front of the garage and pulled down the panelized door. The metal door banged against the concrete floor, sealing up the space from the cold air outside.

Robin stood in the middle of the garage, watching the gray vapor curl up and billow like the breath of a dragon, and the exhaust quickly filled the entire space. She grabbed a ratty towel from the shelf that she used to wipe the boys' winter boots, opened the door to the house, and stepped inside. She noticed that her heart rate was remarkably steady as she rolled up the towel and tucked it at the base of the door to keep the poison at bay.

She sat at the kitchen table and finished her Diet Coke. Stared at some of the boys' drawings hanging on the refrigerator. Eyes drawn to one in particular. A crayon sketch that Mikey had made in kindergarten class. Though crude and hastily done, it was a self-portrait, and the boy looked so sad and lost.

As she made her way down the hallway, she tried to block out the sound of the truck in the garage. She stepped inside the kids' room, flicked off the light, and kissed them on the forehead, one by one. Then she climbed into bed next to Darla, pressed her body against her daughter's, and pulled the blanket tight under her chin.

FIVE DAYS BEFORE GOOD FRIDAY

30

Wade stared up from his office desk, shaking his head at Maggie, whose arms crossed over her chest. "A pistol? In her purse? Are you sure?"

"Yes, Wade. I know what a pistol looks like."

Wade leaned back in his leather chair. "And how exactly do you know that Tess had a pistol in her purse?"

Maggie stared up at the ceiling for a moment. Shifted the weight on her feet. "I didn't know until I saw it."

Wade's head cocked to the left. "So, you were snooping in the woman's purse?"

"I wasn't snooping."

"Looking for chocolate, maybe?"

Maggie marched forward and plopped down on a chair facing the desk. "The woman is carrying a gun in her purse, Wade. Does it really matter how I found it?"

Wade leaned forward. Propped his elbows on his desk. Picked up a pen and clicked the tip in and out a few times. "So? What's the big deal? Everyone we know around here owns a gun. I've got guns in my study at home."

"But why does she carry a pistol in her purse?"

"Hell if I know. Protection maybe?"

Maggie jabbed her index finger toward his face. "She's carrying a *concealed* weapon."

Wade laughed out loud. Shook his head. "Jesus, Maggie. What's gotten into you?"

"I'll tell you what's gotten into me. That woman brought a gun into *our* home, Wade. We know nothing about her. Where she's from. Who she is."

"And what? You think she's a criminal? An outlaw on the run, maybe?"

"That's not funny."

Wade laughed to demonstrate that he thought it was.

"What are you going to do about it?"

Wade stopped laughing. Stared at his wife. Took a deep breath. "Nothing. Absolutely nothing is what I'm going to do about it."

"But what if she's mentally unstable? What if she had taken out that gun and shot someone? What if she shot Butch?"

"Why would she shoot Butch? She hates fourteen-year-old boys?"

Maggie slapped her palm on top of the desk and the sound carried throughout the office. "Damn it, Wade. This is not funny. And you're not funny. I'm being serious. Something needs to be done about this."

Wade sighed. Placed his head between his hands. "Fine, Mags. What is it you want me to do exactly?"

"Talk to the sheriff. Tell him what I saw."

Wade glared at her. "No."

"No?"

"No, Goddamnit. I'm not going to do that. I'm not bothering Lester with this nonsense. I'm not going to talk to the man about you snooping in someone's purse."

"I said I wasn't snooping."

"Whatever. Besides, maybe Tess has a permit to carry a gun. You ever thought about that? Maybe she's from the city. Lived in a bad neighborhood."

Maggie crossed her arms once again.

He stared at his wife. Said nothing. He could tell by the way she sat there and glared at him that she wouldn't let this thing go.

"Christ. Whatever. Fine. I'll look into it."

"What do you mean you'll—"

"But I'm not going to Lester about this. The man's wife is dying. He doesn't need this kind of shit."

"So?"

"So, I'll go and talk with Cap."

"Just the two of you?"

He simply glared at her.

"Are you going to be nice?"

He sighed again. "Yes, Mags. I'll be as nice as apple pie."

"Today."

"Today, what?"

"I want you to go and talk to Cap today. Not tomorrow. Not next week." She pursed her lips. "Otherwise, I'll call the sheriff myself."

Wade's jaw tightened. "Are you sure there isn't something else to this?"

"Like what?"

"Like the fact that you might not like this woman. For whatever reason."

"That's silly. I don't even know her. I'm simply looking out for the safety of my family."

"I bet you are." Wade stood. Grabbed his jacket from a hook behind the door. "Well, so much for getting any damn work done. I guess I'll go and talk with Cap. Find out all about this *concealed* pistol."

"Thank you, Wade. You're doing the right thing here. Protecting your family."

Wade didn't bother responding. He walked out of the office and slammed the door behind him.

31

It wasn't as if Cap regretted what had happened with Tess. Not at all. He hadn't been with a woman for far too long. No, the intimacy was good. He didn't regret the act itself. What nagged at him now were the implications of the unknown.

He opened a new package of 150 grit sandpaper and began to work the top of a bookshelf. He preferred sanding by hand. Maybe it took five times longer to smooth out the wood—and he had a brand-new orbital sander that could do the trick just fine—but there was something about touching wood directly with his fingers that gave Cap a sense of connection. Usually, he got swallowed up in his work, his mind nowhere except in the grain of the wood itself, but today, his mind kept returning to Tess.

The woman was running from something. Running from *somebody*. Maybe an abusive husband or lover. Or maybe she'd done something wrong and was in some kind of trouble.

They'd only known each other for a little over a week. Two strangers really. What did they really know about the other? Not much, that was for sure.

Cap set down the strip of sandpaper, dusted off his hands, and stepped in front of a set of shelves that housed paints and varnishes. He grabbed a fifth of Wild Turkey and poured three fingers worth into a glass.

He took a sip. Then another. He stared out the window that faced the house and scratched at his jaw.

Tess needed to tell him what kind of trouble she was in. She didn't have to tell him everything, but she had to tell him *something*. He deserved that much. And it's not that she owed him anything just because they slept together or that she was staying in his home, but the least she could do was share a little bit about herself. Besides, living with secrets was going to eat her up inside.

Cap laughed out loud—the hypocrisy of his thinking obvious even to himself. He drank down the rest of the bourbon, feeling the warm glow in the pit of his stomach, and refilled his glass.

The truth of the matter was that he wanted Tess in his life, though he wasn't sure how she fit in or how long she would remain. Probably not long—there must be some kind of life for her to get back to. Maybe if he came clean with what he was holding back, she would feel comfortable confiding her own secrets. He wouldn't judge the woman, no matter what kinds of mistakes she had made or what kind of trouble she might be in.

He drank more bourbon and thought about the day they met. How erratically she'd been driving. Her car was all over the road. Almost as if she had intended to drive her Pinto off the road intentionally. Why would she do something like that? Maybe she was distracted. But what if she wasn't?

He swirled his drink, watching the bourbon roll against the sides of the glass.

If Tess wouldn't reveal who she really was, there were other ways of finding out those kinds of things. Lester could help. The sheriff had the means of looking into peoples' pasts. Where they came from. What kind of person they were. Why they might be running from something.

Cap needed to find out her last name. And if she wouldn't tell him, he would look at her driver's license. That's all he needed. Lester was an old friend. He'd be willing to look into who Tess really was.

He finished his drink and filled the glass once again. Picked up the strip of sandpaper and began to follow the grain of the wood in nice, easy strokes.

32

The moment that Tess crossed the threshold, she could tell that Cap had been drinking. A dull-eyed look and slack expression around his mouth. He stood quickly and deliberately as if to mask his drunkenness. And when he smiled at her, Tess could see that it lacked authenticity.

She gestured toward the bookshelf he was working on. *Busy?*

Cap squinted at her. Shook his head and maintained his faux smile. "No. Come in." He pulled out a chair and swept it free of dust. "Sit."

Tess sat and watched as Cap leaned against the bookshelf at a crooked angle. He fidgeted and had a hard time maintaining eye contact with her. For the first time since meeting Cap, Tess felt a slight trace of discomfort.

Cap pointed at the fifth of Wild Turkey. "Would you like a drink?"

No.

He nodded. Wiped his mouth with the back of his hand. "Started a little early today, I guess."

Yes, she replied as a matter of fact rather than judgment.

"I usually don't drink this early . . ." His voice trailed off and he stared down at the piece of sandpaper still clutched in his hand. "No. That's not true."

He pulled out another chair and sat on the edge. "I drink during the day more than I ought to. Especially when I'm wrestling with something."

Tess finally took out her notebook and pencil. *Are you sorry?*

Cap stared at her words for a few moments, and Tess wondered if he was having trouble reading in his condition or if he was thinking on it.

"Sorry? For what?"

Tess merely gave him a look and waited for him to understand.

"About last night?"

Yes.

Cap leaned back in his chair. "No, Tess. Not at all. I'm sorry if I'm giving you that impression."

Tess waited for him to look at her, then wrote in her notebook.

I am.

Cap stared at her. Waited for more.

We should have waited.

"Why?"

We barely know each other.

"That might be true, but it doesn't have to be that way. We can try and be more open with one another."

Okay.

Cap reached for his glass of bourbon.

Why do you drink so much?

Her question caught him off guard. "I don't know exactly."

Some people drink to forget.

"I suppose so."

Or because they're hiding something.

Cap's face grew a little more somber. "Sounds like you're speaking from experience."

My mother.

"And was she hiding something from you?"

Yes.

"I see." He swirled his bourbon in the glass but resisted taking a drink. "You think I'm not telling you something?"

Tess took out her pack of cigarettes, shook one loose, and struck a match under the tip.

Cap set his glass on top of the bookshelf. "You're right, Tess. I drink more than I should. I know that. Didn't always used to be like this. At one time, I was just a social drinker. At parties or at dinner out. Then it became a weekend ritual. And before I knew it, I was drinking every day. Starting earlier and earlier."

You're numbing yourself.

"Yeah. You're probably right." He stared down at his bourbon. "I spend most of my time helping and listening to others. When people see me on the street or call me on the phone, they need something. To talk. To ask questions. To confess." He rubbed at his face with both hands. "After a while, it becomes too much. I can't shut out all of the voices."

Drinking helps?

"It's a Band-Aid, I know."

Both grew quiet, unsure of what to say next.

Do you like living alone?

"It suits me, I guess."

I can leave.

"I want you to stay here as long as you want, Tess. I do. I really do."

She crushed her cigarette out in a tin can.

"You know, you're a lot better at extracting information than giving it."

Although she couldn't detect the tone of his voice, Tess could see in his body language that there was an accusatory element to his statement. As she stepped out of the shop, Cap reached for the bottle of bourbon once again.

33

Wade had no idea what exactly he was supposed to say to Cap. The entire situation was nothing less than awkward. Should he come right out and tell him that Maggie found a gun in Tess's purse? Or should he just see if he could find out a little more about the woman? Or—the third option—turn around and drink a few beers at Red's and forget about the whole damn thing?

He strummed his thumbs atop the steering wheel and thought deep and hard. He knew the third option was out because Maggie wouldn't rest until she got an answer—some kind of satisfaction.

Why did she have to be so damned difficult? It seemed like she made everything more difficult than it had to be. Life sure would be easier without his wife around. No one nagging him. No one bossing him around. No one checking on his every move.

He drove up Route 367 and stopped at the turnoff to Marbaker Road.

Dusk was falling fast, so he flicked on his headlights but kept his foot pressed to the brake pedal.

He couldn't tell Cap that Maggie had been snooping in Tess's purse. That would be embarrassing as hell. The best thing to do was talk to him man-to-man. Find out a little more about the woman. Where she was from. How long she was staying. Aside from all of Maggie's drama and nonsense, Wade had to admit he was curious about Tess. And it wasn't like some of the other women he was drawn to. Maybe it was because he didn't know a damn thing about her. Whatever it was, she sure held his interest.

Snow began to tumble from the sky. A little at first, then with each passing moment, it grew thicker and thicker. He released the brake pedal and made his way the last mile to Cap's.

The sight of the church always made him feel edgy. It's not that he didn't believe in God. Of course, he did. He had attended church ever since he was five years old. He never questioned the whole thing really. It was what it was. Show up once a week at church. Say amen and pretend to sing along with a few hymns.

But sometimes—no, *all the time*—driving up to the church and opening those front doors and smelling the candles and the rose petal perfume from all the white-haired women, Wade's stomach locked up and a pang of paralyzing guilt gripped him by the throat.

He didn't know why, but something about being in church made him feel exposed. As if he was standing naked in the center of town. Everyone staring at him and judging him and seeing him for what he really was: a big, fat hypocrite that cheats on his own wife.

"Goddamnit, Maggie."

As he rode down the hill leading toward the church, Wade noticed the lights inside the rectory, ordinarily dark and unoccupied.

Before he realized what he was doing, his hand slipped down and killed the headlights, and the truck coasted the last twenty yards before stopping next to the church. He cut the ignition and stared at the rectory windows. The curtains were partially drawn, but he could see someone moving around inside.

He shifted his gaze up the hill toward the house and then at the workshop past that. Cap hunched over a workbench, unaware of Wade's arrival. He took a deep breath before returning his gaze toward the rectory. The familiar tingling sensation started down below his belt. That nervous energy starting to simmer and boil.

He licked his lips. Opened the truck door. Stepped out onto the gravel driveway coated with a few inches of snow. He kept his eyes on the rectory window and eased the door closed.

He took a few steps toward the rectory. Stopped. Reconsidered what the hell he was thinking of doing.

Snow continued to fall, sticking to his hair and melting against cheeks that burned hot. He remained rooted in the spot for maybe thirty seconds, halfway between his truck and the side of the church. If anyone saw him standing out in the middle of the yard, they would know that he was up to no good.

A shadow moved past the window and the tingling sensation grew more intense.

The war waging inside his head ended right then and there. He crept forward and moved under the window. The curtains had a few inches between them. Plenty of space to see through. Wade pressed his face closer to the panel of glass, held his breath, and peered inside.

34

Butch hoped that his mother would be off running another one of her lame errands and not fussing around the house. That was the last thing he needed right now. She'd take one look at his busted lip and swollen cheek and end up giving him the third degree. She'd want to know *what* happened, *who* did it, *why* he got himself involved in another situation like that in the first place. Then, after the interrogation, she'd dote on him, treating him like a baby.

But unlike his mother, Butch's father would want to know if he got any good punches in, proud that his son was involved in a playground brawl. He'd press Butch for details, then only be disappointed that his boy didn't fight back, didn't swing a single punch, that he ended up on the ground crying in front of all the other kids.

He was sick of the abuse. Getting worse and worse. And this time, the pastor wasn't there to protect him.

Butch wanted to get inside the house, grab some ice from the freezer, go straight to his room and hope the swelling would go down before dinner. When he spotted his mother's car in the driveway, his heart dropped. He stopped in the middle of the yard and considered his options: the front door or the kitchen door. It was too early for dinner, so his mother probably wouldn't be in the kitchen cooking. There was a good chance she'd be in the living room watching the news or one of her game shows.

He opted for the kitchen door.

As soon as Butch stepped inside, his mother peered up from the kitchen table, her Easter parade to-do list and a cup of coffee in front of her. Her eyes locked on his damaged face and her smile went flat instantly.

"Butch? What happened?"

"Nothing."

"Nothing? Nothing?!" Maggie jumped out of her seat and rushed to inspect his face. "Oh, my Butch. You're bleeding."

He tried to pull away from his mother's prying hands, but she gripped him by the shoulders and checked him over a few more times. "It's nothing."

"It's *not* nothing. Who did this to you?"

"Nobody."

"Don't *nobody* me. Give me names."

"It was an accident. We were just messing around outside."

"I want names, Butch."

Butch pulled away from his mother. "I said it's fine."

"Did Brian and Monte do this?"

"No," he lied.

"Did you tell someone?"

"It's not a big deal."

"Why didn't you tell a teacher?"

"Because."

"You need to go to a teacher or the principal when those boys are picking on you."

Butch didn't bother responding and felt his face grow hot with equal parts shame and frustration.

Maggie marched to the sink and dabbed a paper towel under the faucet. "Come here."

He remained rooted in his spot.

"I mean it."

He rolled his eyes and stomped to the sink.

"Hold still." Maggie cleaned the welt on his cheek. "Well, your daddy's going to want some answers."

"He doesn't have to find out."

"You were in a fight, Butch. Your daddy will want to know what happened."

Butch pulled away from his mother. "Can you not tell him? Please?"

"Why not?"

He sighed again and his eyes rimmed red. "Just because. Okay? I don't want him to know. That's why."

Maggie grabbed a bottle of peroxide from under the sink and poured a little on the paper towel. "Oh, Butch. He might not show it, but your dad cares about you."

A shrug from Butch.

"Your daddy might have certain expectations, but he means well. The two of you are just . . . a little different."

He took his mother by the wrist. "I can take care of it. I know what I'm gonna do. Okay?"

Maggie opened her mouth to argue the point, but she sighed after seeing the unwavering look in his eye. "Fine.

Neither of his parents understood anything. His mom acted like she knew what it felt like to be a teenager growing up in a small town, but she didn't—things were different now than when she grew up. Besides, all she really cared about was how the house looked, her clothes, and shopping.

And his dad was no better. Distracted by his work. Always rushing in and out. The only time his father paid any attention to him was when he got into trouble or didn't do his chores.

The swelling on Butch's cheek and upper lip had barely gone down, but his father didn't seem to notice during dinner. In fact, his father didn't ask him a single question. He merely sat there and shoveled food into his mouth like a race to finish. His mom had babbled on about the Easter parade—seemed like that's all she talked about lately—trying to overcompensate for his dad's lack of interest, but nobody really listened to her or answered any of her questions.

After dinner, Butch retreated to his bedroom to do his homework and waited for his parents to go to bed. He heard them watch television for a little while, then the TV clicked off, and they walked down the hallway in mutual silence. When his mom poked her head into his room, she asked if he was doing okay, and he said yes.

He waited until he was pretty sure everyone would be asleep.

He tiptoed past his parent's room and made his way downstairs. Walked in the dark, feeling his way through the living room and down the hallway toward the back of the house. Slipped into his father's study and smelled pipe tobacco and wood polish. Locked the door behind him, found the small desk lamp and clicked on the light, sending a soft glow of white throughout the room.

Two buck heads hung from the walls, their glass eyes watching him closely. A wet bar in the corner, fully stocked with bottles of vodka, whiskey, gin, and different kinds of wine. A stack of hunting magazines was fanned out on his father's solid oak desk.

Butch marched straight to the gun cabinet and swung open unlocked doors. All the rifles and shotguns were well-polished and gleamed with oil. A Marlin 336, a Winchester 70, a Savage 99, and Remington 12-gauge and 10-gauge shotguns. His fingers traced the stocks of each gun before finally selecting the 12-gauge. It felt heavy in his grip as he shouldered the gun tight against his cheek and pointed the barrel across the room toward the buck heads. He imagined the bucks to be Monte Canfield and Brian Schorr. Calling him names and shoving him around. Harassing him every single day.

Butch's finger wrapped around the trigger, then squeezed.

"Boom."

35

Tess couldn't sleep. Her mind swirled with various images, one blurring into the next. The photograph of her father, Aaron, emerging from the hotel closet dressed in blue, the last moments before her car veered off the road, Chuck slapping the wine glass from her hand, and Cap's body on top of hers.

She sat up and stared into the darkness. It felt strange to be sleeping back in the rectory. She hadn't seen Cap since she left his woodshop. She had thought—hoped—that he might wander down and ask her to join him for dinner. But more importantly, she wanted him to ask her to lie at his side once again.

She climbed out of bed and peered through the window toward the house—not a single light burning. She felt the sudden urge to tell Cap everything. Who she was. What she had done. Why she had run away. But if she revealed all those shameful things, there'd be no turning back. Cap might judge her. Might be disgusted by her actions.

Or maybe he would understand.

She slipped on her jacket and punched her feet into her shoes. She walked through the darkness. Out of the rectory, down the hallway, and through the back door of the church.

A shock of cold air greeted her and squeezed the air from her lungs. Snow tumbled down from the black sky—clouds obscured the light of the moon, and she could barely see two feet in front of her. In the pitch of black, she felt a sudden sense of being in limbo. In between two places of the unknown—her past and her present. She also felt horribly alone.

She mounted the steps to the porch, and for a moment, she wondered if Cap had locked the front door. When she turned the handle, the door swung open, and she slipped inside the house.

She felt her way across the foyer. Climbed the stairs and approached Cap's room. The door was ajar and she could smell bourbon in the air. She walked to the bed and could see Cap lying on top of the blankets, still wearing his clothes and shoes. She untied his laces and when she removed his boots, he didn't stir.

Tess lay down beside him. Rested her head on the steady rise and fall of his chest. Heard the rapid thumping of his heart—beating faster than it should. He mumbled in his sleep, and his body jerked, in the throes of a bad dream.

She stroked his cheek and tried to shush away whatever nightmare Cap was trapped inside. His body trembled, and his head rocked from side to side. Tess began to hum *Camptown Races,* a song that her mother used to coax her to sleep. She kept caressing his cheek and humming the sweet tune until he finally settled, drawing slow and steady breaths.

Tess felt the beating of his heart, and after a few minutes, her eyes flickered shut, and she, too, drifted away.

FOUR DAYS BEFORE GOOD FRIDAY

36

Cap drove with no clear destination in mind. Traveling rutted dirt roads packed down with ice and snow. White birch and hemlock trees hugged close to the road, their limbs weighed down with pristine powder and looking so majestic.

He'd been driving around for a few hours, trying to clear his head of the residual hangover, while at the same time trying to make sense of how much his life had transformed over the last two weeks.

He had woken to find Tess sleeping at his side. He didn't remember going to bed or when she had come into his room. And although blackouts weren't uncommon, he felt the tug of guilt that always accompanied his hangovers. He knew he needed to get a handle on his drinking, or Tess would be one more loss that he'd be forced to endure.

A flock of wild turkeys, a forty-pound tom and a handful of hens, edged out from the woods and strutted toward the road. He pumped the brakes and slowed to a stop in the middle of the road, watching the birds navigate across the snow-covered bank. One by one, the birds took a running start before taking flight, their wings beating against the cold air.

He reached inside the glove compartment for his binoculars and found them sitting next to a pint flask, one that he'd forgotten all about. He hesitated for a moment, considering the inevitable, but closed the glove compartment instead.

When he glanced back through the windshield, the flock of turkeys was long gone, disappearing somewhere into the woods like they had never been there in the first place. He put the truck into gear and noticed a small-framed figure emerge from the trees. It looked to be a boy, bundled up in a down jacket, gloves, and woolen cap stretched over his head. The boy's attention focused on the turkey tracks, and he had a shotgun clutched in his hands.

Cap watched the boy tromp up the embankment to the road, his eyes searching for a trace of the flock, when he finally noticed Cap's truck sitting in the middle of the road. White billowed from the boy's lips, his cheeks marked cherry-red from the wind, and despite being wrapped up in winter clothes, Cap recognized those blue eyes in an instant.

The boy's body language suggested that he'd done something wrong. His shoulders cinched up tight and he glanced behind him as if considering slipping into the woods and taking flight like the flock of turkeys.

Cap pulled the truck up next to the boy, then leaned across the seat and popped open the passenger side door. "Morning, Butch. I'm afraid that old tom took his flock deep into the woods. Long gone by now."

Butch stared in the direction that Cap indicated, then wiped his leaking nose with the sleeve of his jacket.

"I thought spring turkey season wasn't until May. Or maybe you're hunting squirrel?"

Butch wiped his nose again.

"And if you're hunting squirrel, a twelve-gauge is a little much, isn't it?"

Butch stared down at his boots. "You gonna tell my dad?"

"Tell him what exactly? Looks to me like you're just taking a little hike."

Butch started to answer, then realized what Cap meant.

"Pretty cold out there. How about I give you a lift home?"

Butch glanced down the road before shrugging okay.

"You got the safety switched on that shotgun of yours?"

"Yes, sir."

"Fine. Why don't you go ahead and set her in the bed of the truck?"

Butch did just that before climbing into the cab next to Cap. They drove for a minute or so before Cap struck up a conversation.

"How's the eighth grade treating you?"

"Okay, I guess."

"If memory serves me right, you must have Mr. Bradley for algebra."

Butch nodded.

"He still wiping that chalkboard with his hands instead of an eraser? Getting chalk dust all over his face and hair in the process?"

Butch offered a hint of a grin.

"Believe it or not, Mr. Bradley was my eighth-grade math teacher, too. That man must be seventy if he's a day."

"He's pretty old."

They drove down Tewksbury Hollow Road that had been recently plowed and salted, patches of brown peeking through sections of ice.

"Guess you'll be a freshman next year. Excited about that?"

"Nah. Not really."

"And why's that?"

Butch stared out the window, watching the trees blur past. "My dad says once I'm in high school, I gotta join the baseball team."

"That right? Not something you're interested in doing?"

"No."

"You tell him that?"

Butch rolled his shoulders. "Doesn't matter what I tell him."

"I see." Cap found himself tugging on his whiskers. "Things getting any better at school?"

"I dunno. I guess."

"Brian and Monte still giving you a hard time?"

Butch didn't respond.

"Well, not that it'll make you feel any better, but I had my share of dealing with bullies in school. But back then, we'd just call them jackasses."

A bigger grin from Butch.

They drove for a mile in silence, and Cap thought the subject to be closed.

"Why'd kids pick on you?"

Cap rubbed at his jaw before responding. "Lots of reasons. Because my father was a pastor. Because I have a harelip. And because I was different than everybody else, I guess."

"What did you do?" Butch half-whispered as if asking about some kind of shameful secret. "To make them stop?"

Cap sighed. "Shoot, I tried everything. Ignoring them. Telling a teacher. Skipping school. Everything."

Butch seemed to perk up at the admission. "And it worked?"

"No. Those things did not."

"You tell your parents?"

"No. Never did."

"Why?"

"Guess I was embarrassed. And besides that, I didn't think they would understand."

"Did they finally leave you alone?"

"Eventually."

"How?"

"Boys—or jackasses—like that are worse around their friends. Trying to prove how tough they are. Picking on other kids to get a laugh. So, I confronted them one-on-one. Told them that I wasn't afraid of them and that if they didn't stop, I would fight back. That I'd fight back and make them sorry."

"And they believed you?"

"They did, yeah." Cap laughed out loud. "And do you know who one of the bullies was?"

Butch stared at him. "My dad?"

"Bingo."

"Really?"

"Going to school was like riding a roller-coaster. Up and down. One day enemies, the next day the best of friends. I don't think that will ever change."

Butch thought about that for a second. "But you're not friends anymore."

It was Cap's turn to think for a moment. "We grew apart, I guess. That kind of thing happens."

They both grew quiet as they drove through Black Walnut, down Main Street behind a yellow snowplow spreading salt and cinders on the road. They went past the fire hall where a group of volunteer firemen hosed down one of the trucks, then continued up Old Route 6. Cap pulled his truck off to the side of the road, fifty yards shy of Maggie and Wade's house.

"How about I let you off here? Let you sneak into the back of the house and put that shotgun away, and nobody will be the wiser."

"Okay."

"Good. And do me a favor. Wait until May before you go hunting turkeys again."

"Yes, sir."

Cap watched the boy sling the shotgun over his shoulder and make his way home. Butch looked back at Cap one final time like there might be something on his mind before slipping along the side of his house and disappearing inside.

THREE DAYS BEFORE GOOD FRIDAY

37

Cap's heart went out to poor Robin, losing her husband like she did, in the manner that she did. But truth be told, Cap wasn't shocked that Chuck's drinking finally did him in—just in the fashion that death took him.

He glanced around his living room filled with two dozen mourners, most dressed in funeral black or as close as their wardrobe offered. The townspeople had walked up from the church after the service to drink and eat and offer their condolences to Robin. Cap sipped at a black coffee and nodded repeatedly to Terry Ann Bartel, who had him and Tess trapped in the corner, bending their ears about her theory on death.

"It always happens in threes. First Teddie, then poor, old Alice Hunsinger, God bless her heart, and now Chuck. One-two-three."

Cap attempted to get a word in edgewise, but Terry Ann chattered on.

"I don't know why it happens like that, but death always seems to come in threes. Not in pairs. Not in fours or fives. So peculiar. Why do you think it's like that, Cap? Why would God do that?"

"Don't have an answer to that one, Terry Ann. I guess it's like they say: God works in mysterious ways."

Terry Ann seemed satisfied with Cap's response, then turned her attention to Tess. "So, dear, what's it like to be deaf?"

Cap spotted Lester across the room talking with Wade, and when he raised his eyebrows at the sheriff, Lester grinned, knowing precisely the predicament Cap found himself trapped in. Lester said something to Wade, then made his way through the mourners and placed a hand on Terry Ann's elbow.

"I hate to interrupt you folks, but would you mind if I borrowed Cap and Tess here for a second, Terry Ann?"

Terry Ann said that she wouldn't, then moved off, searching for someone else to talk at.

Cap patted Lester on the back. "I owe you one."

"Been on the receiving end of that plenty of times myself." He winked at Tess. "And you, young lady, are the talk of the town."

Is that good or bad?

"Hell, it gives us something to go on about. The only thing that changes around here is the weather. You probably think we're nothing but a bunch of country hicks."

Everyone has been real nice.

"Most everybody is. But Cap here will tell you which ones to steer clear of."

Lester tilted his beer bottle and drank slow. "Your service was nice, Cap. Almost made Chuck look like a beacon of the community."

"Creative embellishments."

"That boy needed a few of those."

"I feel bad for Robin and her kids."

"Me, too. As much as Chuck was a handful, it can't be easy on a young family to lose a husband and father."

Cap said that he agreed and went after his mustache. "Coroner's office up in Towanda confirm that it was carbon monoxide poisoning?"

"Not yet. They're slow as hell up there, but I'm about ninety-nine percent on the certain side that carbon monoxide was the cause. Took one look at that muffler of Chuck's and it leaked like a sieve. He'd been drinking all night at Red's, got himself home somehow. Closed the garage door, then got back in his truck for some reason."

"Robin the one to find him?"

"Handled it pretty well. Gotta admit that."

"I'm not sure how Robin's going to get by. Church only pays her for two days a week."

"Well, even though Chuck was fired from Taylor Beef, his life insurance policy carried over. Robin won't exactly be set for life, but it'll buy her some time to sort through what comes next."

"I guess if there's a silver lining in this whole thing, that might be it."

Lester agreed and finished his beer.

Stacks of dirty dishes filled the sink and littered the counters. Glasses everywhere, half-eaten casserole dishes, empty pie tins, beer bottles, ashtrays, and amongst it all, Tess searched for her purse. She needed a cigarette and a moment away from the locals. Away from all their questions of where she came from, how she met Cap, when she became deaf. Two different women even asked if she intended to have babies. Most of the townspeople were generally well-meaning, but she sensed an element of judgment behind their questions—like what they were really asking was, *Why are you here and what are you running from?*

She finally spotted her purse behind some empty shopping bags and snuck out the back door off the kitchen for a quick smoke. When she closed the door behind her, she noticed Robin sitting on the concrete landing, looking a little worse for the wear.

Sorry, she signed.

Robin peered up at Tess, her brown eyes rimmed red, skin pale and broken out, and her long, unwashed hair hung in a greasy tangle.

Tess withdrew her notebook from her purse. *You want to be alone?*

"From everyone else maybe."

Tess took a seat next to her. Tapped out a cigarette, offered one to Robin, then lit both their smokes.

Tired of talking to people?

"A little. But they mean well."

They sat side by side in silence, smoking and staring down at the church for a minute, maybe longer.

"I'm not sorry," Robin abruptly announced.

Tess stared at the woman but didn't know how to respond precisely.

"That Chuck's gone. I'm not. You saw what kind of man he was."

I'm sure he had a good side.

Robin let out a cynical laugh. "He was a drunk and an asshole. Don't know why I didn't leave him a long time ago."

Relationships can be complicated.

"Maybe. I dunno." Robin drew on her cigarette. "The love slipped out of our marriage a long time ago. After both boys were born. Sometimes, I'm not even sure we were ever in love. We were so young. Got married because it was something you were expected to do around here. Have babies and raise a family. Besides all that, I had to get away from my father."

Tess continued to smoke her cigarette.

"I feel like everyone inside this house expects to see me cry and carry on like a wife is supposed to after their husband dies. They expect all that even though they knew what kind of man Chuck was."

The gray sky above them began to spit a little snow. Tiny flakes floated and twirled in the still air, the countryside quiet all around them.

"Chuck hated himself as much as he hated everyone else around him. He was nothing but mean and resentful of everything he didn't have. You ever know a man like that?"

Tess kept her gaze for a moment before staring back at the falling snow. She flicked her cigarette over the railing and watched it tumble down to the frozen earth below. Then she began to write in her notebook. She flipped to a new page and kept on writing. When she finished, she stared at what she had written before handing the notebook to Robin.

I was with a man who was sick, but he didn't know it. Or if he did, he hid it well. I didn't know what he really was deep down inside. Not at first. I thought he was everything I had ever wanted. He seemed kind. Charming. I felt safe around him. But he wasn't those things. What he was . . . what he is, *destroyed me. My childhood. Every part of me. And now I'm afraid. I ran away from him and everything I knew because I think he will hurt me if he ever finds me.*

Robin gave her a knowing smile. "But you got away. Right? You're safe here."

Tess tapped out another cigarette and tucked it between her lips. *I hope so.*

"From the sounds of it, Tess, you deserve better than you had. You deserve happiness."

Don't you deserve happiness, too?

Robin brushed back a wisp of hair that kept blowing in her eyes. "Maybe. But I don't know if I can find it here. In this town. I don't know if it's possible for someone like me."

I bet you'll find a way.

Robin stared at Tess and shook her head. Then, as she spoke, her voice was barely a whisper. "You don't know me, Tess. Don't know what I am."

I'd like to find out if you let me.

Robin asked for another cigarette and Tess tapped one out of the pack. They both smoked and stared out into the starless sky.

"I let it happen, Tess. I *wanted* it to happen." Tears leaked down cheeks naked from makeup. "I left him in the truck. I knew what I was doing. Do you understand?"

No.

The cigarette rattled between Robin's fingers as she took more smoke into her lungs. "I didn't try and wake him up. Didn't shut off the engine. I let my kids' daddy die . . . and the thing is . . . I'm not sorry. And I don't feel sad. I don't know what I feel exactly, but it's not sadness." Her eyes cut away for a moment. "Does that make me some kind of monster?"

No.

"I let my own husband die because I thought it would make my life easier."

Tess reached over and squeezed her hand.

Robin almost smiled. She stared into Tess's eyes. Leaned forward. Pressed her lips against Tess's.

Tess didn't resist at first. She let it happen. Didn't pull back. But then Robin's tongue slipped inside her mouth. She could taste wine and cigarettes. She pulled away. Shook her head.

Robin stared at her. The rejection slowly transforming her face.

I'm sorry, Tess signed. She stood. Backed away. Kept signing. *I'm sorry. I'm sorry.*

38

Cap stood at the kitchen sink watching the snow come tumbling down in sheets, a wall of white so thick it completely obscured the church. Crystallized flakes stuck to the panel of glass, creating a round portal that would get smaller and smaller until there'd be no view left at all.

He washed dishes and Tess dried. The last of the funeral-goers had left an hour ago, and the two of them had slowly and meticulously restored order to the house—threw away trash, emptied cans of beer, stored leftover food in plastic Tupperware, scraped dishes, and washed about a dozen casserole pans.

Tess had been quiet the latter half of the night. Distracted and inside that bubble she carried around her. Cap wrung out the washrag, dried his hands, and took her by the elbow to gain her attention.

"Thanks for helping with all this. I can't go to bed with the house a mess."

Tess tried to smile.

"Nightcap?"

Okay.

"Glass of wine or something stronger?"

She pointed to a bottle of vodka on the counter.

"Sounds good."

He poured her a screwdriver and bourbon and water for himself.

They both sipped their cocktails for a moment, and then Cap led her into the living room. As they sank onto the sofa, Cap let out a weary sigh.

"It's going to be tough on Robin raising all those kids by herself."

Tess nodded. Looked away. Drank half of her screwdriver.

"You okay?"

No.

"Anything that I can do?"

Tess didn't answer. Instead, she finished the rest of her cocktail. Took the notepad out of her purse and began to write.

Cap watched her for a minute, and she didn't stop writing, not a single pause. Her pencil scraped against paper, filling one line after another. He got up, took both of their glasses into the kitchen and poured them fresh drinks. When he sat back beside her, Tess handed him the notebook, stared down at her hands, and waited for him to read.

Tess had been sitting in her car for two hours. Waiting. And for those two hours, her eyes never wandered from the entrance to Crouse Hospital. She wasn't even sure if this was the right one—Syracuse had so many. But something in her gut told her that this was the right hospital. That this was the place where Aaron worked.

Dozens of people came and went—patients, visitors, doctors, nurses, and a few priests. She had always hated hospitals. Spent too much time in and out of various hospitals when she was first diagnosed with meningitis. Everything white and sterile. The unreadable expressions on the nurses' faces. Always waiting in a small room, sitting on exam tables that were cold and stiff, and staring at charts of human anatomy on the walls. Glass and tile and plastic. No plants. Nothing organic.

And the sounds unnatural as well. Beeping from machines. The squeak of rubber soles against tile. Phones ringing. People whispering, always whispering. Hospital sounds—these were the last sounds that Tess remembered before her world went completely silent.

She crushed a cigarette into the ashtray and lit up another—she had already smoked nearly a full pack. She peered back toward the hospital and her stomach lurched when she spotted who she had been waiting for.

Aaron. Dressed in blue scrubs. A bag slung across his shoulder. Wearing a pair of aviator sunglasses. He walked in that same confident stride that drew Tess to the man in the first place. Now it made her sick. Now all she could see was lies and deceit and manipulation.

She tracked him as he walked to the employee parking lot and climbed into a brand-new Volvo. She watched him check his reflection in the rearview mirror. Then, as Aaron pulled out of the parking lot, Tess fired up the engine.

She followed Aaron's car down one street and onto the next. Through every stop sign and traffic light. She kept her distance, always two or three car lengths behind. Her hands shook so badly she thought that she might swerve into oncoming traffic. Her vision blurred and streaked from crying.

Nothing made sense. How could this happen? Her own father. He tracked her down. Found her. Used her.

She noticed white spots of light creep into her peripheral vision. Her face felt hot. Flushed. She rolled down her window. Sucked in fresh winter air. Willed herself to remain focused.

Her eyes stayed on Aaron's Volvo as he drove through the city and pulled onto the 690-freeway heading north. Tess kept following him for a few miles and Onondaga Lake appeared on the right. People jogging and walking dogs, enjoying the sun, and not having to think about what it must be like to be in a romantic relationship with their own father.

The Volvo took the exit to Lakeland and cruised through the small town. Passed by stores and restaurants and auto repair shops before arriving in the suburbs. Big brick houses with big yards. Bicycles and minivans parked in driveways. The Volvo finally pulled into a driveway next to another car—a Cadillac that looked recently washed and waxed.

Tess slowed to a stop a few houses away. Watched Aaron step out of his car and stride toward the two-story house. The home had a warmth to it and looked well lived-in. She didn't know why, but she could tell that a family was raised within those walls.

A scream burst out of her chest as if launched from a cannon. Loud and violent. She screamed and pounded her palms against the steering wheel, but Aaron didn't look toward the car.

Tess kept screaming and slamming her hand on the horn. Again and again and again.

Aaron watched Tess climb out of her car and his mask dissolved. Gone was his reassuring smile. Gone was the kindness in his eyes. Gone was his glow of confidence. Anger replaced all that. Anger and a coldness transformed his face.

He shot a quick glance toward the house before marching down the sidewalk. He grabbed her by the arm and pulled her toward the street.

"You can't be here," he hissed.

How could you?

"Leave, Tess. Get in your car and go. Now."

She signed again. *How could you?*

He guided her toward her car, but she jerked her arm free of his grip.

"Why'd you follow me here?"

You have a wife? A family?

Aaron's hand shot forward and Tess flinched, expecting to be slapped. Instead, he signed.

Yes. Three sons.

Tess's legs shook beneath her. *You know how to sign?*

I learned because of you. I learned for *you.*

Tess struggled to process everything. So many lies. So much betrayal. She stared toward Aaron's home and a spike of anger replaced her devastation. She felt the sting upon the palm of her hand as she slapped Aaron's cheek. Once. Twice.

You think this is about being married?

He didn't respond.

You know who I am.

"Tess—"

You know what *I am.*

Something shifted in Aaron's face. Darkness exposed.

How could you?

Aaron's jaw tightened.

How could you do this to your own daughter?

Aaron recoiled. His body tensed. Hand shot out. Gripped her by the shoulder. Slammed her against the side of her car.

Tess tried to scream. Maybe she did scream—she wasn't sure. She brought both hands to his face. Dug her fingernails against his skin and yanked down hard.

Aaron staggered away. Covered his face. Blood leaked down his cheeks.

Tess stumbled around her car, sucking in desperate takes of air. She couldn't hear Aaron's howls. Couldn't hear his words, but she felt his rage. Her fingers fumbled with the keys. Turned the ignition but the car was already running. She felt the vibration of the grinding engine. Threw it into drive and sped down the street. When she glanced in the rearview mirror, Aaron stood in the middle of the road, and the look in his eyes was unsettling.

Tess drove through a stop sign and pressed the gas pedal harder.

Cap stared at the last sentence and closed the notebook. He reached for his drink, but the glass was empty.

Tess sat next to him. Huddled and trembling. He lifted her chin and stared into those green eyes. "You were a victim, Tess."

Tears leaked down her cheeks.

"None of that was your fault."

She picked up her pencil. Fingers trembling. *I feel broken.*

"I understand."

How do you come back from something like this?

"I don't know, Tess. I don't. But I want to help you try."

39

Wade stared up at the trailer's popcorn ceiling and couldn't help but notice that one of the bulbs in the light fixture had burned out. Then he glanced around the bedroom filled with nothing but cheap, second-hand crap—a mattress and box spring without a bed frame, a thrift store dresser, the nightstand missing all its knobs, and a metal folding chair piled high with unfolded clothes sat next to a cracked window patched with duct tape.

He hated trailers. He really did. This was the third time he'd been in this tin box, and he still hated the goddamn place. Amy slept beside him, curled up and looking so young. Her porcelain-white skin flawless as a baby's. Perfect in every way.

He picked up his bottle of Yuengling off the nightstand and drank down the rest of it even though it was piss warm.

A full moon peeked through the tattered blinds. He checked his wristwatch—a little before eleven. After attending Chuck's memorial, he'd told Maggie he was heading over to Red's to drink a few beers, but he could tell by the way his wife stared at him that she didn't believe him for a second.

He looked back at Amy and watched her sleep. Definitely the youngest woman he'd been with. In many ways, Amy was perfect. Beautiful, inexperienced, didn't run her mouth much, and best of all, seemed completely enamored by him. He could tell by how she watched him that she was falling hook, line, and sinker.

He grabbed her bottle of beer and finished that off, as well.

Amy rolled on her back and Wade stared at her profile. He had a good thing going with the girl and damn well knew it. She wasn't the type to go yapping to her girlfriends about their relationship. Never wanted him to take her anywhere but to bed. Never wanted him to buy her anything. What more could he ask for?

He stared up at the ceiling again, and his mind went to Tess. The entire time he was inside Amy, all he could think about was being inside Tess. He wanted to kiss *her* lips, *her* neck, *her* breasts. That's what he wanted more than anything else. Fucking Amy only reminded him of how much he really wanted to fuck Tess.

He swung his legs out of bed and rubbed at his jaw.

Amy's eyes cracked open and she smiled that sweet, naive smile of hers. "You leaving?"

"Yeah. Need to be getting back home."

He pulled on his T-shirt.

"When am I going to see you again? Tomorrow?"

Picked his underwear and trousers up off the floor but didn't respond.

"Something the matter?"

"No. It's getting late is all."

She took his manhood in her hand. "You make me feel good."

It didn't take long for him to harden between her fingers.

"Can you come by on Friday? After work?"

"Don't think so, Amy."

"Why?" She stroked him faster.

Wade pulled her hand away despite how good it felt. "I think we should lay low for a while." And before she could ask him why Wade hiked up his underwear. "Maggie's been getting wise to us, I think."

Amy tugged the sheet across her breasts and glanced toward the bedroom door like Maggie might come barging in any second. "She say something?"

Wade pulled on his pants and cinched his belt. "She didn't have to. I can just tell she suspects something."

"Oh." She pouted for a moment. "How long do we have to lay low?"

"I don't know, Amy. A week. Maybe longer."

She leaned up on one elbow, processing everything. "How come you're telling me now?"

"When did you want me to tell you?"

"I don't know. Before we made love?"

Wade couldn't stop the laugh from escaping his throat.

"What?"

"We've been fucking, Amy. Not making love."

Amy cringed at his words and pursed her perfect lips.

"Look. I'm sorry. I didn't mean it like that."

"So that's it? Like we're not gonna see each other again?"

He walked to the bedroom door. "Let's take a break for a few weeks. Okay? We'll see what happens after that."

"It's not Maggie, is it?"

"What?"

"I can tell you're lying. It's that new woman in town, isn't it?"

"What in the hell are you talking about?"

"The deaf one. You like her, don't you?"

Wade stood at the doorway and couldn't hold back a patronizing laugh.

"Stop it," Amy hissed.

But he kept on laughing. "Christ almighty, Amy."

She picked up a Yuengling bottle and chucked it at his head. It missed him by a mile and that made Wade laugh even harder.

"Fuck you, Wade. Fuck you."

"Stop with all this, Amy. You're acting like a damn child."

Amy leapt out of bed and stood in front of him stark naked. "How would you like it if I told Maggie about us? How would you like that?"

He folded his arms across his chest and shook his head. "She already knows, Amy. I told you that."

She lost a little bit of her bluster. "You're done with me and now you're gonna try and fuck that deaf woman, aren't you? *Aren't you?*"

Wade didn't bother replying. Instead, he walked out of the bedroom, and before he made it to the front door, he heard glass shatter, followed by the sounds of Amy screaming words he hadn't heard her utter before.

TWO DAYS BEFORE GOOD FRIDAY

40

He sat behind the wheel of the Volvo across the street from June's house like he'd done every day since the confrontation with Tess. Hours sitting in his car, watching and waiting. But Tess had yet to show. He had stopped by the library numerous times, but her coworkers hadn't seen her and were worried sick. It was so unlike her to not show up for work. She had simply disappeared.

A few days earlier, a moving van rumbled up to the house and backed up the driveway. And for the first time in twenty-two years, Aaron spotted his ex-wife. June stepped onto the porch, looking thinner than he remembered, face and hair ravaged. She smoked a cigarette and spoke to the driver of the moving van, barely making eye contact with the man. She shook her head and gestured toward his truck. The driver, in turn, shook his head. Looked at his rig before returning his attention to June. The driver said something, but June merely turned her back to him and retreated into the house. Aaron watched the man struggle to understand his predicament. After a few moments, the driver climbed into his truck and drove down the street.

Aaron didn't see June again after that day. Nor did he see the person he needed to find.

He spit out a piece of chewing gum and unwrapped another. Kept watching the house. Kept waiting. He caught his reflection in the rearview mirror and traced the set of scratches that extended from his cheekbones to his jawline. The scratches refused to fade—marking him like a brand.

A mail carrier walked down the sidewalk, dropping bundles of envelopes into mailboxes. One by one. House by house. Aaron watched her deposit a few envelopes in June's mailbox before continuing down the street.

He didn't wait long to step out of the car and stride up the sidewalk. Climbed up the porch and without hesitating, opened June's mailbox.

He looked at each envelope—bills, fliers, notices—and then stopped on one envelope in particular. A letter with no return address. He looked at the postmark over the stamp—*Black Walnut, Pennsylvania.*

Aaron tore open the letter and began to read.

41

More than anything else, Robin felt exposed. Rejected? *Yes.* Humiliated? *Yes.* But the vulnerability of being exposed was what bothered her the most. Now Tess knew her deepest, darkest secrets—*both of them.*

She had dropped off the boys at school and drove the back roads until Darla finally fell asleep in her booster seat a few minutes ago. She didn't feel like going back to the house—Chuck's presence was still there. No matter how much Robin vacuumed and dusted, the house still smelled of her husband. Everywhere she looked, he remained behind. His clothes in the bedroom closet. His boots next to the garage door. His gun cabinet in the living room. He was there. Chuck was everywhere.

Darla kept asking when her daddy would come back home, and couldn't understand no matter how many times, and how many ways, that Robin explained the reality to her. Both boys had been unusually quiet since she told them that he wasn't coming back. They didn't quite comprehend the finality of the concept but knew enough to be sad and lost.

Robin gazed out the window and stared at Tanner's Pond, frozen over with six inches of ice. It was the same pond that she and Chuck used to skate upon when they first started dating, back when Chuck enjoyed her company and tried his hardest to make her laugh. Back when she felt love and infatuation and being around Chuck caused the butterflies in her stomach to flutter like a flock of crows.

She gripped the steering wheel and her mind wandered back to Tess. Why did she tell Tess what she had done? It was stupid. Reckless. And to make matters even worse, why did she try to kiss her? Did she really expect Tess to be attracted to her?

Robin hated this feeling deep in her stomach, causing it to ache and cramp. It felt like her insides were toxic and rotting. It wasn't fair. None of it. Just when she was finally unburdened, released from the wrath of Chuck, now she had to think about Tess and what she might do. What she might say.

She stared at Darla for a moment. Her little face so sweet. So innocent of all the awfulness in the world. Robin would do anything to protect her daughter. Anything.

She kept driving with no destination in mind. It was strange to be riding around in the truck, the last place that Chuck drew breath, but she didn't have much choice. At least Scott and Skeeter had repaired the muffler leak. They had towed the truck to their garage, made the repairs, and refused to accept a nickel for the parts and labor.

Mile after mile of trees rushed past her. Everything coated in white. Everything cold and buried. She finally recognized where she was driving: down Marbaker Road, toward the church. She looked at Darla, chin resting on her chest, her nose leaking yellow. Robin wiped her daughter's face with a Kleenex, but the girl didn't stir.

With each passing mile, she became more determined about what needed to be done. She guided the truck down the final turn leading to the church. She didn't see Cap's truck, but the house lights were on. She parked in her usual spot, cranked the heater up to high, checked on Darla one last time, then stepped out of the truck.

Tess watched Robin stride across the snow. Saw that the truck was still running. Noticed the little girl asleep in the passenger seat.

She knew what this was about. Of course, she did. She opened the front door and stepped outside.

Robin stood in the middle of the porch. Her arms crossed over her chest and there was a harshness set in her eyes. "Are you going to tell people what I did to Chuck?"

Tess gestured for Robin to come inside.

"Just answer the question."

Tess shook her head. Started to open her notebook when she felt Robin's hand clamp on her wrist.

"I'm not gonna have my babies taken away from me." Robin squeezed Tess's arm even harder. "You understand? I won't let that happen."

Tess signed—*I'm sorry.*

"Why are you even here? In this town? What do you want?"

Tess backed toward the house. Toward the threshold.

Robin matched her step for step. Pressed her face close to Tess's and poked a finger against her chest. "You don't belong here, Tess. You don't. You know that."

Tess stepped inside the house. Grabbed the door handle with a trembling hand. Began to swing the door closed when Robin's hand slapped against the wood.

"Leave!"

Tess pushed the door closed. Flipped the deadbolt. But she felt the vibration against the wood as Robin struck the door again and again and again.

42

A dozen or so regulars huddled in green vinyl booths or sat at the Friedenshutten's long counter, drinking coffee and digging into plates of fried eggs, thick-cut bacon, and hash browns. Cap knew most of them—farmers, truck drivers, and men and women that worked at the slaughterhouse.

On any other day, Cap would shake some hands and make small talk, but on this morning, he felt like keeping to himself, drinking a few mugs of coffee, and trying to make sense of what to do about Tess. The woman was damaged, and despite his attraction to her, he wasn't sure whether the two of them were good for each other. Or was he merely overthinking the whole thing and making something complicated that was supposed to be simple?

He sat down on a stool at the end of the counter next to a mountain of a man. Tall and wide, his three-hundred-pound girth spread across the stool, causing the seat to disappear under his considerable mass. He sported short-cropped, red hair and a face so clean-shaven that his skin shined under the fluorescent lighting. Despite the man's massive size and unreadable expression, there was a doe-like quality to him. Attempting to project neither menace nor intimidation, the way he held himself gave the appearance that he was there but not there to be seen.

Although the big man didn't attend church or participate in any social functions that Cap might be a part of, he knew Danny Bedford. Most folks in the area either knew Danny or knew *of* Danny.

"How's your day going, Danny?"

Danny's head pivoted toward Cap on a thick neck. "Pretty good, I guess, Pastor." His voice was low and monotone, and his words were delivered with great deliberation.

"What have I told you about that, Danny? Just call me Cap like everybody else does."

Danny nodded like he understood and that it wouldn't happen again, then returned his attention to his plate of breakfast.

"Hmm. What do you think? Should I go with the eggs or flapjacks this morning?"

"Guess I kinda like the eggs better."

"All right. Thank you, Danny."

Danny replied with what sounded like a cross between a grunt and a one-syllable word.

When the waitress approached, Cap ordered a plate of eggs sunny side up, a couple strips of bacon, and a cup of coffee. After his mug was filled, he blew at the steam and watched Danny from the corner of his eye. The oversized man mopped up every bit of his eggs with a slice of toast, nothing wasted. He pulled out a few crinkled dollar bills and a handful of quarters and dimes and proceeded to count out the money slowly and carefully.

"Laundromat keeping you busy, Danny?"

Danny folded his hands together and let them rest on the counter in front of him. "Yes, Pastor. Keeping it clean and stocked the best I can."

"I bet you do." Although Cap tried not to, he felt a dull pang of pity for the overgrown child. Danny's life had never been easy—he had suffered permanent brain damage due to a near-drowning accident when he was ice-skating as a boy of five or six, and his mind had never grown to match his size.

Cap was jarred from his thoughts when Danny swiveled on his stool and spoke a few simple words. "Do folks stay in heaven forever?"

"What do you mean, Danny?"

"My folks are up in heaven. Can they come down and visit? Or do they have to stay up there?"

Cap wanted to tell Danny the truth—that he didn't really know. "When people go to heaven . . . well, there's no better place to be. But your mother and father, they can see you right now. They can hear you talking. They don't need to come down to be with you. You understand?"

Danny didn't respond. His brow creased as he thought about what Cap said.

"What I mean to say is that your parents are always with you. Watching you. You might not see them, but they're here. Here with you every day."

Danny stared down at his hands as he processed these words. When he returned his attention to Cap, he seemed like he wanted to ask another question but couldn't quite bring himself to say it out loud.

"What is it, Danny?"

His eyes went back to his hands as he mustered the courage. "Is it true? That your new friend can't hear nothing?"

"You mean Tess?"

Danny said yes.

"Well, yeah, Tess lost her hearing when she was a little girl."

"How do you talk to her then?"

"She can understand what I'm saying."

"How? If she ain't able to hear?"

"She can read lips."

"Can she talk?"

"I don't know, Danny. I've never heard her try."

Danny seemed satisfied with that answer. "Well, I best be getting back to the Wash N Dry."

"Okay. You take care of yourself now."

Danny said that he would and left without another word.

The other customers watched Danny over the tops of mugs of coffee, staring at the man like he was a bull in a pasture.

The waitress placed a plate of eggs and bacon in front of Cap, wisps of steam lifting off the yolks. Cap doused the eggs with some hot sauce, and as he ate his breakfast, all he could think about were Danny and the father he never got to know.

ONE DAY BEFORE GOOD FRIDAY

43

Wade never came home from work early. Not once in their eighteen years of marriage. Agway only closed its doors three days a year: Easter, Thanksgiving, and Christmas. Wade would stay home on those three days and take a few days off here and there during deer and turkey season, but he never came home before the store closed its doors for the day.

So, when he walked into the house a little after two o'clock, Maggie stared at him as if he were a home intruder. "What's the matter? Something happen at the store?"

"No. Nothing happened at the store."

"You sick?"

"No."

Maggie put away the dish she was drying and placed her hands on her hips. "Well? Why are you home so early, then?"

"We need to talk."

Maggie picked up a rag and a bottle of Windex. "Not now. I'm in the middle of cleaning."

"The house is clean enough. I've got something to say."

Maggie didn't recognize the expression on Wade's face—she had never seen him look so resolved. "Somebody we know die?"

He didn't respond. Instead, he sat down at the kitchen table and waited for her to do the same.

"Would you say something, Wade? You're scaring me."

"Sit down, Maggie."

She didn't like taking orders from anyone—especially her husband—but Maggie sat across from Wade, still clutching the rag and bottle of Windex.

"Is this about Butch? Is he—"

"I want out, Maggie."

She stared at him. Processing his words. "Out of what?"

"You know exactly what I mean."

Maggie stood, then sat right back down. "You want out of our marriage?"

"Yes."

She blinked. Straightened her posture. "Why?"

"Why?" He sounded genuinely shocked. "Come on, Maggie. Are you really happy?"

When Maggie offered no response, Wade continued with his train of thought. "Are you getting anything out of being married to me? Anything at all?"

Maggie started to say something, then her mouth snapped shut.

"Other than the obvious, what do you get out of our marriage? Sure, we have a nice home. Nice cars. Closets full of new clothes. We're comfortable. If we want something, we buy it. Butch has everything a teenager needs. We could take vacations if we wanted to, but we don't. And do you know why? Because we don't want to spend time together. Because we have nothing in common anymore. You and I both know it. We coexist, Maggie. We live under the same roof. Eat at the same table. Sleep in the same bed. That's all. So, why should we stay together? What's the point? Because of Butch? If that's the only reason, we're not doing him, or *us* for that matter, any favors. The honest truth of the matter is that we would all be better off if you and I weren't married."

Maggie hadn't flinched or looked away during Wade's entire monologue. She maintained eye contact and sat upright. She nodded. Even produced an unsettling smile. "Are you done?"

Wade sighed. "Let's not be petty, Maggie. This is our life I'm talking about."

"I understand."

Wade waited for the explosion. Waited for her wrath. Waited for the insults.

But she gave him none of that.

"Well? You have anything to say? I think it's important that we're honest with one another."

"You're right, Wade."

"About?"

"About everything. Everything that you said is true."

Wade finally leaned back in his chair and crossed his arms. "So that's it? You've got nothing to say?"

"No."

"No?"

Maggie stood. "Lawyers are expensive, and I don't trust them. I think we can settle this between ourselves. Butch and I will stay here at the house until he graduates, then we'll sell it. We'll divide everything in two. You'll give me half of what we're making at the store until we sell that, too."

"Fine. Is that it?"

"No. I have one last question."

She made him wait and quietly relished his discomfort.

"Well?"

"Are you leaving me for someone else?"

His eyes cut away and he shifted the weight on his feet.

"I guess that's my answer."

Wade cleared his throat. "It's not what you might think."

"Well, that makes me feel much better."

All Wade could do was stare at her.

"I'm going to finish cleaning, then get dinner started unless there's something else you want to talk about."

"What about Butch?"

"What about him?"

"What do we tell him?"

Maggie crossed to the sink and sprayed Windex on the window. "We tell him the truth. That we're getting a divorce." She commenced wiping down the window and didn't turn around as Wade left the kitchen.

44

Butch listened to his father's footsteps echo down the hallway, followed by the front door banging shut. He heard the rumble of a truck engine barking to life and tires chewing up chunks of snow.

He waited before stepping toward the kitchen doorway and peering inside. His mother scrubbed the window above the sink with a rag, her hands moving in rapid circles, scrubbing and scrubbing even though the window looked perfectly clean, and she rubbed so hard he thought she might break the glass.

She stopped abruptly, leaned against the counter, and lowered her head. Motionless at first, then her shoulders shook, and she made a sound completely unfamiliar to him. Her chin pressed against her chest, and she appeared broken and vulnerable. For the very first time, Butch felt sorry for his mother. He had never seen her so exposed and vulnerable. Never seen her display sadness. Over the years, he felt many ways toward his mother: embarrassed, intolerant, ambivalent, but never pity.

As his mother cried harder, louder, Butch felt his pity shift, slowly turning into anger. Dull, raging anger.

He backed away from the kitchen and crept down the hallway. He went past the steps that led upstairs and entered his father's study. Closed the door behind him and took a seat behind the desk. His eyes scanned the framed photos that his mother had placed there: a picture of the three of them standing at the edge of Niagara Falls when he was five; one with his parents at his sixth-grade graduation; and another of his mother and father posing for their fifteenth wedding anniversary.

He stared at the pictures, and all he could think was fake family. Fake happiness. Fake love. Everything *fake, fake, fake.*

He leaned back in his father's leather chair and gazed at the gun cabinet.

Butch took his time deciding which gun to use.

45

"You said a couple of things the other day that have really stuck with me. That some people drink to forget something painful, and others drink because they're hiding something."

Cap poured two strong drinks. Bourbon and a splash of water for himself. A vodka and orange juice for Tess. He set the glasses on the kitchen table and sat across from her.

"I guess what I'm trying to say is that I'm doing both."

Tess lit a cigarette.

"To be honest with you, I don't quite know what's going on between the two of us. I feel like there's something here, but at the same time, something is holding us back."

Tess didn't disagree. She smoked and waited for more.

"And I've always been better at listening—at least when it comes to what

I'm thinking. What I'm feeling." He took a sip of his bourbon. "Well, if you and I have a chance at whatever this thing is, then I need to tell you something."

She watched as Cap drank from his glass.

"I've been living lies most of my adult life. Two specifically. Both of them my choices. My decisions. I'm not going to blame them on anyone else. I used to. Easier to blame someone else, but at the end of the day, that doesn't get you anywhere."

Cap stood. Poured another inch of bourbon into his glass.

"The first lie, I think you're well aware of. Living here. In this house. Preaching in the church. I don't believe in half of what I say. The other half, I either question or don't quite understand."

He drank some more.

"I don't think that I can do it anymore. I really don't."

I understand.

"The other lie . . . well, it's complicated. It would be easier if it was just about me, but it isn't. It's a lie that affects other people, and it won't ever go away, and there's not a damn thing I can do about it."

Maggie?

Cap stared at the name written on the paper before looking back at Tess.

"Yeah, she's part of it." He rubbed at weary eyes.

Are you in love with her?

"No. I wish it were that easy, but it isn't." He struggled to form words that he had never spoken aloud. "Butch. Maggie's son. Well. Butch is my son, too."

He brought the glass to his lips and emptied the bourbon into his mouth.

"It was a one-time encounter. But I didn't try and stop it. I let it happen. She was already married to Wade. For a few years, I guess. The day after my mother died, she came to see me. To talk. To comfort me. Then it happened. Blame it on grief. Blame it on two people that once felt something for one another. Whichever one, it doesn't really matter. We promised each other that it would never happen again. That we made a mistake. That we would live with the secret."

He stood. Grabbed the bottle of Wild Turkey and set it on the table.

"When Maggie told me she was pregnant, she didn't have to tell me that it was my baby."

Wade doesn't know?

"Maggie wanted a family in the worst way. She and Wade had been trying for a while. She wanted that baby. We didn't talk about it. Didn't make a plan. It was unspoken. I did it for Maggie. Didn't want to destroy her marriage. And I guess I thought the baby would be better off in a real family."

And now?

Cap stared off into the distance. Not looking at anything in particular. It was quiet for some time before he answered the question.

"After Butch was born, I did everything I could to avoid laying eyes on him. But that didn't last long. Not in a town like this."

He sipped bourbon.

"It's been killing me slowly for fourteen years. My own son living a few miles from me. Being raised by another man. That's part of why I drink, I guess. To try and help me forget that I have a son."

And does it help?

He didn't answer.

Tess scratched in her notebook. *He has the right to know who his real father is.*

Cap read her words. He didn't respond and drank instead.

It's not fair to you. To Butch. Or to Wade.

"No. It's not fair at all."

You need to tell them.

He stared at her for a moment with incredulous eyes. "I can't do that, Tess. I *won't* do that."

Why?

"Because I can't. It would ruin that family."

What about you?

Cap's eyes began to shift. Glazing over, becoming dull and unresponsive. "It's a burden I'll have to bear."

Tess began to write again, but he placed his hand on hers.

"I made this confession so that you might understand. To be honest with you. Not to be persuaded to do something I simply won't do."

Tess pulled her hand from his and began to write. *Haven't you suffered long enough?*

Cap shook his head as he read her words. "And what about you? Haven't you suffered enough?"

Tess wasn't sure how to respond.

"You suffered because of your father, right?" His words began to slur a little. "Are you going to tell your mother about what your father has done to you?"

She didn't answer.

"No. You won't. And you know why? Because it would devastate her. Just like the truth would devastate Butch's world."

You're drunk.

"And you're not being truthful with yourself, Tess."

She stood. Shook her head.

"It's true. And we might not like it, but the fact is, sometimes it's better to hang onto a secret rather than destroy the lives of others."

No.

Cap stood up as well. "You really think I should do that to Butch? To Wade?"

He took a step toward her, but Tess backed away.

"I was the one that made the mistake fourteen years ago. Not Butch. Don't you understand that?"

Tess kept backing away.

"And what happened to you with your father isn't your mother's fault. Telling her the truth won't change a damn thing."

He reached for her hand, but Tess wouldn't allow it.

"Tess. You and I . . . we have to live with the part we played in these situations. We have to keep the secret. Don't you think that Butch and your mother deserve that?"

Tess's hand shot forward. Her open palm slapped Cap's cheek hard enough to knock him off balance.

Cap stared at her. Rubbed his jaw. "You might not be able to admit it, but you know I'm right, Tess."

He grabbed the bottle of Wild Turkey and walked out the front door. He shuffled across the front lawn, his feet swallowed by snow, and disappeared inside his woodshop.

46

Robin had Darla inside the shopping cart, distracted by a box of animal crackers. Chuck Junior and Mikey took off running down the aisle in front of her, making a beeline for the selection of boxed cereal. She told all the kids that they could pick out one treat in the market, and all three of them were wound up like it was Christmas morning.

She knew she needed to be careful with money, but her babies had been through so much in the last few days and deserved something special. Besides, she had two hundred and twenty-five dollars in her purse from the collection that Cap had gathered at Chuck's service. Maybe folks hated Chuck, but they sure were generous in giving a few dollars to her and the kids. Or maybe folks dug deep into their pockets because they *did* hate Chuck. Whichever way, she had plenty of money to pay for groceries for a while—or at least enough to last her until Chuck's life insurance policy paid out.

Darla watched her brothers pick up a box of Cap'n Crunch, then a box of Fruit Loops, searching for the one that had the best toy inside. She whined like a caged dog, so Robin scooped her out and sent her on her way.

She pushed the cart down the aisle. Grabbed a bag of sugar and a six-pack of diet soda and wheeled into the next aisle when she noticed a stranger standing at the front of the store, talking with Joe. The man wore a long wool jacket that looked expensive. As did his shoes and leather gloves. His haircut, too. The man stood out like a sore thumb.

The stranger stood with perfect posture and looked serious—like he rarely allowed himself to smile. Joe seemed slightly uncomfortable, not able to look the stranger in the eye. Robin couldn't help herself—she was curious what this was all about. She pushed her cart forward, pretending to browse.

The stranger turned away from Joe, his mouth drawn straight. He gazed around the market until his eyes fell on Robin.

Robin's stomach tightened at the look in his eyes. Then she noticed the scratch marks on both his cheeks. The marks were a light shade of crimson, barely visible, and there was something about the scratches made Robin think that they had been inflicted by someone—a deliberate act.

The stranger maintained Robin's gaze and attempted to smile, but the facial expression appeared artificial, almost painful.

"Excuse me, but do you live here?"

Robin said that she did.

"Good. I was hoping that you might be able to help me. I'm looking for a woman that's about your age that might be staying here in town or possibly passed through recently."

The stranger proceeded to describe the woman he was looking for—first a physical description, but then he paused before continuing.

Robin blurted out three words before she could stop herself. "Is she deaf?"

The stranger simply nodded and the look in his eyes darkened.

"Then you must be looking for Tess."

47

Tess removed the pillowcase draped over the painting of Christ and stared up at the depiction—his eyes cast toward the heavens, looking solemn and pensive. She wondered if she'd ever be able to understand why the concept of religion made her so uncomfortable. Maybe it was because her mother never took her to church. Religion was never discussed, God never considered. Or maybe it was because she had been stricken with meningitis—what kind of god would allow a child to bear that burden?

She made the bed, folded her sweater and a few extra shirts that Cap had picked up for her in town, and placed them in a brown shopping bag. She opened the bottom drawer of the dresser and returned the Bible to its spot on the top of the wood dresser.

She gazed around the rectory bedroom and made sure it looked restored—all signs of her temporary presence removed. It was as if she had never spent a single night in the rectory. She picked up her purse and the paper bag and took one final look at the painting of Christ before stepping out of the room.

Tess felt the presence—a frenetic energy somewhere in the church.

Maybe Cap, but it didn't feel like Cap. Someone else. Someone that wasn't supposed to be there.

She stood motionless in the middle of the hallway that led to Cap's study, peered into the shadows, waited for something to move, for something to shift. She waited for fifteen, twenty seconds, and although no one approached, she was convinced that someone else was lurking somewhere inside.

She inched forward and stopped in front of Cap's study—the door slightly ajar. Her heart hammered in her chest, and she attempted to steady her breath. She pressed her palm against the wood and felt for a vibration produced by footsteps, or a cough, or any kind of sound. But there was nothing.

Her heart thudded faster as she eased the door open and peered inside. Shadows masked the corners of the study, but there was no movement, no sign of another.

Tess tried to shake off this nagging feeling. Tried to tell herself that she was being jumpy and nervous. She looked at Cap's desk and wondered if she should leave him a note of explanation. A letter of gratitude for his kindness and for helping her. An explanation of why she didn't belong there and why she needed to leave.

But that kind of letter would take too long to write. She needed to give herself enough time to walk to town before it got too dark and before Cap realized that she was missing.

She stepped into the sanctuary and gazed up at the stained-glass windows.

Light from outside lit up the panes like a giant kaleidoscope. She was halfway down the aisle when something shifted in the back pew. She froze but could not repress the gasp that slipped from her mouth.

Tess's heart thudded hard enough that she could feel the thump of her own eardrums as someone stood up and stepped out from behind the pew. Her feet wouldn't move, stuck to the carpet as if cemented in place, and she clutched her purse tight to her chest.

The figure emerged from the shadows.

It was Maggie, her eyes red and swollen, tears trailing down her cheeks. "I didn't know where else to go."

48

The drunker he became, the angrier Cap felt. At Tess. At his father. At himself for allowing himself to lead a life that wasn't his.

He gazed around his shop—at the tables and chairs and bookshelves that he had crafted with his own two hands. A dull, throbbing headache began to creep up the back of his neck, so he poured another inch of bourbon into his glass and drank it down.

Cap had thought that telling Tess his darkest secrets would help free him from all the lies. He had hoped that in sharing his deceit, she would understand why he had become what he became.

But Tess didn't understand. Not at all. She wanted him to tell Butch and Wade the truth, which was simply something he would never do.

He poured more bourbon.

As his brain grew duller, Cap wondered if Tess might take it upon herself to let his secret out. Would she do that? He honestly didn't know the answer to that question. He barely knew the woman.

He lifted the glass to his lips. Felt the burn of bourbon on his eyes. His mind raced this way and that, one thought bleeding into the next until finally, he wondered what the hell he should do about Tess.

49

"Wade wants a divorce." The words blurted out of Maggie's mouth before she could stop them.

She and Tess sat side-by-side in the front church pew. Maggie clasped her hands together on her lap. She tried to smile but failed.

I'm sorry.

"You'd think I'd be relieved. Wade has been cheating on me for as long as I can remember." Her eyes threatened to spill over again. "I've always acted like his affairs didn't bother me, but they did. They still do. It's devastating knowing that your husband is sleeping with another woman. That he chooses someone else over you."

Maggie stopped herself. Shook her head. "I honestly don't know why I'm telling you all this."

We are in a perfect place to confess.

Maggie found herself smiling, but the moment was short-lived.

"What is this going to do to Butch? He's such a sensitive child."

Tess didn't respond.

"Wade and I used to be happy. We really did." She found a Kleenex in her purse and dabbed her eyes. "I know that I'm not perfect. Far from it. I'm moody and bossy, and I got caught up in being the perfect homemaker and mother and lost sight of being a good wife."

It's not your fault that Wade cheats on you.

Maggie smiled at first but ended up crying instead. "But letting my marriage grow sour is. I'm partially responsible for that."

She blew her nose. Took a deep breath.

"Robin and I didn't exactly have the most stable environment growing up. Our parents were both heavy drinkers. Always fighting. We moved from one house to the next. Smaller. Cheaper. More depressing."

By talking about her childhood out loud, the memories of her father came bubbling to the surface. "It was no surprise that Robin married a man like Chuck. He was just like our father. Mean and nasty." Her voice cracked. "My father wanted boys but got two girls instead. Robin got the worst of it. With me, he was verbally abusive. But with Robin . . . he did things to her. I knew it. My mother knew it. But we didn't talk about it. We pretended that nothing was wrong."

She grew quiet for a moment and stared up at the pulpit.

"When I got married to Wade, I was determined to create a normal, stable household. For the first few years, it was blissful. Then Butch was born, and he brought even more love into the house. Years flew by, and I didn't realize it at the time, but Wade and I started to drift apart. He threw himself into his work, and I took care of everything else—Butch, the house, shopping, and cooking. All of it."

She stared down at her hands. "Then I woke up one morning and didn't even know who I was anymore. I had changed, but you can't blame your family for that."

She blew her nose again. Stared at Tess and shook her head. "I'm sorry that I haven't been nicer to you, Tess. I really am."

That's okay.

"No, it's not. You're new to town and hardly know anybody besides Cap." She looked down and noticed Tess's purse and a bag of clothes and knew in an instant what that meant. "You're not leaving, are you?"

Maggie watched Tess's lips pull tight.

Yes.

"Why?"

I don't belong here.

Maggie started to say something, but Tess wrote something else in her notebook.

I'm running away from a problem that won't go away.

"I've aired all my dirty laundry. Most of it, at least. Might make you feel better to do the same."

Tess's eyes burned red as she considered Maggie's words.

Would you like a glass of wine?

"Depending on your story, Tess, maybe I'll have two."

50

Cap slept in a chair that he had made with his own two hands. The bottle of Wild Turkey nestled between his feet. An empty glass beside it.

Cap dreamed. He dreamed of things that felt real, but he wouldn't remember them in the morning.

He drove his parents' Dodge Coronet station wagon. The snow so thick outside that he couldn't see anything but a wall of white. He felt anxious about something, but it wasn't the dangerous conditions—not the snow or wind or driving blind. Instead, he was worried about not getting to his destination on time. A destination that escaped him, but he knew that he needed to drive faster before it was too late.

Over the howl of violent winds outside, Cap heard distressed voices whispering from the back seat.

He peered into the rearview mirror and saw his mother, father, and Max, leaning forward, staring back at his reflection. Each of them wore a grim expression. When his mother began to cry, Cap noticed that she only had one eye; beside it, only wrinkled folds of a wasted lid remained.

"You're not going the right way, boy," his father hissed. He was dressed in black clerical clothing, complete with a white starched collar. "When are you ever going to learn?"

Cap tried to respond. Tried to tell his father that he was going the right way. But he was unable to speak. The words were there, but he couldn't utter them aloud.

His father reached forward and gripped his shoulder. "Take us home, son." He squeezed him tighter. "You need to get back home before it's too late."

The station wagon began to drift, and all sound faded away in an instant. No longer could he hear the howling wind or the hum of tires upon the road. His father's lips moved faster, more urgently, but Cap couldn't hear a single word. Trapped in silence. He stared out the windshield, everything white and swirling, and they floated without direction. He tried to regain control of the car, but it kept drifting, spinning faster and faster.

A shape materialized in front of him, emerging from behind a curtain of driving snow. At first, Cap thought it was a tree or perhaps a sign, but the shape slowly took form. It was a woman.

As the Dodge Coronet barreled forward, Cap saw that it was Tess running down the middle of the road as if she was trying to get away from someone. She flailed her arms for him to stop. Her mouth pulled back in terror. Cap tried jerking the steering wheel to avoid crashing into her, but the car sped straight ahead. Twenty feet. Ten feet. A collision inevitable.

Then silence inside the car shattered when his parents and Max began to scream.

51

Tess sipped her wine and felt Maggie's eyes on her. It was strange to be alone with Maggie in the house. They barely knew one another. But she was glad that Cap was still in his workshop. She didn't know why exactly, but she felt more comfortable opening up to another woman.

They sat in silence. Both drinking their wine. Tess peered at her notebook on the coffee table but seemed hesitant to pick it up.

"It's okay, Tess. You can tell me anything you want."

Tess's hand trembled as she picked up her notebook and began to write.

Before she climbed into bed, before she picked out her favorite book, *Where the Wild Things Are*, and before arranging her collection of stuffed animals—Harry the Hippo, Wolfie, Orangie, and the Three Teddies—Tess made sure that the closet light was on, the door fully open, and that she scanned for legs and feet that might be lurking behind rows of dresses and winter coats. She did the same thing every night—checking for the Man in Blue.

Her mother entered the room holding a glass of white wine. It made her breath smell funny, but Tess didn't mind. She tucked the blankets around Tess's legs, swept the hair from her face, and gave her a hand-tickle, which Tess preferred more than all the other tickles.

Tess tried to let her eyes close, but she couldn't help herself and kept looking toward the closet.

"There's no such thing as the Blue Man, sweet pea."

"Man in Blue," Tess corrected.

"Him either."

"He's real, mama."

"He is?"

Tess's chubby cheeks nodded earnestly.

"Are you sure?"

More nodding.

"What does he look like?"

"Very tall."

"Bigger than me?"

"Much bigger."

Tess's mother sipped from her glass of wine. "What else?"

"He is always dressed in blue. Blue pants. Blue shirt."

"That doesn't sound so bad."

"He has blue feet, too."

"That's silly."

"It's not silly, mama. It's true. He says that his blue feet make him walk real quiet."

Tess's mother drank some more wine and tickled Tess's other hand. "Maybe he's a good fairy. Like the tooth fairy."

"He's not. He's not good at all."

"Well, I won't let him hurt you."

"You promise?"

"Cross my heart. Goodnight, baby."

Tess watched her mother cross the room and pull the bedroom door half-closed behind her.

She stuck her thumb in her mouth and thought about anything but the bedroom closet. About Harry the Hippo, about her first-grade teacher, Miss Salgado, and about the chocolate chip cookies she had had for a snack that day. She'd eaten two even though her mama had told her she could only have one. Then she thought about snow and hoped that there would be a few inches on the ground in the morning so she could build a snowman. After a few minutes, her eyes fluttered closed, and she fell into a light sleep.

She didn't remember what she dreamed about or whether she dreamed about anything at all. She didn't hear the set of voices carry down the hallway just after midnight. She didn't know that at 2:30 a.m., the Man in Blue came to visit her once again. She didn't see him poke his head inside her room and move into the closet, listening for the sounds of her mama's footsteps. She didn't notice the closet light snapping off. She couldn't hear the whisper of the blue polyester fabric that covered his shoes. She didn't smell the sanitizer on his skin.

Tess didn't remember her mama coming into the room. Didn't remember the pitch of shock or the horror in her voice or the way her mother lunged at the Man in Blue.

What Tess *did* come to know many years later was that her mother finally believed in the Man in Blue.

52

Darkness. Pitch black in every direction, the moon and a million stars obscured by passing storm clouds. The drone of an eighteen-wheeler laboring down Sugar Run pricked the silence for a few moments. Then everything slipped back into absolute quiet once again.

Butch stumbled through a grove of knotted black walnut trees, fingers and toes throbbing and burning from the cold. His nose ran, and his eyes blurred from tears that wouldn't stop, but he kept his feet moving forward.

A hard wind swept through the limbs of barren trees, trunks groaning against the resistance and branches rattling. From somewhere in the night, a barred owl hooted, sounding lonely and lost.

Butch knew he was lost as well, but it didn't matter.

He wondered if his parents even knew he was gone. But that didn't matter either.

Nothing would ever matter.

His eyes roamed the woods, searching for one specific tree—the black walnut tree scarred by a strike of lightning that he had discovered years earlier. He considered it *his* tree. *His* special place. He'd sit under the canopy of its dark green leaves and dream of the day that he could move from this town forever and away from these people. He would live in a city where no one knew who he was, and he would be left alone. No one telling him what to do or making fun of him. And he would never come back to Black Walnut. Never.

But he knew his search for that specific tree to be pointless.

He stopped walking. This was far enough. His legs shook under him, so he dropped to his knees and could feel the frozen dirt press through his jeans. His breath hitched in his chest as he stared up at the outline of the moon peeked out from behind thick clouds overhead. When he was little, maybe seven or eight, his father told him that a rabbit lived on the moon and pointed to the markings of a hare pounding a mortar with a pestle, but Butch could never make out that image. And even though all he ever saw were dark, random shadows, Butch pretended that he could see the moon rabbit to share a connection with his father.

Butch placed the single barrel twelve-gauge shotgun on his lap, his fingers finding the safety and switching it off. He had loaded two shells into the chamber, but one was all it would take.

His parents would probably think that it was their fault. That their divorce pushed him over the edge. Or maybe that it was because he hated going to school, was bullied every day, and didn't have a single friend. His parents would never really understand why. They would never understand that he felt different than everyone else—an outsider. At school. At home. Everywhere he turned.

He dug the stock of the shotgun in the dirt at a forty-five-degree angle. Pressed the tip of the barrel under his chin and felt the spike of cold from the steel.

The wind picked up again and cut right through his jacket. His eyes burned, and tears continued to stream down acne-marked cheeks. He cried not because he was scared. Not because he felt sad. Not because of the sense of unknown. It was the unbearable weight of loneliness.

Thoughts of his parents and school, teachers, and classmates swirled through his mind. Then he thought about his tormentors—Brian and Monte.

Everything would be over in a split second. No more pain. No more shame. No more being lost and alone.

His thumb traced the trigger guard's polished steel, and Butch thought about the shotgun. That thought brought him to the memory of hunting turkeys, and from there his mind went to riding in the truck with Cap.

He saw the pastor every Sunday but never really talked to him other than to say hello and goodbye. He thought it would be strange riding with a man he didn't really know, but it hadn't been. Cap spoke to him like a real person—not like how older people usually talk to kids, asking questions they didn't care about hearing the answer. And most grown-ups would have given him a lecture about hunting during the off-season or gone straight to his parents and gotten him into trouble.

But Cap didn't.

Butch had never told anyone else about Brian and Monte. Certainly not his parents. He didn't know what compelled him to tell Cap something like that.

Well, not that it'll make you feel any better, but I had my share of dealing with bullies back in school.

Butch tried blocking out thoughts about Cap, but his mind kept returning to the man he barely knew.

"No," he whispered into the woods. The sound of his own voice sickened him. He sounded weak. "No," he said again, but louder. "NO. NO. NO." His words echoed through the forest before fading away into nothingness.

He pressed his eyes closed and forced himself to think about his fourteen-year-old life, knowing in his heart that it would never get better, and nothing would ever change.

His hands trembled from the cold. He took a breath and slipped his thumb against the trigger and waited for everything to come to an end.

53

Robin had difficulty focusing on anything for more than a few seconds. She burned the pork chops. Spilled bleach all over a load of laundry. Accidentally threw away a drawing that Mikey had made at school, which caused the boy to have a full-blown meltdown. She couldn't think straight, her mind replaying the encounter with the stranger, the man looking for Tess—the man that Tess was afraid of.

She sat at the kitchen table drinking a Diet Coke and smoked one cigarette after another. The television blared a cartoon in the living room. Chuck Jr., Mikey, and Darla scooped cereal, their replacement dinner, from plastic bowls, their eyes glued to the screen.

Robin had tried calling Cap's house at six, but no one answered. Then at seven, seven-thirty, and a few times after that. Each time the phone just rang and rang. She tried the church as well, but with the same result.

She couldn't take it anymore. Thinking the worst. Feeling a wave of shame and guilt slap her across the face. She stared at her babies, all of them blissfully unaware of what kind of mother they shared.

Robin jumped up. Grabbed her purse and stepped into the living room. "Put on your shoes. We're leaving. We're leaving right now."

Darla nodded, but the boys were too caught up in the cartoon.

Robin snapped off the television. "Chuck. Mikey. I want you to put on your shoes and a jacket. Let's go."

"I don't want to. I wanna watch cartoons," Mikey pouted.

Robin didn't respond. She knelt down and shoved a pair of sneakers on Darla's feet.

"Where we going?" Chuck Jr. demanded.

"Out. Now put on your shoes."

"Will Papa be here when we get back?" Darla asked.

She laced up her daughter's shoes. Stared at her little face. "No, baby. He won't."

Robin ushered all three of her kids to the front door. Took one final look inside the house before pulling the door closed behind them. All the lights were on. Clutter on every surface. Everything she owned was in the house, and part of her wondered if she'd ever walk through the front door again.

Darla squeezed her hand tight. Her eyes wide and on the verge of spilling tears. "When are we gonna come back home, Mama?"

"I don't know, baby. I just don't know." Either the tone of her voice or what she said set Darla off. Then both boys broke down into tears as well. By the time she got the kids into the truck, Robin found herself crying right along with all three of her children.

The cab of the truck was cold, the vinyl seats stiff and uncomfortable. It took Robin a few tries before the engine turned over, and by that time, her kids' cries progressed into unstoppable howls.

The truck lurched down the driveway, but Robin refused to look back at the house, at the home that had offered so little happiness.

54

Maggie could barely steady her hands as she read the final words on the page. Her entire body shook, and her throat burned dry. She snatched her glass. Drank down the wine, and when she looked at Tess, all she could think of was her younger sister. Flashes of repressed memories from their childhood came bubbling forward like boiling water overflowing a pot.

Maggie felt the guilt and shame wash over her. She had allowed her little sister to be molested and never lifted a finger to help her. She could have told someone. Could have run away with Robin. Anything would have been better than sticking her head in the sand and pretending that awful things weren't happening.

She wasn't quite sure what to say as she watched tears roll down Tess's cheeks.

"I'm sorry."

Those two words sounded useless and empty.

Tess wiped her face before writing once again in her notebook.

I don't know what to do.

"You're safe now."

Not really.

"But it's all over now, right?"

No.

"I don't understand."

Maggie watched as Tess broke down and began to cry harder. She waited for the storm to pass. Waited for Tess to compose herself.

He came back into my life a month ago. I didn't know who he was. What *he was.*

Tess struggled to form words on the page.

We started dating.

"And he knew who you were?"

Yes.

Maggie stood. Her legs trembling beneath her. She poured more wine into their glasses. They sat in silence, and Maggie didn't notice the headlights cut across the church lawn. Didn't hear the hum of the motor or the footsteps crunching atop the snow. She wasn't aware of the presence moving up the stairs.

Only when a fist pounded on the door did Maggie know that she and Tess were no longer alone.

55

It could have been anyone, but Tess knew exactly who it would be. She opened the door anyway.

Aaron towered in front of her, hands clenching and unclenching at his sides.

Tess's entire body hummed, but she tried to mask her paralyzing fear. She stood her ground and signed.

What are you doing here?

Aaron's eyes cut past her before settling back on Tess.

"We need to talk."

There's nothing to talk about.

"Please listen. I know I was deceitful. And I know that was wrong. I realize that now. I should have been honest with you about who I am."

Blood rushed to her head. Her throat contracted. She tried to suck in air.

"I'm sorry, Tess. I really am."

Leave-me-alone.

She swung the door closed, but Aaron's foot shot forward.

He signed instead of speaking. *We belong together.*

Tess didn't respond. She had the overwhelming impulse to find a dark place to curl up and escape into sleep.

"You can't deny that we have something between us, Tess. We both felt it. Can't you see that?"

Tess's knees buckled, but Maggie caught her and stepped in front of her.

"You need to leave. Right now." Maggie jabbed her finger toward Aaron's chest. "Or I swear I'll call the sheriff."

Aaron stared at Maggie for a moment with an unreadable expression. "This doesn't concern you."

His gaze settled back on Tess. He crossed the threshold and closed the door behind him.

"Please. Hear me out." He held his hands out in front of him, palms up. "I'll leave my wife, Tess. Anything. We can go wherever you want. Just the two of us. Nothing else matters."

Tess's heart whooshed in her chest, and she was seized with the urge to empty the contents of her stomach.

"I'm willing to give up everything for you, Tess. My family. My career. Everything."

Tess felt disconnected from her body. Floating away. Further and further. The disconnect growing. She could only watch as Maggie continued to jab her finger at her father.

"How dare you. How dare you come here. You destroyed her childhood, and now you want to ruin her as an adult?"

Aaron's dull expression didn't shift. He reached for Tess, but Maggie clutched her by the arm and guided her back a half step.

A wave of cold air rippled across her skin, and Tess watched the front door bang open. There stood Robin, silhouetted by the night sky. She locked eyes with Tess, her face knotted and twisted.

The energy in the room shifted. On the precipice of combustion. An extended moment of unsettling quiet.

"I did this. This is all my fault," Robin finally whispered.

Tess understood Robin's words but not their meaning.

"He was looking for you." Robin thudded to her knees, tears streaming down her face. "I'm sorry, Tess. I was angry. Frustrated with my life. I wanted to hurt you. I am so sorry."

The room fell silent once again. All eyes on Aaron. But his gaze remained only on Tess.

"What are you even doing here, Tess?"

Getting away from you.

"I understand. Maybe all this doesn't make sense. Maybe it's wrong—"

"Maybe it's wrong?" Maggie blurted. "You're sick. Pathetic and twisted."

Aaron ignored both Maggie and Robin like they weren't even present.

Nothing made sense. Maggie screaming. Robin wailing. Aaron looming before her.

Tess stared at all of them—their mouths moving, pitted in silence—but all she could think about was Cap. *Please come back inside.*

"Come with me, Tess. Please."

Tess recoiled. Her feet moved beneath her. She stumbled into the kitchen. Reached for the back door. Swung it open and a blast of cold wind shocked her system.

She needed to run. Needed to get away.

She moved down the steps, but a hand snatched her by the wrist and, Aaron yanked her back inside the kitchen.

He was talking, but she couldn't understand what he was saying. His lips moved rapidly. She could smell his aftershave—that familiar scent from her childhood.

The Man in Blue.

She stared into his eyes.

The Man in Blue.

Years of fear and confusion and anger came bubbling up. Images of the awful things done to her when she was five flashed in Tess's mind—his hands, the smell of his breath, the cold look in his eyes. Her hand snatched a wine glass from the counter. She swung it like a hammer, the glass shattering on the side of Aaron's head. Blood began to leak from his temple.

Tess watched him stumble onto the concrete landing, clutching at the wound. Everything in her silent world began to move more slowly, and her vision twisted and blurred.

Maggie gripped Robin by the shoulder and pointed at Aaron. "He's just like Daddy. Just like Daddy."

Tess swayed on her feet. She watched Robin's face transform. Her eyes clouded over. She sprang forward and lunged at Aaron. Clawed at his face. Slapped his cheeks. Screamed vile, hateful words at him.

Aaron pushed her away. His lips pulled back, baring his teeth.

Robin went after him again. Punching, slapping, scratching.

This time, Aaron fought back. He swung his hand, and it connected with the side of Robin's face. Her head snapped back, and she collapsed to the floor.

Everything moved so fast.

Aaron drew back his hand once again. Brought it forward. Tess felt a sharp percussion reverberate all around her, then the side of her father's head blossomed red, and a warm mist dotted her face.

Aaron's body went limp, and he teetered backward. She watched him fall down the concrete steps. Arms and legs cartwheeling and crashing into the darkness below.

Tess rocked on the balls of her feet. Stared down to where her father had fallen.

Maggie and Robin stepped on either side of her, and they, too, stared down the steps.

Tess noticed the pistol clutched in Maggie's hands—*her* pistol.

All three women gasped for air. Eyes wide, barely blinking.

Tess noticed Maggie's lips moving.

"Just like our daddy."

The urge to be swept away from all of this was finally too much. Tess's legs went out from under her, and darkness ushered her away.

GOOD FRIDAY

56

Did I do this?

Although a flock of crows flapped from one tree to the next, restless and agitated, Cap didn't register the hoarse call of their forlorn bird song. He didn't hear the crows or the wind or the rustle of barren limbs. All he heard was the thudding of his own heart.

He stared down at the face of a man he had never seen prior to this day. The snow had turned black next to what remained of the right side of the stranger's skull—his eye sockets nothing but two darkened pits as the result of the crows.

A dead man. A dead man shot in the head. A dead man murdered on his church grounds.

Cap felt a sharp flash of mounting panic as he tried to remember the previous night.

Did I do this?

The flock of crows took flight in unison—dozens and dozens—swooping in a slow circle above his head. Some fluttering and perching on the limbs of trees, others disappearing into the woods behind the house. Shrieking and cawing with excitement over the death of the stranger lying on the snow and ice.

Cap backpedaled from the body, unable to tear his gaze away from where the dead man's eyes used to be.

His mind swirled, damaged from booze and compromised by a mounting panic.

Where was Tess?

Was she safe?

Had something happened to her, too?

It was then that he noticed a set of footprints in the snow. They led from the crown of the dead man's skull toward the church.

Tess. He needed to find Tess.

He didn't feel the bite of the wind or the throbbing of his bare feet upon the frozen ground as he followed the footprints to his church.

57

Butch hadn't slept all night. His fingers and toes still throbbed from the cold. He still wore the clothes from the previous day, and he could smell the odors of the woods on his shirt and pants, dirt and moss and decayed leaves. Sleep evaded him. Too much had happened. Too much of his life flipped upside down, not making sense.

He curled up in a tight ball at the edge of his bed. Pulled the blankets under his chin and listened to his mother cry from down the hallway. It wasn't the fragile sound of sobbing he'd heard before, but rather, loud, uncontrollable wailing. It had been like that for the last few hours.

Something awful happened, and for the first time in his life, Butch felt a sense of fear for his mother's mental health.

He pressed his eyes closed, and under the wrenching howls coming from his parents' bedroom, Butch could hear his father's voice—his tone steady and calming. No anger or impatience. In fact, his father's manner of speech was utterly unfamiliar.

Though he could not hear the words themselves, Butch understood that they were filled with compassion.

58

The quiet in the church felt unsettling—raw and piercing.

Cap swung the bedroom door open and peered inside. The bed was made, everything in its place. Everything except for Tess. Her purse was gone, as was everything she had to her name.

His knees were unreliable, almost foreign under him, but he kept searching, terrified at what he might discover.

He checked his study, both restrooms, then the administrative office. But no sign of Tess.

Growing panic caused his chest to tighten. He had to find Tess. He would get in his truck and drive the roads, go into town, into every store, search everywhere until he found her.

Cap stepped into the sanctuary and saw Tess rolled into a fetal position on the front pew, but he couldn't tell whether she was asleep or in a condition much worse.

He called out her name, then remembered that she couldn't hear his voice.

Tess must have sensed his presence because she lifted her head. Cap saw her red and swollen eyes. She stood, unsteady at first, then threw her arms around his neck and buried her face against his chest.

He let her cry it out. Her body trembled in his embrace, and he could feel tears leak through his shirt. After a minute, maybe longer, Tess's breathing steadied, and she dropped back down onto the pew.

"That man out there. Did he hurt you?"

Tess removed her notebook from her purse, but her hands could barely grip the pencil.

"Do you know him? Do you know who he is?"

She proceeded to cry once again. Quiet at first, but then she had difficulty catching her breath.

Cap looked toward the church doors before settling his gaze back on Tess. "Your father?"

Yes.

He sat down beside her, his mind reeling with so many questions. "Okay. It's going to be okay. It's over now."

No.

"You were protecting yourself."

Tess rocked on the pew and refused to look him in the eye.

Cap lifted her chin. "Listen to me, Tess. If he came here to hurt you, you had no other choice.

No. Her hand struggled to keep the pencil on the paper.

Cap watched as she scrawled one word, barely legible, but he could read the six letters. He stared at the word, trying to process and understand.

"Maggie did this?"

Yes.

"Maggie was here last night? At the house?"

Yes.

"I don't understand, Tess. I don't—"

The sound of tires crunching upon the driveway stopped him mid-sentence. He stood. Gawked at the church doors and wondered what else this day might bring.

59

Wade peered down at the dead man. Half of him still not understanding how this happened—*why* this happened. But this was real. Maggie hadn't made it up. Hadn't exaggerated one damn bit.

He looked up as Cap approached, and the two of them locked eyes.

They stood shoulder to shoulder. Both men staring down at the body.

"Where the hell were you last night, Cap?"

Cap's first instinct was to make something up, but in his current state, he couldn't wrap his head around lying. "I was drunk. When I woke up this morning, this is what I found."

"Christ almighty."

A gust of wind pulled across the yard, lifted a flurry of light snow off the ground, and sent it swirling in the air like a million tiny dancers.

"What happened, Wade? Did Maggie really do this?"

Wade looked him straight in the eye. "It wasn't self-defense."

"She told you that?"

"She's a mess right now. I gave her a Valium, but she's a damn mess. Didn't sleep one bit last night."

"How did it happen? I mean, why would she do something like this?"

Wade didn't answer for a long time. He simply stared down at the dead man, trying to process everything. "Maggie and Robin had been abused by their father growing up. Verbally. Physically. Did you know that?"

"No. I didn't."

"Their old man was a sick son of a bitch. He started molesting Robin when she was seven or eight years old." He rubbed at his eyes. "Maggie hid it from people here in town. She was ashamed. Ashamed of her father. Her mother. Herself. And she was scared about what could happen to Robin if their secret got out." He looked away. Off and into the woods. "She was afraid that they'd take her sister away."

Snow tumbled down all around them, flakes sticking to their hair and clothing.

"Maggie snapped last night, Cap. After Tess told her what this piece of garbage did to her when she was just a kid, it triggered all those memories of what Maggie's father used to do to Robin."

Cap tried to say something but couldn't find the words.

"Maggie knew that Tess carried a pistol in her purse." He peered at Cap. "She could be looking at second-degree murder."

Wade waited for Cap to turn and face him. He hoped that Cap would have something to say. Offer some kind of advice. Offer anything, but Cap simply stared down at the body.

"That's a twenty-five-year sentence, Cap. Twenty-five years." Wade pointed down at the body. "You know what kind of man he was, Cap? Do you know what he did?"

"I do."

"So maybe what happened is for the best."

Cap finally looked at him.

"What are you saying, Wade?"

Wade took a breath. Removed Tess's pistol from his jacket and wiped it down with a handkerchief. He squatted down next to the body and slipped the gun into the dead man's pocket.

"Are you going to help me, or am I gonna have to do it by myself?"

60

It didn't seem real—especially in a world of absolute silence—watching Cap and Wade heft her father onto a tattered canvas tarp and slowly wrap the material around his body. First his legs, then torso and arms. The two men didn't utter a single word as they performed their task. They worked in unison, almost casually, as if it was perfectly normal to wrap a dead man in a tarp. Tess had no idea as to what would come next. She would not ask or interfere. She would only watch and wait.

Cap had asked her to stay in the church, but Tess wanted to see her father one last time. She felt a sense of obligation. Or maybe she needed to confirm that this was real, that her father was indeed dead.

She watched the snow fall. Noticed how the wind tugged at Cap and Wade's hair. A handful of crows stared back at her from the limbs of black walnut trees, their beaks opening and closing as they called down with some urgent message.

As the tarp slipped over her father's face, Tess didn't feel anger, sadness nor remorse. Instead, she felt a sense of peculiar relief—a weight that she had carried for the last twenty-five years lifted.

And although she hadn't slept for twenty-four hours, she didn't feel tired. Instead, she felt more alive than she had ever felt before.

The Man in Blue is gone. The Man in Blue is gone forever.

61

Cap tried blocking out all the doubts racing through his mind. Tried to not think about what he and Wade were doing.

Wade's words replayed over and over again. *Maybe what happened is for the best.*

The dead man's feet started to slip from his grip, so Cap hooked his arm around the ankles and pulled them tight to his chest. It was a cumbersome, awkward task to carry two hundred pounds of dead weight. Like lugging a roll of carpet.

Wade clutched the man by the neck and head. Neither of them had spoken since setting off from the church. Wade didn't tell him where they were headed. But he didn't have to—Cap knew.

Maybe what happened is for the best.

Even though the temperature dipped below thirty degrees, Cap could see the perspiration on the back of Wade's neck. "You want to rest for a minute?"

Wade said that he didn't.

Clouds crept in front of the sun, and the forest dimmed around them, and for a moment, he thought he was on the verge of passing out. But then a swath of sunlight cut through the canopy of branches to guide him forward.

Cap tried to think of a reason why they shouldn't be doing what they were doing but couldn't come up with a single one.

The dead man had sexually abused Tess.

The dead man had tried to have an affair with his own daughter.

The dead man had showed up at his home looking for Tess.

Maybe what happened is for the best.

They crested a knoll, and Cap spotted the mouth of the bear cave.

Wade stopped by the entrance to the underground tunnels, and they set the dead man to the frozen earth. Then both he and Cap sat down to catch their breath.

They'd been mulling over their task in silence for a while. Neither of them in any hurry to get started on what needed to be done.

A wind blew in from the north, and a light rain began to fall. The smell of snow and rain—clean, natural, and wholesome—didn't fit their current predicament.

Cap thought about how long it had been since the two of them had been alone together but couldn't remember the last time.

Wade was the first to break the quiet. He pointed toward the mouth of the cave. "Remember playing down there?"

"How could I forget?"

"We were just a couple of kids. Thought we were invincible."

"Those were good times."

Wade shook his head. "What the hell happened to us, Cap?"

"I don't know, Wade. We grew up. Grew apart. Made some mistakes along the way, I guess."

Wade leaned forward, stared at the body, and rubbed at weary eyes. "Shit. I still can't quite believe all this." His voice turned soft and unsteady. "What we're doing here, Cap, it's the right thing to do, isn't it?"

Cap had rarely seen cracks in the man's exterior, but he saw them now, and they were on the verge of breaking wide open. "If we don't, Maggie's life, Butch's life, changes forever. We're protecting them is all, Wade."

Wade grew quiet, and Cap thought the conversation to be finished.

"I've tried, Cap. I really have."

He looked at Wade, and the man stared straight at him.

"I've tried to be a good father to Butch. It hasn't been easy, and I've made a helluva lot of mistakes, but I've tried." Wade looked down at his hands. "I've tried to be a good father to a son that isn't mine."

Cap felt as if he had been punched in the gut. He processed Wade's words. Tried to respond but failed. Fourteen years of deceit and loss swirled and pressed down upon his shoulders, but more than that, the realization of his betrayal of Wade shook him hard. His childhood friend had been burdened with the same unspoken truth. Never saying a word and carrying the shameful secret that Cap thought he alone had carried.

"Butch is lost, Cap. I failed him and I'll be damned if I know how to help him."

Wade removed a pint of Wild Turkey from his jacket. Cracked the seal, took a pull on the bottle, and held it out to Cap.

Cap accepted the whiskey. Stared at the amber liquid. More than anything else, he wanted to press the bottle to his lips and drink deep and drink long. Drink every damn drop. He wanted to mask the pain unspooling inside him.

But he didn't. Instead, he handed the whiskey back to Wade. "How long have you known?"

Wade took another pull on the bottle. "I don't know. Since Butch was about six or seven, I guess."

"Why haven't you ever said anything?"

Wade let out a broken laugh. "Shit. And what exactly would I say?"

Cap stared at the bottle of Wild Turkey, every part of him wanting to feel the burn and glow in his stomach.

"Besides, I guess I didn't want to lose him. Thought if I said anything, all the ugly truth would come spilling out, and I'd lose my son. My family. Hell, my entire life, I guess."

"I'm sorry, Wade. I really am. We made a mistake. Not that it makes one damn bit of difference, but it only happened the one time—"

Wade held his hand up for Cap to stop. "Hell, I should be the one apologizing. Especially to Maggie. It's not like I've exactly been a saint in my marriage."

Both men grew quiet. Rain fell on them, slow at first, but then it seemed as if the sky split open and a torrent pounded down without mercy.

Wade tossed a rock into the mouth of the cave and listened to the clatter fade away. "What a damn mess. You think that Maggie will ever be able to recover from this? Will any of us?"

Cap's eyes fell upon the body in front of him. He still had a difficult time wrapping his head around the reality of what they were preparing to do. He thought about Wade's question, and he had no way of knowing what might happen next for any of them—not tomorrow or the next day, let alone a few weeks down the road. Despite all that, he felt a sense of steadfast resolve wash across him.

"We'll find our way."

Wade recapped the whiskey bottle and slipped it back into his jacket. "You really believe that?"

"I do." Cap stood. Extended his hand to Wade. "Let's get this done with."

Wade accepted Cap's hand. Let him pull him to his feet. He hefted the dead man's legs, and Cap lifted the head, and they crawled into the mouth of the cave.

EASTER SUNDAY

62

Red, white, and blue banners snapped from the front of store awnings. Balloons in assorted Easter colors pulled at their strings as a steady breeze whipped down Main Street. Mounds of blackened snow slowly melted under the midday sun, and rivulets of water crept onto the asphalt like liquid snakes. Despite the wind and the chill in the air, the sidewalks were filled with a few hundred townspeople watching the Easter procession that marched down the center of Main Street.

The Black Walnut High School marching band performed *Here Comes Peter Cottontail*, drums thumping, trumpets and trombones blaring to the beat. Young girls in floral dresses pranced along the street. Boys with slicked-back hair wore their Sunday's best and waved to the crowd. A handful of dogs wore rabbit ears. Fire trucks rumbled past, occasionally sounding their sirens to the thrill of the children. And a flatbed truck with stacks of hay gained the most attention as a six-foot bunny rabbit tossed handfuls of chocolates and saltwater taffy to the eager crowd.

Cap and Tess huddled next to one another on the west side of the street between Lacey's Hardware and the IGA. Maggie, Wade, and Butch stood across from them on the east side of Main Street in front of the Agway store. And a little way down the street, Robin attempted to wrangle her three kids, who ran around and squealed nonstop. Each of them watching but not watching. Despite the smattering of *oohhs* and *aahhs*, the squeal of young laughter, the yipping of dogs, and the occasional shout, neither Cap nor Tess nor Maggie nor Wade nor Butch nor Robin heard specific sounds. All that was drowned out by scattered memories replaying the events of the last forty-eight hours.

It had been an unspoken understanding between them to attempt to go about their lives as if nothing happened. To go to church, school, work and attend social functions, all the while pretending that blood had not been spilled and death concealed.

When someone marching in the parade waved at them, they lifted their hand automatically and waved in return. They attempted a smile. To appear in the moment of their small-town celebration. But they were not. Too much had happened. Not enough time had passed. And maybe time would never fade the series of individual events from their minds.

Even Maggie, who had planned and organized every detail of the festivity, was unaware that not a single child carried the Easter baskets that she had been so insistent on. Her typical watchful, critical eyes were now vacant and glassy from sedation. Wade's arm wrapped around her shoulder, and it appeared that he was responsible for holding her upright.

Cap and Wade made eye contact. Briefly. Each man nodded to the other. Their message clear—*Everything will be fine.*

Cap felt Tess's hand wrap around his, and he squeezed it tight, never wanting to let go.

63

Under the pungent smell of litter boxes, Cap caught the unmistakable odor of disease as soon as he and Tess crossed the threshold into Lester's home. He'd grown accustomed to that smell when visiting folks in the area who were nearing the end of their lives. It reminded him of boiled cabbage left in the pot too long, but he had learned to mask his discomfort from the odor over the years. No one wants to see their pastor wincing at the smell of impending death.

Lester appeared genuinely taken aback as he escorted Cap and Tess inside. "Well, this sure is a surprise. Thought Easter Sunday would be your busiest day of the year."

"We missed you at the parade." Cap dragged his boots across the mat and tried to shake off the cold. "Besides, I wanted to bring Tess by so that she could finally meet Bonnie."

"That sure is kind of you." Lester peered at Tess. "Bonnie has been eager to meet you, young lady."

Lester took their jackets as they walked into the living room. Flames crackled blue and orange in the fireplace, chunks of embers dropping off the logs and smoldering in ash.

"Get you folks a drink?"

Cap blew on his hands. "Maybe a little coffee, if you have it."

"You bet. How about a little splash of bourbon to warm you up?"

"Just coffee will be fine. Thank you, though."

"How about you, Tess? A little bourbon kick?"

No, thank you.

"All right, then. Guess I'll be drinking alone. Make yourself comfortable, and I'll go rustle up those drinks."

Cap and Tess looked at a pair of worn recliner chairs where two cats, a calico and a Siamese, took up the better part of the cushions. With a mutual understanding, they opted to sit on the couch instead.

They could feel the smoky heat from the fireplace upon their faces, and they not only savored the warmth but the quiet and normalcy of Bonnie and Lester's home. Tess peered around the room and couldn't help but notice the cat figurines. There had to be two dozen of them. On the coffee table and end tables and lined up in rows on a bookshelf. Ceramic cats curled into balls, cats playing with yarn, a cat chasing a mouse, a mama cat with a litter of kittens.

"Quite a collection, isn't it?" Lester asked as he handed them each a mug of coffee.

"Didn't realize you were such a cat person."

"Neither did I. Neither-did-I."

"Are you all making fun of my cats?" a woman's feeble voice whispered from behind them.

There stood Bonnie, wrapped up in a thick, baby blue terry cloth robe that threatened to swallow her entirely. A knit cap that had seen better days covered her head. And even though she only weighed around eighty pounds, she stood straight, and there was little doubt that she ruled the roost.

Lester winked at Tess before addressing his wife. "We were just admiring these things of beauty."

Bonnie snorted. "You wouldn't know a piece of art if it crawled up your leg and bit you on the backside."

Bonnie stepped in front of Tess and took her hand between hers. "And you must be Tess."

Yes.

"I've been wanting to meet you for the longest time."

Thank you.

"And I can take one look at you and know that Cap is one lucky man."

Tess reddened at the cheeks.

"Hell, Bonnie. Don't go scaring off our guests in the first few minutes," Lester protested.

Bonnie gave Lester a playfully withering look. "How about pouring me a little of that bourbon you're sneaking?"

"I ain't sneaking." Lester set his mug on the mantle. "And to answer your question: no. Make you a tea, though."

"You're no fun."

"Doctor's orders."

"Fine. I guess I'll have to settle for a tea, then. Chamomile, I suppose."

"Either that or peppermint."

"Surprise me."

Cap watched the man shuffle out of the room, looking tired and used up, and felt Bonnie squeeze his hand. When he gazed into her eyes, there was a clarity and sense of purpose that made him know that Bonnie had more on her mind than a social visit.

"I worry about Lester."

"He seems to be managing."

"Not now. I can still look after him. I'm talking about after I'm gone."

"Well—"

"Speak straight with me, Cap. None of that pastor pep talk business."

"What would you like to know?"

"Tell me what to expect . . . or what Lester should expect after I'm gone."

He tugged at his mustache for a moment before speaking. "It's never easy on the spouse. Especially after being married as long as the two of you have been."

Bonnie kept her eyes locked on Cap, tears welling up in the corners.

"I've seen it dozens of times. The husband or wife can't seem to find their way after losing the other. They become lost without a sense of purpose."

"I see," she whispered.

"But the thing is—with someone like Lester—what makes him different is that he has another purpose. He's got responsibilities. Something to wake up to in the morning. That will help guide him."

"You really believe that, Cap? You're not just saying it to try and make me feel better?"

"I do, Bonnie. I really do."

Bonnie laughed, then cried. She found a Kleenex in her robe pocket and went about cleaning up her face. "I'm sorry to be carrying on in front of you, Tess. Just meeting and all."

Tess leaned forward and placed her hand on Bonnie's knee, and her smile said it all: *Don't worry. It's okay.*

Bonnie patted Tess's hand in gratitude and asked Cap, "Will you check on him from time to time? See how he's doing? The man can't even boil water on his own."

"I'm real fond of that husband of yours. And if there's one thing I'm good at, it's boiling a pot of water."

A fresh batch of tears rolled down Bonnie's cheeks, and she wiped those away, too. "Enough about all this kind of talk." The calico jumped up on her lap and commenced grooming itself. "So, Tess, are you planning to stay in Black Walnut for a while?"

Cap could feel his stomach clench and his breathing almost stop—he was surprised by how much hung on her answer.

Tess gave him a quick look before answering Bonnie's question. *Yes.*

"That's good to hear. Cap here has been a bachelor for far too long. Isn't that right, Cap?"

Cap wasn't quite sure how to respond.

"I think it's about time you settled down and got yourself married."

"I'm not sure that we're at that stage quite yet, Bonnie. We'll see what the future holds."

"Don't argue with a dying woman, Cap."

Cap held his hands up in mock surrender.

Bonnie winked at Tess. "Cap's a good man. This community is lucky to have him."

"I don't know about that."

Bonnie's face grew solemn and she looked Cap dead in the eye. "Let me tell you something. I knew your folks well. They were good people. Salt of the earth. And your daddy was a good pastor. Don't get me wrong. Your daddy, for better or worse, was more of a fire and brimstone man of God. But you, Cap, are cut from a different cloth."

Cap tried to protest.

"I'm not done yet. You just sit there and listen to me." She leaned back in her chair and pulled the collar of her robe around her neck. "Maybe most folks don't know that you didn't want to come back to Black Walnut and take over your father's church, but I did. You came back home out of a sense of duty. And that's what makes you special and your own kind of pastor. You're a man of the people. Instead of walking in front of us, you walk with us. Folks respect that, Cap. And don't you forget it."

SIX DAYS AFTER EASTER SUNDAY

64

Gray skies above the cemetery grounds threatened to open up. The temperature dipped below forty, and a mighty wind from an approaching storm front blew through a grove of century-old black walnut trees, snapping at the slacks and dresses of mourners gathered at Sturdevant Cemetery.

Cap stood at the edge of a freshly dug grave, wearing his stole and gown. He held neither notes nor a Bible. They would not be needed here today. He scanned the faces of both the young and old. He knew every one of them by name. Benny Hunsinger, Carol and Glenn from the Agway store, and Scott and Skeeter. Wade and Butch stood shoulder to shoulder while Maggie and Robin pressed close to one another, and Robin's kids clung to the hem of her dress. Tess stood beside Lester with her arm hooked through his. He wasn't wearing his uniform. Instead, the sheriff wore a suit and tie and black dress shoes that looked recently purchased. Lester appeared tired and a little lost, but he stood straight, his eyes never straying from Bonnie's casket.

At the back of the crowd of mourners, Cap spotted Danny Bedford standing off by himself, like a mountain in the distance. The big man wore green work pants and a dress shirt that wouldn't button at the collar. Cap nodded to Danny, and Danny nodded back before staring down at his work boots.

Cap heard the call of crows from the edge of the cemetery, but he blocked out their cries, cleared his throat, and began to speak about Bonnie.

"When do the dead die?" Cap paused as he gazed out at his friends and neighbors. "When they are forgotten."

He locked eyes with Lester. "Bonnie will not be forgotten. Not by me. Not by Lester. Not by any of you standing here today. Bonnie will remain in our hearts and minds until we meet her once again."

Cap grew silent for a moment, searching for the right things to say—the truthful words to express.

"Bonnie was not only a member of the church, but she was also my friend. She was a straightforward woman who spoke her mind. And she was kind in her words, and her actions as well. She volunteered countless hours to the church, the library, and even though she did not have children, she also gave her time to our schools."

He stared at the casket before continuing.

"Over the last few days, I've been asking myself why Bonnie was so giving of herself. Why was she willing to volunteer so much of her time?" His voice cracked and he took a moment to compose himself. "I believe it was because Bonnie genuinely cared about people in this community. And she knew she was part of something bigger than herself. Community was important to her. It *was* her family."

He looked back toward the collection of townspeople.

"I think sometimes we lose sight of the power of community and take one another for granted. Or, at least, I have been guilty of that. At times we get caught up in the very struggle of living. Our jobs. Our spouses. Our children. Sometimes it can feel overpowering, and we lose our way." A strong gust of wind blew across the cemetery grounds, rustling both clothing and hair. "And that is why we need our neighbors. Why we rely on our neighbors. In many ways, the people we live amongst are more important than anything else."

His eyes settled on Maggie and Wade.

"I think it would put a smile on Bonnie's face if she knew that her passing reminded us of the importance of community and that maybe we all could try and mend a few fences and forge friendships, new and old." He paused for a moment, allowing his words to resonate with those gathered before him.

"I've presided over many funerals. Too many. And to be honest, it doesn't get any easier. I feel each and every loss. Bonnie's is no different. I feel a powerful loss. I mourn for her. I miss her. But I'm also comforted by knowing that she is no longer in pain. She is free from that now."

His eyes burned hot, and his voice trembled.

"Let's leave here today not only mourning Bonnie's passing but celebrating what she left behind." Cap thought those would be his final words, but as he peered out at his friends and neighbors, he began to speak once again. "Even though I walk through the valley of the shadow of death, I will fear no evil, for you are with me; your rod and staff, they comfort me."

65

Butch's stomach tightened the moment his mother knocked on his bedroom door and asked him to come down to his father's study. *A family meeting*, she announced.

He yanked off his dress shirt, then his trousers, and tossed them under the bed. While he slipped on a pair of blue jeans and a sweatshirt, he could hear his parents' voices from downstairs and thought about the family meeting. He knew what this was about. And he knew the kind of things they were probably going to say: *We've grown apart. It's not your fault. It will be better for everyone. We'll still be a family. It's okay to feel angry.*

But Butch didn't feel angry anymore. He didn't feel much of anything the last few days.

Ever since last Friday, after his mother had been so hysterical, both of his parents had been unusually quiet. They didn't really talk, but more importantly, they didn't argue, didn't nag, didn't seem to hate one another.

He wasn't sure how he'd respond to their announcement. He wouldn't be able to fake surprise and didn't think that he would cry. Besides, it'd probably be for the best for everyone.

His parents still wore their dress clothes from the funeral. His father sat behind his desk with his tie loosened, and his mother stood beside him, stiff and rigid.

"Sit down for a minute, Butch," his mother requested.

He sat. Crossed his arms.

His father cleared his throat. "Butch—" But his voice trailed off and could not look Butch in the eye.

The knot in his stomach clenched tighter.

He noticed that his mother had her hand on his father's back. They rarely touched one another. He couldn't remember the last time he saw them hug or kiss or display any form of affection.

His mother took a breath and began to speak. "I think that the three of us have been moving in opposite directions for far too long. And even though we live in the same house, I feel like we've been living separate lives. Maybe some things have been broken for a while, and maybe they can't be fixed, but we'd still like to try."

Butch's eyes went to his father. His callous exterior had been replaced by something else. He seemed uncomfortable and unsure of himself. Butch watched as his mother gripped his father's shoulder. She squeezed it tight and spoke softly.

"It's okay, Wade."

His father finally peered at Butch with red-rimmed eyes. His jaw tightened as he attempted to form words.

"Butch. This isn't easy for me—"

"You're getting a divorce," Butch blurted.

His father appeared genuinely surprised by the comment. "No. No, Butch, we're not." He stood and came around his desk. "Look, son, I know I've been selfish and not here for you for a long time, and I'm sorry for that. You deserve better. And the only way I can see being better at both those things is to be honest with you."

His parents locked eyes, and they exchanged an unspoken understanding. His mother nodded her head and reached for his father's hand.

"Go ahead, Wade. It's time to stop with the lies we've created."

EIGHT DAYS AFTER EASTER SUNDAY

66

"I wanted to thank you again for your words at Bonnie's service."

"I meant every word, Lester. You know that I did."

Lester stood in the middle of the porch. Took off his hat and waited to see if Cap would invite him inside.

"You holding up, okay?"

"I'd be lying if I said I was. Still doesn't seem quite real. The house feels empty and just plain wrong. Everywhere I turn, Bonnie's there, but not there."

"Not that it makes it any easier, but those feelings are natural."

"One day at a time, I suppose."

Cap finally propped open the door a little more. "Offer you a cup of coffee?"

"I won't say no."

Lester followed Cap inside the house and took a seat on the couch.

"Let me put on a fresh pot."

As Cap headed toward the kitchen, Lester cleared his throat. "Cap?"

Cap stopped. Peered back at him.

"I think it might be a good idea for Tess to join us. Something's come up that she may have some insight on."

Lester noticed Cap's body language—his shoulders pulled up slightly and his eyes shifted. "Take your time. I'll just sit here and rest my legs."

Cap and Tess sat in chairs across from Lester—their coffee cups before them, untouched. They both attempted to appear at ease, but their discomfort was obvious. Rigid posture, arms folded, averted eyes.

"You know, I have to admit, there's one thing that Bonnie left behind that I wasn't quite prepared for." He removed his hat and played with the brim for a moment. "Her cats. Apparently, they need to be fed and have their litter box changed. Guess they don't do those kinds of things themselves. And if they didn't have name tags, I wouldn't know what in the hell to call them."

Cap and Tess both smiled and seemed to relax a bit.

"I'm not sure if you would be interested, Tess, but Cap here told me that you used to work in a library. Is that right?"

Yes.

"Well, Andi Cavallo, the librarian in Wyalusing, is fixing to retire here pretty soon. Maybe you could stop by and see if that's something you might be interested in."

Thank you.

"You bet. Hope it works out for you. Whereabouts did you work at a library?"

Lester watched her write in her notebook.

Syracuse.

"A New Yorker, huh? Well, I won't hold it against you."

Lester picked up his coffee and took a sip. "I was curious about something else. Does the name Aaron Douglas ring a bell for either one of you?" He intentionally kept his eyes on Cap but noticed Tess stiffen in her chair.

"Someone new to town?" Cap asked.

Lester shook his head. "No. Nothing like that."

"I've never heard the name before, Lester."

"I kinda figured as much." He peered at Tess. "How about you, Tess? You know a man by the name of Aaron Douglas?"

Tess stared back at him, rigid and unresponsive.

"What's this all about, Lester?"

He placed his hat back onto his head. "Well, we pulled a Volvo out of Tanner's Pond yesterday. No damage to the car. Looks like someone just drove it straight into the water."

"Roads have been slick. Maybe they lost control."

"Could be. Could be. But the odd thing is that there wasn't a body in the car. It was empty. Doors closed. Windows shut. Very strange."

Cap said nothing this time.

"It belongs to an Aaron Douglas from Syracuse, who was reported as missing a week ago by his wife. Hasn't called. Nothing. Apparently, he just up and disappeared one day."

"You think his body will turn up in the pond?"

"Yeah. Maybe. We'll see what happens."

Lester swirled his mug of coffee. "Could I get a refill, Cap? Haven't been sleeping well and I could use a little jolt to keep me moving."

Cap almost seemed unsure about leaving Tess alone. "You bet." He took Lester's cup and headed into the kitchen.

Lester smiled at Tess, and she attempted a smile in return.

"Working in a library must be peaceful."

Yes.

"So, you're not itching to get back to Syracuse?"

No.

"Why's that?"

He waited for her to write in her notebook.

It wasn't a good place for me.

"And Black Walnut is?"

I think so.

"Well, I hope so. You'd be doing us all a favor by keeping Cap company. That man needs somebody to keep him honest."

I'll try.

Lester nodded like he expected nothing less. "It occurred to me when I was driving over here that I don't even know your last name, Tess."

He watched her reaction. Her rigidness.

Tess wrote down a single word and slid the notebook across the coffee table. Lester read the name before leaning back into the sofa cushion.

"I guess Douglas is a pretty common name."

Tess maintained eye contact but didn't respond.

"Who knows? Maybe this Aaron Douglas fella was bad news or got himself into some kind of trouble."

Maybe.

"Well, will you let me know if anything comes to you that I might want to know about?"

Yes.

"Good." He patted her knee and stood with some effort. "I'm sure looking forward to getting to know you better, Tess."

Tess stepped forward and kissed Lester on the cheek.

"I see. I leave you two alone for a few minutes, and this is what I find?" Cap stood in the middle of the room holding a cup of steaming coffee.

"Competition is a good thing, Cap. You remember that." Lester returned his hat to his head. "I think I'll take a rain check on that coffee. I need to be getting back home. Duty calls. I've got cats waiting on me."

MAY 4TH — OPENING DAY FOR SPRING TURKEY SEASON

67

Cap cleared the condensation from the bathroom mirror and stared at his reflection. The clarity in his eyes struck him—no dullness, no hint of the nightly damage he had been accustomed to waking to every day. For the first time in as long as he could remember, the sight of his reflection did not disappoint him.

One thing that had not changed was morning rituals.

He opened the medicine cabinet and found a can of Barbasol shaving cream and a double-edged safety razor. He pulled up the sink stopper and ran the water until it was good and hot. Applied white foam to his cheeks, chin, and throat, avoiding the whiskers on his upper lip.

He started the razor upon his cheeks like he always did. After he completed one side, he cleaned the razor in the water, then began the process on the other side.

As he grabbed a hand towel, his eyes fell upon his reflection and the fullness of his ever-present mustache. He stared at the facial hair for a moment when the impulse seized him.

Cap didn't hesitate or second-guess the decision. He used a pair of scissors to trim the whiskers as close to the skin as possible, then massaged a fair amount of shaving cream on his upper lip. Rinsed the razor and began. The effort was slow going and painful, the whiskers too thick and too long to be removed in a few strokes. When the blade turned dull, Cap stopped and replaced it with a new one.

After rinsing the freshly shaved area with cold water, Cap noticed how white the skin was above his upper lip, concealed since he was an eighteen-year-old boy. He stared at a new face foreign to his eyes. The absence of a mustache made him appear younger and so very different as well.

His fingers traced his flaw—the tiny cleft in the skin exposed for the first time in many years. In his mind's eye, the imperfection had been something hideous and shameful. Something that others either couldn't bear to look upon or were unable to keep themselves from staring at.

He went to the bedroom closet and pushed aside all the black-collared shirts reserved for Sunday mornings, selecting a green flannel button-up shirt that he hadn't worn in a long time.

Tess knocked on the bedroom door. She wore a lavender dress that suited her. Cap liked the way she looked.

Tess did a double take when she noticed his bare lip.

Cap rubbed the soft, tender skin. "I thought it was time for a change. Does it look as strange as it feels?"

No.

"You don't hate it?"

No.

"That's good. Because I don't plan on growing it back anytime soon." Cap took a final look at his reflection in the mirror. "Well, you ready?"

Yes.

"Good. Because I don't know if I am."

Tess took his hand in hers and gave it a squeeze. "Nervous?" The sound of her voice was soft yet clear.

"Nervous. Excited. And a little bit scared, to be honest."

"You'll be fine." She squeezed his hand again. "Let's go meet your son."

68

The sky glowed powder blue, and the sun burned bright above the canopy of black walnut trees overhead. Buds sprouted from limbs, gray and fuzzy, spring finally upon them.

They walked side by side through the woods, brittle leaves and twigs snapping beneath their footsteps. Clutched at their sides, they both carried twelve-gauge shotguns. Neither of them had spoken much for the last thirty minutes or so. Neither felt compelled to say something that didn't mean anything. The forest sounds were conversation enough: a gentle breeze tugging at branches, the crunch of leaves underfoot, and the melodic chirping of nuthatches, robins, and warblers.

Butch slowed his pace as he approached a black walnut tree permanently marked by a strike of lightning. He traced his fingers against the disfigured bark, and a hint of a smile creased his lips. Despite the scarring, the black walnut tree was well and thriving.

He took one last look before catching up with Cap. "I did what you said."

"And what was that exactly?"

"I talked to Brian and Monte."

"Yeah? How'd it go?"

Butch ran the back of his hand under his nose. "I was nervous, but I told them that I wasn't afraid of them and that if they didn't leave me alone, I would fight back."

"And?"

"So far, so good."

From somewhere in front of them, father and son heard a distinct call. They froze in their tracks, switching off the safeties of their shotguns in unison. Cap gestured to Butch to stand flush against a twisted oak tree, and he did the same.

Cap winked at the boy as the rustling of leaves became louder and louder. Then they brought the stocks of their shotguns to their shoulders and watched as a forty-pound tom stepped into the clearing of black walnut trees.

Thank you so much for reading *Come Away From Her*. If you've enjoyed the book, we would be grateful if you would post a review on the bookseller's website. Just a few words is all it takes!

Acknowledgments

I am grateful for the support, kindness, and expertise of many.

To author Ayn Carrillo-Gailey, for her skilled reading of every draft, her skilled editing, and constant inspiration.

Appreciation to Esmond Harmsworth and the Aevitas Creative Management team; Amy Schiffman and Echo Lake Entertainment; my editor, Scott Bury; and Sheri Williams and Ashley Carlson at TouchPoint.

Thank you, Charles Brock, for your book jacket design—you rocked it.

A heartfelt thanks to my Orcas Island writing pod—Joe Thoron, Guy Woods, Alex Callen, Theresa Harris, Angela Saxe, and Ayn Carrillo-Gailey; to fellow author, Bruce Holbert, for reading an early draft and providing insight and inspiration through his own written words; to Michael McClary, Stu Sheldon Smith, and Shelley "Squirrel" McAndrew for providing feedback and a watchful eye; and to Andy Lynn for his unwavering support of my work.

I owe a debt of gratitude to Reverend David Evans for his assistance in developing Cap's spiritual struggle; Kathleen Tudor for sharing her personal experience within the deaf community; and Kiki Smith for her etching, *Come Away From Her*, that inspired the title.

A shout out to the Darvill's Bookstore team and to the staff at the Orcas Island Library, my homes away from home.

And finally, my gratitude to Orcas Island, a creative and generous community.

CPSIA information can be obtained
at www.ICGtesting.com
Printed in the USA
BVHW030233080223
658054BV00008B/1038